BRAVELY

MAGGIE STIEFVATER

BRAVELY

DISNEP PRESS

Los Angeles • New York

For information address
Disney Press, 1200 Grand Central Avenue,
Glendale, California 91201.

Printed in the United States of America
First Hardcover Edition, May 2022
1 3 5 7 9 10 8 6 4 2
FAC-021131-22077

Library of Congress Control Number: 2021944036
ISBN 978-1-368-07134-5

Designed by Margie Peng

Visit disneybooks.com

TO THE ISLANDERS

PROLOGUE

THIS is a story about two gods and a girl.

It takes place a very long time ago, when Scotland was only beginning to be called Scotland, at a castle called DunBroch.

The first god, the Cailleach, was very old. In fact, one of her other names was the Old Woman of Scotland, although most humans never saw her in that form. Instead, those with the Sight merely felt her invisible presence in a wild storm or a rushing waterfall or even in the melted snow that pools in fresh-plowed spring fields. The Cailleach was a goddess of creation. She made trees bud. Grass thicken. Calves grow inside cows. Fruit ripen on the vine. Her work was the ancient business of making and renewing.

Oh, she was a wily old woman.

She was a rule-bending, shape-shifting, trick-playing, truth-splitting old crone, and she'd do whatever she could to get her way.

The second god, Feradach, was very young. It wasn't that he hadn't been around as long as the Cailleach, because he had, in his own way. But unlike the Cailleach, who had the same physical form every time she became visible, Feradach appeared as something different to every person who saw him. It meant he was always learning himself new, over and over and over, a kind of eternal youth.

Feradach was a god of ruin. His work was the ancient business of destruction. Under his attention, fires seared landscapes, plagues harrowed communities, and floods erased civilizations.

Feradach destroyed the obsolete; the Cailleach prompted renewal.

Together, they kept the balance.

Unfortunately, they didn't always agree on what the *balance* required. Or rather, the Cailleach didn't always agree. Young Feradach was unflinchingly fair, because it's easier to have unclouded justice before experience complicates things. The Cailleach, on the other hand, was old enough to have preferences. Biases. Favorites. This meant that sometimes, even when ruin was perfectly merited, she wanted *her* side to win instead.

And that was usually when she cheated. She'd been playing tricks on Feradach for ages.

Some years she managed to save a warrior or a family or even an entire village from him. Some years, she lost them all. Some years, when the tricks didn't work, she used a miracle, although she didn't get many of those to spend. The Cailleach was old, but wherever the miracles came from was even older, from a deep part of Scotland that has always favored healing and creation. Miracle years were rare ones.

This story takes place in a miracle year.

On the day it begins, DunBroch looked particularly splendid on its perch above the glittering loch. In that sharp winter weather, everything that wasn't green and red was black and white. Black water, white-heaped shore. Black road to the castle, white-shouldered bracken on either side. Black walls, white capped battlements. A powdered sugar layer of snow rendered all the courtyard's divots smooth as an iced bun. Red berries popped brightly in the holly and bay leaf boughs hung over every threshold. Old green banners flapped elegantly from the tall towers.

DunBroch was getting ready for a Christmas wedding. Yes, they had Christmas back then, and weddings, too, although neither looked exactly as they do now. The part of weddings we spend a lot of time on these days—the bride and the groom, the picking of flowers and matching of dresses, showers and stag parties, flower girls and ring boys, the kiss, the kiss—that was the least involved part back then. A DunBroch wedding ceremony was just a couple quickly exchanging a ring or a brooch in front of a cleric, then getting on with it all. No kiss. No romance. Just a perfunctory transaction. But the celebration that came after—now that was really something. It could go on for days. Pantomime plays, courtly dancing, feats of strength, silly games, and, of course, the food. The food, oh, the food! To modern eyes, it would have looked much more like a festival than a wedding.

Now, a DunBroch Christmas was more like its modern-day cousin. The Christmas turkey was more likely to be a boar or a swan, and the board games played before the fire were ones that have long since gone extinct, but the seasonal trimmings were the same. Holly wreaths and ivy boughs, mischievous mistletoe and merry carols, twelve short winter days of gifts, twelve long winter nights of treats and spiced wine. It was a natural companion to the revelry of wedding feasting.

The Christmas wedding was Leezie's. Foolish, lovable young Leezie, who had been a member of the DunBroch household staff so long that she was like family. She loved ritual and religion. The Christians, the druids, the Jews, the witches, the Cistercians, the Lads of Cernunnos, the Ladies of the Morrigan, the Tironensians, the Cluniacs, she had tried them all. Recently, she'd dedicated herself to Minerva, the Roman goddess of wisdom and crafts, and spent weeks weaving and writing songs about owls. It was a trying time. Luckily she'd moved on to astrology and then, on to getting married. Leezie had always wanted a Christmas wedding—a perfect combination of ritual and religion—and now she'd finally found a man to star in it with her. The others at DunBroch called him the Cabbage.

Cabbage is not exciting, but it is nutritious. He would do.

Leezie is not the girl this story is about, however. It is about another DunBroch girl.

Now, there are three DunBrochs: the *castle* DunBroch, gazing watchfully over the wooded hillsides. The *kingdom* DunBroch, with its lochs and burns, its lowland fields and highland shielings, its coven of white-haired mountains and sliver of black-tongued sea. And the *Clan* DunBroch: King Fergus, Queen Elinor, Princess Merida, and three triplet princes, Hubert, Harris, and Hamish.

This story belongs to the Princess Merida.

Merida was less like the mannered royal you're imagining and more like a struck match, although matches did not yet exist. Red hair, keen eyes, quick brain, built to start fires but not to put them out. She was an absolute wizard with a bow and arrow. For over a decade, before the wee devil triplet princes arrived, she'd been the only child, and where other children might have had friends, Merida had her bow. She practiced her archery breathlessly, automatically, in every moment her mother hadn't scheduled her for lessons in embroidery, music, and reading. There was a stillness to archery she couldn't get anywhere else. Whenever she had a problem she couldn't solve, she went out to practice. Whenever she had a feeling she didn't understand, she went out to practice. Hour upon hour, she collected calluses on fingertips and bruises on forearms. At night, when she dreamt, she still sighted between trees and adjusted for strong highland winds.

In the months before the wedding, Merida took her bow and traveled the kingdom. In spring she'd gone with the villagers and their herds up to the temporary bothies in the shielings. In late summer she went down to Morventon to study letters and geography with the nuns. By fall, she was traveling with a handful of her father's old confidants who had vowed to map the varied terrain of DunBroch.

In winter, she returned for Leezie's wedding. She hung up her bow. How safe and unchanged she found DunBroch after her months of wandering.

She didn't know that Feradach—and disaster—was approaching.

But the Cailleach knew. That wily old goddess.

She also knew that DunBroch had earned Feradach's ruin. But the Cailleach was old, and she was biased, and she had a stake in the Clan DunBroch.

So she cheated.

This is that story.

PART I

WINTER

1
THREE KNOCKS

MERIDA had been eating bread rolls for an hour when the first knock came.

The rolls were wonderful. Fresh baked. Crisp on the outside, pillowy and warm on the inside. Merida had finished off all the wonky-shaped ones, and had now moved on to some of the perfectly shaped ones. There were still hundreds of them piled on the rough-hewn kitchen table, far outnumbering the planned guests for the Christmas feast. The bread was destined for a silly wedding ritual: Leezie and the Cabbage were supposed to try to exchange a kiss over the top of a wall of buns. Merida was doing them a favor by making the wall just that bit shorter.

Leezie, getting married! Merida couldn't really believe it.

As she munched bread in the dim midnight kitchen, she used her bare foot to trace her name through the flour dusting the stone floor. How pleasant to feel the chill of the floor on the bottom of her foot and the heat of the smoldering hearth on the top. How pleasant to feel the squish of the roll's interior against the roof of her mouth and the crisp mountain crust against her tongue. How pleasant to just let her mind prattle, as her mother Elinor called it, to just let it play over nonsense like how her name spelled backward was Adirem, which wasn't half bad, really. Adirem of DunBroch. Her mirror self, she thought. Her shadow self. As dark and pensive as Merida was bright and active.

Merida traced *DunBroch* into the flour. Hcorbnud didn't look at all appealing backward.

Then came the first knock.

Tap–tap–tap.

Merida stopped chewing.

She listened.

Could it be one of the triplets? Hubert had had a mischievous look in his eye as Merida pinched the triplets' candle out at bedtime.

But the castle was silent in the way that only castles can be. The stone stopped most sound dead in its tracks and the wall tapestries drowned the rest of it. Everyone besides Merida was dreaming of Leezie's wedding and the Christmas feast to follow. The knock had probably just been one of the fireplaces popping.

Merida finished her roll. She took her time selecting another, resisting a somewhat triplet-like impulse to pull one from the bottom of the heap to watch it collapse across

4

the floor. Picking a perfectly round one, she tore it open to admire the structured crevices and crannies inside. Over the past several months, she'd eaten a fair bit of bread, but none could compare to Aileen's. Aileen, the family cook, was irritable, territorial, and foulmouthed, but Scotland's kitchens had no better. Merida's mother Elinor went to great lengths to find the most modern of recipes for Aileen, often all the way from France, and every time a new one came via messenger or pigeon, Aileen closed herself up in the kitchen for days, testing and retesting it before she was willing to let any of the royal family try the result. Well, most of the royal family.

This wasn't the first time Merida had snuck down to sample Aileen's handiwork.

As she ate this roll, she thought back over her grand homecoming earlier that day. There'd been hugs and tears, the works. DunBroch was very enthusiastic about stories, about legends, and Merida had delivered the Ballad of Merida's Year, at volume, from atop one of the tables in the Great Hall, feinting around Christmas decorations. The triplets and her father and Leezie had hooted with delight, and her mother had pretended to look disapproving.

Ah, home! It was so nice to be back among DunBroch's creature comforts: its bellowing fireplaces and plentiful candles, its worm-free snacks and discreet privy, its flea-free blankets and luxurious bedrooms. Nice, too, to find the little things unchanged: the herbal smell of the kitchen. The chaos of her triplet brothers caterwauling in the halls. The percussive clearing of her father's throat as he sat in his chair by the fire. The ritual of kissing her mother's cheek good night as Elinor wrote down the day's events in her journal.

Tap-tap-tap.

Was that a second knock?

It seemed like it might have been. A soft triple tap, just like she thought she'd heard before.

"Hubert, I hear you," she whispered.

But it didn't seem to be Hubert. Was it coming from the door? The castle gate was barred at nightfall, so no one could have gotten into the courtyard, and even if they could, the closest civilization was the wee blackhouse village, which was a twenty-five-minute walk even when the road wasn't bad-tempered with snow and ice as it was that Christmas Eve.

Merida waited. She listened. There was nothing.

She got another piece of bread.

The strange restlessness that had driven her out of bed in the first place was beginning to rise again.

Why was it even there?

She should have felt marvelous. She loved her family. She loved her home. She loved it more than she had words to say. It was wonderful to be back, to find it almost exactly as she'd left it.

But up in her tower bedroom, she'd lain awake in the cold moonlight that snuck around the window tapestry and wished desperately that it wasn't dark so that she could go outside to the exercise fields and shoot her bow until her body and mind felt perfectly still. Instead, she fidgeted, her feet itching to take her away on an exciting journey.

Exactly how she'd felt the night before she'd left months before.

But she'd *gone* on the journey already. Something should have changed. She should have changed.

Then came the third knock.

Tap-tap-tap.

This one was definitely not coming from a fireplace. It was coming from the door. Not the main one, but the little ugly one around back, for deliveries, where the carts wouldn't tear up the grass. But who would be out there on a night like this?

Merida had a sudden, hideous thought that perhaps it *was* one of the triplets, somehow trapped outside for hours, able to manage only that feeble tap. Leaping across the kitchen, she turned the enormous key in the lock and heaved the heavy door open.

Outside, the courtyard was brighter than she'd expected. The huge moon, although out of sight behind the castle, lit all the snow to daylight brilliance. Freezing air, scented with woodsmoke, blew into the kitchen around Merida. Every star was so bright and shimmering that they seemed as if they'd be wet to the touch.

There was no one standing on the doorstep. There weren't even footprints in the snow. But she knew she had not imagined the knocks.

A very peculiar and particular prickling was rising inside her. She could tell that *this* feeling had been hiding among her other restlessness all along, only now it had

7

become big enough for her to recognize its unmistakable timbre. It was like the wet, sharp shimmering of the stars overhead, but in her chest.

Magic, it whispered. *Magic is near.*

It had been a very long time since she'd felt that call.

And that was when she saw him.

In the deep blue shadow near the castle wall stood a hunched figure, although he couldn't have been the one who knocked—there were no footprints leading from him to the door. He was paused in the act of tugging one of his gloves off, absolutely motionless, hoping she wouldn't notice him.

This was no visitor. This was an intruder.

"Hey!" she called. "I can *see* you!"

The figure didn't move.

Merida would have preferred her bow and arrow for effect, but she used what she had in her hand already: bread. With her perfect aim, she railed it right off the figure's head.

"Hey!" she said again. "Announce yourself, stranger!"

He turned his head. What was his expression? Merida couldn't see; it was hidden in shadow.

Merida snatched up a weapon; the closest to hand was a fireplace shovel. She crossed the courtyard in several massive strides. "I said, announce yourself!"

The stranger's voice was scornful. "You can't hurt me—*ow!*"

Merida hit him right behind his knees, a trick she'd learned not from battle training, but rather from her fiendish brother Hubert, who'd hidden for weeks beneath the Great Hall table, perfecting the technique on Merida and anyone else foolish enough to wander close.

It worked just as well on mysterious strangers. He fell to his knees. His gloved hands disappeared right up to his wrists in the snow. He shot Merida a single, astonished look.

"You can't stop me," he told her.

This was not at all the reply she'd been expecting. "Stop you from *what*?"

But he simply took off running.

Around DunBroch, Merida was considered hot-tempered. She felt this was unfair and only because she was a girl, as she had three redheaded triplet brothers who were far more likely to pop off in anger than she was, and they never got called hot-tempered. What *she* was, she felt, was quick-witted. She didn't take a lot of time to put her reactions together. Sure, sometimes that reaction was a blunt reply, but sometimes, that was what was deserved. For instance, sometimes you were a stranger in the night and what was needed was a fireplace shovel to the back of the knee and then a pursuit.

In the back of her head, she heard a tiny voice that sounded a lot like her mother's saying, *Merida, princesses do not chase strangers barefoot through the night!*

Merida narrowed her eyes.

She gave chase.

2

The Black Raven

ERIDA realized very quickly this was no ordinary pursuit.

One moment she was chasing a man, his cloak twirling. And then she was chasing a deer.

Or something like a deer, something large as a deer, its flanks silvery in the starlight as it leapt over the bracken into the snow-light woods.

No, she thought, she was mistaken. It was a fox, surely. She saw its tail whipping gray through that black-and-white landscape.

A wolf, ears pricked as it cleared a creek.

A stretched, lanky hare, incredibly spry.

A sinewy mink, teeth flashing in the moonlight.

A floppy rabbit pillowing into the brush.

Oh, she thought. *It* is *magic after all.*

Scottish magic was not much different than Scottish wildcats: both were pretty rare, and a person could go their whole life without encountering either, if one wasn't paying attention. Most people paid magic (and wildcats) as much thought as they did songbirds or fruit that grew in funny shapes; there were more concrete things that required their attention. Some people didn't even believe in magic (or wildcats).

Merida believed. She had to. A few years before, it had called to her, she had answered it, a world of trouble ensued, lessons were learned. It had turned out for the best, but ultimately, she understood that the world of humans and the world of magic were separate for good reason. They followed different rules. Her mother had told her there were two kinds of people with the Sight: people who were interested in magic, and people magic was interested in. After the last experience, Merida had decided she was certainly not the first.

Yet here she was again, chasing magic through the woods.

Could she turn back?

You can't stop me, he'd said.

She had to know what he was doing in the courtyard in the middle of the night.

But it was clear she was never going to catch him in a one-on-one chase, so she turned her attention to trapping him instead. This was *her* DunBroch. She knew the low boggy areas and the sudden rises. She knew where the mossy boulders became untraversable and where the trees were knit too close for fast travel. She knew the way to a treacherous burnside, a place where the river cut through the ground so swiftly that the banks were steep and unfor-giving. Impassable.

A good trap.

The two of them angled and circled, bounded and shifted. Her shimmering quarry thought he was being pursued. But he was being driven. He fled right to the field that ended at the burnside, and not a moment too soon, because her lungs were bursting with this cold air and her feet stinging from running over the rough ground.

Drawing to a halt, hand pressed to the stitch in her side, she watched the stranger, now vaguely hound-shaped, leaping away across the field. Over the thump of her heart-beat in her ears, she could just barely hear the complicated sound of the cold river charging fast in the burn beyond, and she doubted he could hear it at all over his progress through the dry grass.

Sure enough, the burnside took the stranger by sur-prise.

He slid, slid, slid, legs wheeling, then: stopped. Just in time, right at the edge.

Slowly, he turned to face her.

Now he was neither a stag nor a fox, hare nor rabbit, mink nor wolf. He was a comely young man with a blond mane of hair like a wild pony's. His heavy cloak, powdered with snow, was held shut by a brooch engraved with a tree with both the branches and the roots visible. He had no visible weapon.

"You're—you're trapped," Merida gasped. She was still

too out of breath to sound commanding, but she gave the fireplace shovel a threatening sort of twirl. "I've seen two cows drown in this river, and *they* weren't wearing a cloak to drag them down. Now: who are you?"

His gaze dropped to her bare feet, which were bright red from the cold, then back to her makeshift weapon.

"I am not a thing you fight," he said. "Why do you think you can?"

"Why were you in our courtyard?" Merida shot back.

"How did you know I was there?"

"You knocked!"

"Knocked? I certainly did not."

"Someone knocked!"

"It wasn't me!"

"Why did you run from me?"

"Why did you run *after* me?"

"I thought you knocked!"

"I wouldn't knock! You weren't supposed to see me doing my work."

"What work?"

He didn't answer.

With a great *pwang* against the cold rock, Merida knocked the head of the shovel right off, exposing the rather pointier metal end. She directed this pointy end at him. Not like a sword, but like an arrow without a bow, drawn back and resting on her shoulder, waiting for her to send it right through his eye. "I demand you tell me what your business was at DunBroch."

The stranger shook his head as if he were clearing

cobwebs from it. "No. No, this is a distraction. This is a trick." He didn't seem to be talking to her. "I told myself I'd be wiser."

He leapt neatly over the edge into the roaring burn below.

Just like that, not a bit of hesitation; he'd never been trapped at all. He had simply let himself be stopped out of what—curiosity? And now he was gone.

Maybe she should just go home. Maybe it would be all right.

But the knock, she thought.

It hadn't been the stranger, according to him, and she couldn't imagine why he would lie about that. If not him, then who? Someone who wanted her to see him out there, to catch him in the act of—what? *You can't stop me,* he'd said. She had to know. That's all there was to it.

Merida jumped after him.

It was madness, of course. The river, wild with winter, was in the sort of mood to devour bridges, and from the feel of the debris-ridden water, it already had. Merida swam and tumbled. She hit boulders. Wood hit her. Her fireplace shovel swam away from her grip to start its own adventure somewhere else.

"I'm not leaving you!" she shouted, getting a mouthful of icy water. Who knew if the stranger could hear; possibly he'd turned himself into a fish. She barked her knee on a boulder. "You might as well give up now and answer my questions!"

Suddenly she was *flying.*

She fell—

    fell—

        fell—

Midair, she realized she was going over a waterfall. She knew this waterfall! She'd seen it many times during the day, and it had always appeared quaint, small, and picturesque. It didn't feel that way at all when she was going over it. She fell for countable seconds, hit the surface of the shallow pool at the fall's base, and then smashed her shoulder against the gravel bottom. There was just enough current left to unceremoniously wash her up to the pool's edge. Her mouth felt gritty with river water. Her lungs felt pierced with icicles. Every limb was completely numb with cold.

Footsteps crunched on the brittle rushes by her head.

The stranger stood inches away, looking down at her where she lay on her stomach, completely robbed of any royal dignity she may have possessed before. "Just when I think I understand mortals. What do you want out of this?"

Mortal! It was shocking to hear him say it, even though she already knew after this chase that he was no ordinary human.

She licked her frozen lips to warm them just enough to speak. Her voice sounded thin as ice as she said, "I demand an answer. I *caught* you."

He said, "You haven't caught me."

Merida reached out to snatch his ankle.

The stranger recoiled.

Not the calculated move of someone avoiding capture, but rather the involuntary jerk of someone leaping back from an adder. Stiffly, he said, "I don't think you'd like that, Princess."

Princess! It was as shocking to hear this as *mortal*.

"Why not?" she asked. She got to her feet, slower than she would have liked. Her bare feet were still completely numb, and a bit of a worrisome color. "Or is that another question you won't have an answer for? Are you only a thing that runs away?"

"How do you know you want answers?" he shot back. "How do you know you want your prey? Are you only a thing that gives chase?"

"More questions? And still no answers," Merida said, but as she did, she wondered if perhaps he *couldn't* answer. Magic was funny that way, sometimes, according to some of the women she'd met at the shielings. Around the fires at night, they'd told her many half-believed stories about the fey beasts and uncanny entities that roamed their kingdom. In these legends, the magical creatures often had limits upon them, especially the human-shaped ones. They could speak, but they could only repeat what humans said to them, or they were extremely beautiful, except for an ugly rat's tail, or they couldn't touch water or sunlight lest they turn to dust. There were always consequences to appearing human. Maybe he was magically forbidden to confess his purpose. Or perhaps he had none. She mused, "Perhaps you're just a bogle playing silly tricks."

"You think I'm a *bogle*?" he replied, in disbelief.

"Or a pooka," she suggested.

"A *pooka*?"

She could tell this needled him, so she went on. "A brag, a shellycoat." She was running out of creatures who sometimes took human form. Her teeth were starting to chatter. "A . . . a . . . hobgoblin."

His mouth puckered. "You want an answer. Here is an answer."

She was mystified when he followed this statement by showing her his hands. They were covered by wonderfully made gloves, thin and supple as a second skin, stitched with oxblood thread.

He began to take one off now. Slowly. Dramatically. She was reminded that he'd been in the process of removing his gloves when she first saw him.

"Don't look away, Princess," he ordered. With his newly bare hand, he seized the narrow trunk of a sapling close to him. Skin to trunk, fingers immediately pinking in the bitter cold. He squeezed tight.

Merida just had time to think, *Wait, maybe I* didn't *want an answer,* and then a sharp wind shouldered past her.

It was clearly on its way to the sapling.

Spiky white frost prickled up from the ground like colorless weeds. Frost wasn't supposed to appear that quickly, but this frost did—only around the tree. Ice scoured the tender bark. And, worst of all, a wretched, wild dread surrounded them all.

Magic, magic, magic.

The sapling began to die.

The bark went dull, then dry, then colorless as every bit of green life went from deep within it. The very ends of its branches seemed shrunk in on themselves.

Merida could tell that if she put any pressure on the narrow trunk, it would simply snap.

The sapling was dead.

The frost vanished. The harsh wind subsided. The dread remained.

The stranger tugged his glove back on, his gaze fixed knowingly on Merida all the while.

Magic, magic, magic.

Oh no, Merida thought, but she didn't even quite know why. She fought back her shivers. She did not want to appear to be afraid, even though she was. *Oh no, oh no.*

The stranger drew himself up. All the tentative bemusement had gone from his voice as he said, "I am not a bogle or a hobgoblin or a pooka or a brag. I am Feradach, and I am here to ruin DunBroch. I come where there is rot, and I dig it out so that the world can begin again. I ruin that which has fallen into stagnation to clear the way for new growth. I strip the ground and the bones down to new bare earth so the Cailleach can do her work of renewal. Do you understand?"

She did and she didn't. The part of her that was tuned to the uncanny prickling of magic seemed to understand it perfectly. It was her more ordinary human side that couldn't accept what he was saying. No one had threatened DunBroch in years. Danger was a thing Merida had to travel to find, not a thing that came to her home.

"DunBroch is rotten," Feradach said.

"You're—you're mistaken."

Feradach gestured over his shoulder. From where they were, DunBroch was just visible, silhouetted on the rocky outcrop. The night and the distance erased all its finer points, so all that was truly visible was its tattered banners, the sagging roofs, the crumbling battlements. She saw it through a stranger's eyes. Through Feradach's eyes. It looked like a ruin already.

"Ah, but that's not the truth of it," Merida protested uneasily. "It just needs a bit of love, is all. Dad's said he's going to work on those roofs once the weather's good and warm, and Mum'll fix the banners when the rains come and we can't do any more planting outside. And anyway, that's just a building. The people—well, the triplets are growing like horses. Leezie's getting married. Those are big changes."

"Change isn't about getting taller or changing the roof over your head. Change happens in your heart, in your way of thinking, of moving in the world. And if it were present at DunBroch, I wouldn't be called here. Moth to flame, osprey to water, salmon to birthplace; they have their nature, I have my nature."

"You're mistaken," Merida said again.

"I cannot make mistakes." He added, dismissively, "Anyway, look at you."

"Me?"

"You're the daughter of kings, the daughter of queens. Is this all you think you were made for?"

Merida sputtered, "I've been doing things for months! You have no idea—"

"Up to the shielings with the crofters. Reading with the sisters at Morventon. Riding with the mapmakers," Feradach said. His tone was patient. "Yes, I know about all that. How are you any different than when you began? Before you left, you were a person who would do those things. Now that you are back, you are a person who has done those things. You would do them again. What mark has been left on your heart or in the world from the doing of them? You have been learning new skills and riding horses here and there for your entire life." He shrugged. "Some storms make a lot of noise but move no rooftops."

Merida opened her mouth. She closed it. It was the first time in her life anyone had ever said something like that to her. In fact, people were usually saying the *opposite*, that she was moving too fast, asking for things to shift too much.

"This country has lain fallow for too long now," Feradach said. "It is time for a new generation to have its chance. Nothing can stop me now that I am here."

They both looked at the dead, dead sapling between them. She wanted to deny all of it again, but hadn't she just been thinking that she felt exactly the same as before she'd left?

Think, Merida, think. Use your wits.

There was a board game they played at DunBroch called *Brandubh* (a fun word to say out loud, Merida had always thought, the "a" like the "o" in *glob*, the "u" like the "oo" in *oof*, and the "bh" like a "v," all together sort of rhyming with "pond-oove"). The goal in Brandubh was to take control of the tower to free the prisoners within. Usually this was done with some combination of soldier pieces, but sometimes one could take the risky strategy of attempting to win the favor of the Black Raven, the Brandubh, a piece that followed its own rules. It was difficult to employ, but once on the board, good luck to the other fellow.

DunBroch had a Brandubh set that at one point had been very splendid: squat ordinary soldier pieces that felt good in the palm, an agate Brandubh piece that was dark and impressively purple-brown, an even slate board carved intricately with the game-play movement directions. Elinor had told Merida once the set was a gift from a neighboring kingdom, and it did look like the sort of thing people would gift and other people would put on a high shelf so nothing bad happened to it. Only this one hadn't been put on a high shelf, and so bad things *had* happened to it—one of the triplets had done some kind of rebellious picture-making on it with paints and chisels (Merida suspected it was Hubert; he was the only one with the guts for it). Now it was still playable, but only if you knew the rules quite well, which Merida did.

For a long time, she had been terrible at Brandubh. But then, all of a sudden, she had worked out how to unlock the Black Raven instead of trying to win the ordinary way. Each game, she felt a little prickling inside her just before she managed to fetch out the Brandubh. Then she'd just won all the time, until her family had banned her from playing entirely, which she felt was quite unfair.

Brandubh, Brandubh.

Standing on the edge of that pool looking at that uncertain god, Merida felt the same prickle as she felt just before she worked out how to call out the Brandubh. She knew the rules of this game. Feradach, something uncanny and powerful. Her, a mere mortal. She knew she was meant to be outwitted at this point, to go back home to the castle to die.

But something had knocked on that door and brought her out here, and it hadn't been Feradach. Feradach was supposed to kill her, and he hadn't yet. The balance of growth and ruin had been disrupted, and he wouldn't go away until it was corrected. These were all the moves that had been made so far.

Think, Merida, think, she thought. *What's the Black Raven in this game?*

And then she had it.

"Why did you jump away from me so quickly a few moments ago? It's because you thought your touch would kill me, isn't it?" She took a daring step toward him, cold hand outstretched. "So, if I'm supposed to die, why didn't you just get it over with right then? Why not just now?"

Feradach stumbled in his haste to back out of her reach. "That's—that's not how it is supposed to happen."

She asked, "Then what about that sapling?"

"The sapling?"

"You killed that wee little tree just to prove a point. Are you allowed to just go round killing things? Was that how it was 'supposed' to happen?" She could tell from his troubled face that she was on the right track. "You changed the balance, too. So there's got to be room for something positive in exchange."

"You cannot ask me to spare all of DunBroch for just this sapling," Feradach said. "That's not balance."

"No, I'm not asking for you to spare us," Merida said. "I'm asking for a bargain."

"I don't bargain. The balance—"

But before he could finish his thought, the waterfall and the pools began to transform.

3

THE BARGAIN

Y DAY, this place was beautiful and unusual, the shallow pools a jeweled blue green. By night, they were usually a still, secretive black, nearly hidden in the dark landscape.

But after Merida had spoken of a bargain, the water began to gleam, like her words had been yet another question and this was another answer. Orbs of bluish light rose from below the surface, as if the pools were much deeper than they seemed. Will o' the wisps, she thought, those eerie beacons that lured travelers to miracles or to doom. She'd forgotten how impossible they were. How unlike candlelight or sunlight.

Magic, magic, magic.

The clear black sky was changing, too. An intense ribbon of green danced among the stars like cold fire. *Na Fir-Chlis!* The Nimble Men. That was what they called that phenomenon in DunBroch. Merida had seen it before, in both green and purple, but never so close. This glimmering trail seemed low enough for a bird to fly through.

A low, melodic moan began to sound, like wind through a gap in the rocks. It keened and soared from both above and below, as if the sky or the river were singing.

Quite suddenly, the space felt holy.

And then Feradach and Merida were no longer alone.

An old woman stood on the opposite bank. She was crooked and lined like an ancient tree or like the great old boulders around her. Her winter-white hair was matted into huge, strange shapes. Her weight balanced on a dark staff, twisted as a fire-blackened branch. She had only one eye, and it was the swirling dark black-and-green of the starry sky overhead.

Merida's stomach dropped right down to her feet. She might have mistaken Feradach for a mere boggart or goblin, but she couldn't mistake this figure.

What child in DunBroch didn't know the stories? The strong winds of winter were named after her breath. Her wizened likeness, her blackened staff, and her multicolored starry eye—they were stitched into one of the tapestries hanging in DunBroch's Great Hall. Bringer of rain, of life, of justice.

"The Cailleach," Merida whispered, through chattering teeth. She nearly couldn't stand from the awe of it. The goddess of winter. The goddess of *Scotland*. This was bigger magic than Merida had ever thought she might touch in her lifetime. Bigger magic than anyone in Scotland usually touched in their lifetime.

Feradach, however, sounded quite annoyed. "Oh, come on now."

Feradach, the Cailleach said, *is that any way to greet me?*

Her voice still sounded like the moaning, singsong tones Merida had heard as the god had arrived. It was both elemental and wild, nothing like Feradach's.

His voice seemed particularly human now as he complained, "I should have known you had a hand in this. The knock. That was you."

You know I have a stake in this family.

"I won't be tricked," he said.

Of course you won't. But the Cailleach sounded a little amused. *Merida of DunBroch, I see you're out late on this night.*

Merida didn't know what to say to her. Her mother had been trying to teach her how to appear respectful for the better part of twenty years, and the presence of a goddess didn't seem to improve her instincts. She tried, teeth chattering, "H-h-h-h-happy Chr-Chr-Christmas?"

I am from a time before Christmas, the Cailleach said, but she seemed sort of pleased. In any case, she raised her staff in Merida's direction. Merida thought this was just a salute until she realized her entire body was being suffused in agreeable heat. More magic! The supernatural blast dried Merida's soaking dress and hair. Her numb nose and feet warmed to vital pink. Even her thoughts thawed; she hadn't realized how disordered they'd become.

Now Merida could finally remember to curtsy. "Thank you."

Feradach, what are you doing here on this night?

"You must know they have earned my presence here, Old Woman," Feradach said, still sounding vexed. "The balance requires it."

Balance! You speak of balance. Then you must know your arbitrary destruction of that tree has earned my presence here, Young Man. What is this bargain you propose, Merida of DunBroch?

"Choose your words carefully," Feradach muttered to Merida. "She will twist them if she can—she's a wily old creature."

Merida scoffed. "*You* just wanted to kill me! Now you're giving advice?"

"I didn't *want* to kill you," he said stiffly. "It's my duty."

"*My duty* was to marry young and meek and bear lots of princes for my husband, and I didn't do that."

"And now look where you're at!"

Quick-witted Merida became hot-tempered Merida in an instant. "Are you saying that if I'd taken a husband you wouldn't be here?"

"That's not at all what I meant—"

"It certainly sounded like it!"

"If you had thought about other options a little harder, then perhaps—" Feradach said, at the same time that Merida snapped back, "*You* didn't seem willing to consider other possibilities—"

Silence!

The entire surface of the water shimmered with the Cailleach's order.

Propose your bargain, Merida of DunBroch.

Merida didn't want to take Feradach's advice, but it was

true that she'd nearly stuffed it all with her last magical bargain because she hadn't thought about all the ways her own words and desires might be used against her. What did she really need?

"Time," Merida said. "That's all I ask. I can change them. Give me a chance to fix the balance without *his* ruin."

"They have had many years," Feradach interjected. "The world keeps changing around them and they do everything they can to keep from changing with it. No matter what has come to them, they have stayed essentially the same instead of using it to grow. They must be destroyed. They—"

"You've made your stance very clear!" Merida replied.

The Cailleach's voice cut through their quarrel. *Feradach by his right could destroy the Clan DunBroch tonight, but Merida may not be wrong, either. I am willing to allow a bargain.*

"I have never made a bargain," Feradach said. After a pensive pause, he rephrased: "There has never needed to be a bargain."

And so perhaps it is time for a change, the Cailleach noted. *The bargain is this: Merida will try to prove her case: change doesn't require ruin. Feradach will try to prove his: ruin is required.*

"Who will decide?" Feradach asked. "You?"

I will only tolerate so much of your impudence, Young Man.

Feradach bowed.

During the course of the bargain, Feradach will show Merida examples of the ruin he brings about in the name of change. Merida will show Feradach the changes she brings about to avoid ruin. At the end of the bargain, I will decide who has proven their win, and nature will assert its course. You may speak of this bargain only to each other.

Merida and Feradach did not look at each other, but it was clear both intended to spend as little time speaking to each other as possible.

"How long do I have?" Merida asked.

A year.

A year! The whole *world* could change in a year, much less one family. She said, "Oh, *thank* you."

Do not thank me yet. Everyone in your family must change for you to win the bargain. Elinor and Fergus and Harris and Hamish and Hubert, and even Leezie Muireall. All or none.

Feradach made a clucking sound and Merida expected him to object, but all he added was, "And no more cheating. No more knocks." This was directed not at Merida, however, but at the Cailleach. It seemed quite a cheeky reply, but the Cailleach just looked mildly chastened.

I will not cheat. Do you accept this bargain?

"Yes," Merida said at once.

Feradach didn't look happy, but he said, "If this is what I must do, I will do it."

A little change won't hurt you, the Cailleach said, her voice again a little amused. *Now—*

She held her blackened staff up, pointing it straight at the green light twisting through the stars. Her starry eye twinkled and glimmered to match.

Magic began to move once more.

The feeling of dread trickled away from Merida's heart. The orbs began to descend back into the pools. The green light twisting through the stars faded. Feradach sighed and turned away from Merida and from DunBroch.

The Cailleach's withered mouth smiled cunningly as she began to fade away right before Merida's eyes, like the stars disappearing at dawn. Right before the gods took their leave entirely, Merida heard the Cailleach's proclamation:

Then the bargain is made.

4

THISTLEKIN

MERIDA was woken on Christmas Day by a pack of wolves.

Christmas! It seemed ridiculous for Christmas to come as ordinarily scheduled when Merida had only just been conferencing with supernatural entities the night before. Doubly ridiculous that it should arrive as it always did, with some ridiculous prank pulled by the triplets at the very crack of dawn.

Wolves!

They were not really wolves, of course. As soon as she fully woke, she knew they were dogs. A veritable pack of them, all eager to leap on her stomach and press tongues into her ear. Merida's father had three favored hunting dogs allowed to live inside the house, her mother had two, and then the castle itself had one that no one wanted to claim, as all she did was vomit and then eat what she had just vomited. Merida had never understood why the last dog was allowed in the castle, but both parents were adamant about her privileges.

"*Get off!*" howled Merida, which did nothing but get a dog tongue in her mouth and provoke some boyish sniggers from somewhere within her bedroom. The triplets. Merida's younger brothers were often little devils, particularly together. Hubert was the unthinking feet of most operations. Hamish was the uncertain hands. And Harris was the brains.

I hate those little monsters! she'd told her father once, knowing it was untrue the moment she said it.

You're thistlekin, her father had replied, with amusement. *You've all got wee spines all over you, so you stick together even if you prickle each other sometimes, too. Me and my brothers were like that too as lads.*

Thistlekin indeed! Why couldn't the triplets come up with a nicer Christmas tradition? Last year it had been a bucket of flour dumped on her head—who knew how they'd stolen it from under Aileen's watch. The year before that, three geese, all mad as Merida—who knew how they'd gotten up the stairs. And next year—who knew what it would be next year.

If there *was* a next year.

But it was hard to hold the truth of last night in her thoughts as she heard the vomity dog making some experimental vomity noises from somewhere on her bed. A clatter sounded as a whipping tail knocked something off her bedside table. Her blanket twisted as they jumped up and down. She gripped it tightly. If the dogs pulled it free, the triplets would really have it coming, since she'd hung her snow-damp dress before the fireplace to dry last night, and underneath the covers, she was currently clothed in just *Merida*.

One of the dogs stepped hard enough on her hair that her head turned along with it, just in time to see the three ginger brats standing in her doorway, wearing matching grins.

This was the final straw.

She yelled. It began as a wordless howl and resolved into: "Ayyyyyyyyyyyyyyyliiiiiiiiiiiiiiiiiiiiiiii hope you got swan turds for your gifts, you wee maggots!"

The boyish sniggers turned into proper howling laughter as the triplets took to their heels. One called "Happy Christmas!" That had to be Hamish, because surely Hubert was still laughing, and Harris would never say something as sentimental as *Happy Christmas!*

With a grumble, Merida climbed out of bed, wrapping her blanket around herself and wading through dogs. She realized there was a new member of the pack since she'd gone: A lanky, wiry hound puppy with a friendly-looking sparse beard, brindly stripes, and little, intense eyes that never focused on any one thing in particular. Unlike the rest of the dogs, he wasn't trying to lick her, but only because he already had ahold of something small in his mouth.

She asked, "Who are you now? And what have you got?"

The brindly dog made a great deal of fuss as he tried to show her the thing in his mouth while at the same time not wanting to give it up.

"I don't think this was meant to be *your* Christmas gift," Merida told him, once she wrested it free. His treasure was all that remained of a decorative wooden spoon; among the leaves carved intricately on the handle, she spied the name *Merida*. Or rather: *Merid*. The *a* had been eaten. "Unless your name's Merida, too."

The dog began to bark, the high, resentful yelps of a teen hound that felt he had been wronged.

She sighed. It wasn't that she wanted another carved spoon (somewhere along the way, her parents had gotten it into their minds she was collecting them, which she wasn't, and they'd given her so many she had to line them up on the mantel, which made it look even more like she was collecting them, which only generated more, a never-ending cycle of spoons), but she would have rather had the choice of deciding whether or not she wanted it.

Ordinarily, this would be the part of Christmas Day when she began to plot her revenge on the triplets, something to be enacted after the holiday's frantic hub-bub. Unlike the days of family festivities leading up to it, Christmas Day was a public affair. Before the sun rose, cooking and cleaning and decorating began, filling the castle with activity. Once the sun set, the castle opened itself to villagers, crofters, tacksmen, and wanderers to eat until they couldn't eat any more and dance until they couldn't stand. The DunBroch royal family told stories and made merry and generally made certain everyone had a good time as they pretended for at least one night that they, too, lived in the castle. It was ever so much work, and that was without Leezie's Christmas wedding on top of it.

And today, Merida had a family to save. She didn't have time for revenge.

"Out, wolves, out!" She shoved the dogs into the circular stairwell and slammed the door. "Michty *me*."

She also didn't have anything to wear.

A quick examination revealed that her dress was still wet. Leezie hadn't bothered to stoke the fires in the early morning as she was supposed to (she didn't bother with many of her assigned duties), so the remaining sullen embers had only made the back of the dress lukewarm. Moreover, it was filthy. The chase through the woods had needled the off-white fabric with dried thorns and barbs. Merida didn't have another one. Like her mother and Leezie, Merida wore the same garment day in and day out; formal attire simply meant putting a fancier layer over it. She had to wash it.

But of course her kettle was missing, and there was no firewood in the rack. Supplying all this was Leezie's job, but Leezie hadn't done it.

Merida just stood there for several long minutes. The process of acquiring the kettle and remembering wherever her little bit of soap had gone since her last bath and getting the fire going hot and picking all the twigs from her hair so her mother could twist it into wedding-appropriate knots that would fit beneath a wimple seemed like an impossible amount of effort. It wasn't as if she could ask for help, not without explaining how the dress had come to be in its current state, which was impossible under the terms of the bargain. How ridiculous! And she'd thought it such a simple part of the bargain last night.

Quite suddenly, Merida was furious. At Leezie for never

doing her tasks properly. At her mother for letting Leezie always get away with it, when she never let Merida get away with sloppiness. At the devilish triplets for using up too much of Elinor's disciplinary energy. At her father Fergus for not taking up the slack of shouting at the triplets so that her mother had more time to shout at Leezie. And finally, at the fire, for failing to do the only thing expected of it. Burn! Burn! How hard could it be? Merida's cheeks were doing it just fine.

"Ma'am, do you need me to stock your hearth?"

Merida jumped.

The voice had come from behind her, inside her room.

Spinning, she discovered an elegant little girl in a servant's simple dress, her arms piled with firewood and cleaning supplies.

"How'd you get in here?" Merida asked.

"Came in with the dogs, ma'am."

This girl had been in her room this entire time? It felt like a magic trick. Not magic like the Cailleach's knock on the door last night, but a little unsettling nonetheless. Merida asked, "*Who* are you?"

"Ila, ma'am." The girl managed a catlike, sinuous curtsy even with her arms full. "I was supposed to take Leezie's place."

Take.

Leezie's.

Place.

Merida felt an actual burst of physical pain at this phrase—a squeeze, right in her stomach, like her insides were being gripped. She felt betrayed by her own mind. It had tried to convince her she was upset about her filthy dress or the unready fire or even the dueling gods, when really the thing stopped her in her tracks was the knowledge that today was Leezie's wedding day. Leezie! Getting married! *Leezie!* To the *Cabbage!* It had been four years since Elinor had invited Leezie to be the castle's housekeeper. Four years since Leezie had completely failed at anything like housekeeping and had completely succeeded in weaseling her way into the Clan DunBroch's hearts instead. Now, she was like a sister to Merida. An aggravating, vague, silly sister, but a sister nonetheless, her best friend. She was only moving as far as the blackhouse village, barely a mile away, but when the rest of your family lived in a castle, it wasn't physical distance that mattered.

"Ma'am?" Ila said politely. "Is something wrong?"

Merida was uncomfortably aware she had been staring off into space, her face twisted with distress. She tried to organize it into something a bit more royal and drew her blanket robe close around her. "I'm fine. Fine! Fine. My mother hired you? Wait, is that soap you've got there?"

"Aye, and some wee tweezers, ma'am. I saw your dress and thought you might need them for the thorns. Anything else, ma'am?"

Merida, entirely unused to having a housekeeper who actually kept house, had no idea what was reasonable to ask. "Could I get some water for washing? Are you big enough to carry a bucket up these stairs?"

"I'm stronger than I look," Ila said. She transferred the

contents of her arms to the hearth in one neat movement, as if she'd been doing this sort of work her entire young life. Possibly she had. Leezie had only begun once her mother died, but most of the villagers knew their future trades from birth. "Older, too."

Merida said, "And more clever, I suppose."

"Yes, ma'am." There was no hint of a smile to indicate if Ila thought this was a joke. She really was a lot like a cat. Sly. Private. Not conniving, like Harris, just thinking secret thoughts in the way cats do.

"Of course you are," Merida said, watching Ila expertly birth a fire from embers. Amazing how cheering a good little pile of firewood was. Really, Leezie's wedding was a good thing. Last night, the Cailleach's offering of one year had felt generous. Excessive. But now, in the bright, stark light of morning, it seemed obvious that the gift of a year meant the gods were expecting much more sweeping changes than Merida had originally been picturing. Change like Leezie's wedding. Leezie was such an integral part of the household that it was possible her marriage would provoke shifts in the other family members, too. It might do most of Merida's work for her.

Yes, she was starting to feel much better. "Ila—Ila, is it? So you're helping with the feast and the wedding today, right?"

"I am, ma'am, but—"

"You don't have to call me ma'am. I just need to know how much time I have to clean my dress," Merida said. "I wonder if I could boil it. Does that sound reasonable? I thought I heard Leezie say something about boiling bed-sheets, but sometimes her ideas are not very good."

"But, ma'am—"

"Call me Merida. You can call Mum ma'am. She likes it. I suppose my dress doesn't have to be that clean, does it? Just not crunchy. The parts that stick out under the surcoat need to be clean, that's all. I need to stay focused! Lots to do before the wedding and the feast and the revenge on the triplets and all that."

"But, Merida," Ila said, managing to somehow still say "Merida" in a very "ma'am" way. "Didn't you hear, then?"

"Hear what?"

Ila looked a little apologetic. "First thing this morning, Leezie called the wedding off."

5

THEY TOOK THE FEAST

RIGHT off. Leezie had called it right off. She hadn't postponed it to a new date. She hadn't said she needed more time to prepare. She had simply called the wedding right off.

Really this was a very Leezie way to handle things. She often simply didn't do things she decided she didn't like, or decided were too hard. Merida would have lost sleep thinking of all the half-finished projects and shoddily done tasks, the unsolved puzzles and unmarried Cabbages. But not Leezie. Leezie didn't seem to get tangled in things as weightily as most people. She butterflied pleasantly from interest to interest, unfettered by obligation. Tasks, education, hobbies. And Elinor let her get away with it every time! *That's just Leezie,* she'd say. Just Leezie! Merida was always expected to do things properly and thoroughly, even if they annoyed her. Even if they'd been Leezie's job in the first place. No one ever said *that's just Merida!* if she didn't finish a task.

No, they only said it when Merida got a little hot around the collar, as if her losing her temper was the epitome of Merida-ness.

She was *not* often hot around the collar. People just never let her forget when she was.

She did feel a little hot around the collar after hearing about the wedding. She had only just come round to seeing how the wedding was actually a good thing for the bargain, and now she had to start from scratch.

Ila had seemed to anticipate Merida's frustration, because she volunteered to take care of Merida's dress while Merida "took in the news." She'd even helped Merida find something to wear until the dress was dry—a man's nightshirt, pilfered from the servants' quarters. Then she took up Merida's filthy dress while Merida gratefully got her bow and snuck outside to clear her mind with some archery practice.

The high field was frigid, even under the full sun, and the wind was too relentless for predictable shooting, but Merida could feel the ritual working its wonders on her even as she tramped across the snowy field to knock snow off the targets. She paced off her distance and turned around, fast, loosing an arrow from the quiver on her back without giving herself much time to aim. The arrow hit near the center of the target with a satisfying *whuck!* as the arrowhead dug itself into the wood. She knew these first shots would be the best. Her fingers would get too cold to feel exactly when she loosed the string, and her arm would get too tired to demand good distance from the shots, and her mind would wear out from adjusting for the wind over and over.

But that was how the archery calmed her. It emptied her mind by making it work too hard to fret. And somewhere in that calm emptiness, ideas would come from nowhere. She just had to wait long enough.

So she loosed arrow after arrow, trudging back and forth through the snow to retrieve them, making a pile of the ones too damaged to shoot again, and another pile of ones that would be serviceable again with some repair. She needed to repaint these targets, she thought. No one had touched them since she'd left, and they were faded with mildew and sun exposure. It didn't matter on that short winter day, though. She knew the targets like she knew the Brandubh board; she could play it even without the markings for game play. And she did. The only things to interrupt her focus on the exercise were the distant smells coming from the castle; even from here, the lovely, oaky scent of that night's feast roasting away was quite clear. She thought about that bread from the night before and her stomach rumbled.

There truly was nothing like nearly a year's worth of travels to make her newly appreciative of DunBroch's cooking.

That's it! Merida thought.

She should get her family out of the castle. Not forever. But for a bit. The triplets had never traveled. Leezie hadn't traveled since she came to stay with them, and it didn't seem likely that her mother, a midwife, would have traveled far beyond the village and bothies. Merida could take her to see the nuns, maybe! Elinor had been trying to get Leezie to learn to read for ages and it had never stuck, but maybe the nuns could drive it into her. Maybe Leezie would even like the convent itself; how she loved collecting religions.

Bold Hubert would like the mapmakers, surely? It was hard work traveling with them because it was a different camp each night, but he liked lots of noise and action. Shy Hamish would like the bothies and their frolicking baby calves. Surely seeing different ways of life and new landscapes and experiencing the joy and hardships of the road would have to change them all in some fashion. And Harris—well. Harris could come along on whichever journey he was least likely to sneer over. No matter. She didn't have to have all the plan in place, just the beginnings of it. She'd learned this from the mapmakers. Reach the northernmost point of this loch? Check. Verify these bridges hadn't been washed out since last survey? Check. Arrive at the pub in time for plenty of drinks? Check. One step after another.

Under the already-waning winter sun, Merida loosed another arrow.

Bull's-eye.

"Merida, there you are," Elinor said to Merida as she joined them just a short while later. "Gille Peter said something very unusual that I'm *sure* can't be true. He said he saw someone who looked a lot like you, but in a man's nightshirt and one of the old hunters' cloaks, out shooting arrows in the snow. I know it wasn't you, because that would not be the sort of thing a princess would do on a feast day, but isn't that funny?"

The Queen of DunBroch's mouth was pursed just a little. In the past, this would have been the sort of thing that caused a fight, but Elinor and Merida tried their best to meet in the middle these days. Elinor couldn't make Merida much more dignified; Merida couldn't make Elinor much more playful.

"Very funny," agreed Merida. "I'm sure it was an illusion."

Elinor patted the seat beside herself without pressing the question further and Merida sat down in her still slightly damp, soap-smelling dress without explaining herself further.

The entire DunBroch family was currently gathered in the smoky common room, as was tradition. The music room was just as warm with none of the smoke, but Merida's mother preferred the chairs and light of the common room, which meant every Christmas they sat in a romantic haze, eyes watering, enjoying a personal feast before the official public one. This year, Merida saw rashers, poached eggs in a fragrant sauce, canceled wedding buns spread with a bit of dripping butter, boar meat made into warm, onion-scented drinking broth. Tarts golden and fragrant with cheese and scraps of pastry, mushrooms simmered in broth and browned with leeks in goose fat. Preserved pears in bowls, figs soaked in whisky, even little biscuits with rabbits stamped on them.

Their private feast was always all the bits and bobs and failed experiments left over from preparing the public one. If this was the odd-ends, Merida could only imagine what the proper feast would be like later. Cranky Aileen was a wonder.

The triplets piled a plate for Merida and returned to bantering with Leezie over a game of Whips and Hounds that was missing a few pieces. It was all very like an ordinary Christmas Day, as if the wedding had never been on the schedule at all.

"Leezie," Merida said. "Wasn't he very upset?"

Leezie was dressed in some sort of gauzy flowing dress that she had put together herself. It seemed likely it had been either a curtain or a horse sheet before she'd co-opted it. She also wore an outlandish headdress, a brimming bay leaf crown studded with dried flowers and berries. She'd nearly managed to get her hair up by herself—braids followed rules, and Leezie wasn't big on rules—and just a few dusty locks escaped in an attractively messy fashion. She always looked as if she needed help, which always somehow ended up making people help her, even though she never asked for or even seemed to realize she needed it. All of this was what it meant to be Leezie. Like a fancy table, she was more decorative than useful.

That's just Leezie.

"Who?" Leezie asked. "Oh, John?"

"Yes, John!" repeated Merida. "The Cabbage! Husband to be! Master Leezie in Training! Who else? Wasn't he upset?"

"The Cabbage is fine," Merida's father Fergus boomed

45

pleasantly. "I gave him two heifers for his trouble and he was well satisfied."

"Two heifers," echoed Merida. "As in, two cows."

"One would have been rude," her father said.

Merida's father was spread enormously in his equally enormous chair, his big wooden leg on one side, his big flesh-and-bone leg on the other. He had been crowned already with a voluminous green Christmas wreath pebbled with red holly berries. He was a big person. Big beard, big body, big personality, big stories. To meet Fergus of DunBroch was to meet the hugeness of him. *You don't get to be a king by staying small,* he liked to say. In his hand was a mug of one of the best Yule traditions, whipkull, a drink made with lots of eggs, sugar, rum, and cream, and in his beard were the crumbs of one of the biscuits. Like Merida, he thought of his appearance only *after* Elinor pestered him.

"I think two was perfectly fair, especially in the middle of winter," Elinor said. The queen was perched in the chair closest to the fireplace, a place won for her by Fergus, who won everything his queen desired. Unlike her redheaded children and redheaded husband, Elinor's smooth hair was a heathered gray brown. She was quite the opposite of Fergus, all slender and precise, not a single bit louder or more unpleasant than she needed to be. Quite the opposite of Merida, too, come to think of it. She was regal perfection; hard for Merida to imagine what she could possibly need to change.

"How many cows do you think *I'm* worth?" Merida asked, voice tense.

Elinor dipped a toast soldier in her egg with regal splendor. "I pray we never have to find out."

"They'd probably give *us* cows to keep her." This was a whisper from one of the triplets, though Merida couldn't tell which. Their voices remained mostly identical even though their appearances had begun to diverge. Their personalities, too. Aileen had just complained to Merida that they were impossible to tell apart, but to Merida, they seemed distinct now more than ever.

Hubert had a big heart, and big feelings, and a big voice, like Fergus. Since Merida had left for three seasons of wandering, he'd grown nearly a hand taller and also plaited his fiercely red hair like a Norseman. He'd told her when she returned that he planned to also grow a Norseman's huge beard, and then plait *that* as well. When Merida looked too disbelieving, he assured her he'd already picked out the two blue beads he intended to use to finish the plaits.

Hamish, on the other hand, had stayed small. His fingers were delicate things, spiderlike, and colorless as a dead man's, and in the winter, if he put them against Merida's neck when she wasn't looking, she was forced to scream from the cold of them. His red hair, finer than Hubert's and Hamish's, was fluffed up high like a downy seed head. He was a very feathery sort of person altogether, and Merida had an abnormal number of nightmares about him getting broken in some way, an attribute they seemed to share.

Harris looked neither big nor small; he looked *old*. Mature. This was because he always sat very straight and because he wore his long red hair slicked back from his forehead, which made his head look smaller. Between that and his pointy features and slender shoulders, his proportions looked less like a sweet little boy ready for a hug than a conniving thirty-year-old lord come to take your dinner right out of your mouth for lack of tithing. He was also a know-it-all, which was never an attractive trait, particularly when one *did* know it all, as Harris often did. Once upon a time, he and Merida had had long, thoughtful conversations, but yesterday, when she returned, he had only seemed scornful of her attempts to start one with him.

Really, Merida thought, all the triplets had in common was the red hair and the mischief.

"It was a fair transaction," Harris murmured now, in a very Harris-y way, silently moving a piece on the board. It was a winning move, though neither of his brothers had noticed it yet. "Any bad feeling would have simply been ego."

This entire conversation had Merida feeling a little bad for the Cabbage. Lump or not, this all felt a little below the belt. "What about *love*?"

"Yes!" Leezie agreed, her voice dreamy. "What *about* love?"

"You can't just say what I said," Merida said.

"You don't have to be mad," Leezie replied, nearly dragging her sleeve through some gravy. Hubert hurriedly lifted it at the last minute (the urge to help her was so strong it extended even to the triplets, which was strong indeed). "I was agreeing with you. Why not wait for love?"

"You didn't love the Cabbage?" all the triplets roared in unison, even Harris.

With a vague smile, Leezie squished one of her wedding buns into a flower shape. "I think I might have been bored, and that's why I thought of getting married."

"I'm sure the right young man will come along and sweep you off your feet. It simply wasn't the right time," Elinor said, and something about her words made Merida realize that the queen had known all along Leezie wouldn't go through with the wedding.

What a load of tosh! Merida thought. Years ago, Merida had said she didn't want to get married at that moment, and it had caused an enormous fight, the biggest fight, in fact, that she and her mother had ever had, the one that ended up with twenty-four hours of bad feeling, magical curses, and eventually a reconciliation. Merida wasn't sorry it had happened, as it had improved their previously tense relationship immensely, but to see Leezie reaping the benefits of the chaos without having to live through it seemed very unfair.

"Those two heifers will definitely sweep the Cabbage off his feet," snickered one of the triplets. The other two triplets snickered along with him.

"Boys," Fergus said, but in that voice that meant he wished he could snicker, too.

From somewhere deeper in the castle, the dogs began to bark.

"What are they carrying on for?" Elinor mused.

This reminded Merida. She asked, "Who's that new dog, by the way? The one who ate my Christmas present?"

"Harris!" admonished Elinor. "I've told you time and again that dog needs discipline! Your father traded a ewe for that spoon!"

Merida would've preferred a ewe with MERIDA shorn into it to yet another carved spoon, but she tried to look appropriately crushed.

"I've *tried* to teach him," Harris said, a bit of a whinge to his voice. "Brionn's untrainable."

"Brionn is from good stock!" Fergus said. "Comgeall said he was pick of the litter out of Sneachda, and there's no more faithful hound than her." To Merida, he said, "Comgeall remembered how Harris liked his hounds when he visited here three years ago, can you imagine that? What a memory he has, mind like a trap! Sent Brionn this summer. What a lad."

Harris gave Merida a persecuted look that meant he disagreed with some part of this story; it was just a hint of their old secret sibling conversations.

"I'll get you another spoon," Fergus said.

"Oh, you don't have to," Merida interjected quickly. "It's not that munched. With a li'l bit of—"

"Ma'am, sir," interrupted a familiar voice. The new girl, Ila, stood in the doorway of the common room, her gaze firmly fixed on Elinor and Fergus. She still looked catlike, only now she seemed more like when cats have their ears pressed back and tails set to thrashing warily. "There are some men here to talk to you. They demand it, ma'am."

"Demand?" Merida's mother raised a courtly eyebrow. "They can wait by the bonfire in the courtyard, and we will give them an audience before the feast."

"They *took* the feast." This voice came not from Ila, but from Aileen, who had joined Ila in the doorway. There was nothing Aileen liked less than coming out of the kitchen, so the situation couldn't be good. Her hands tensely knotted and unknotted a kitchen rag as she explained, "They threw it to their dogs. Gille Peter got the castle dogs into the armory before there was a fight."

Merida, Leezie, and the triplets all looked at each other. Hubert and Leezie's faces wore two different genres of bewilderment. Hamish looked terrified, of course. Harris, to Merida's surprise, appeared merely pensive.

Violence was not shocking by itself; the kingdom, for all its pleasures, was a dangerous place, as all wild, hard places are. But violence inside the castle? Unheard of.

Merida thought, *First Feradach and then Leezie's wedding and now this! Does this count as change?*

But she knew what Feradach had said. External change wasn't the same as internal change.

Fergus rose from his chair. "Did they say who sent them?"

"The Dásachtach, sir," Aileen said. "About—"

Elinor swept the rest of the words away with her hand. "We will see them in the Great Hall. Aileen, please take the children to the tapestry room. Ila and Leezie, please let the other servants know where we are and tell them not to take orders from anyone but us."

The Dásachtach? An ominous-sounding word, Merida thought. *The Madman.*

"Come along," Aileen said in her brusque way as Elinor and Fergus went one way and Leezie and Ila another. "Up we go."

It took Merida a moment to realize that they'd counted Merida as one of the "children." After she'd been roaming about all this time, she still got lumped with the babies. Maybe she was beginning to see what Feradach meant about stagnation; they were set in their ways. Leezie canceling her wedding and returning to the way she always was, Merida returning here and becoming a child once again.

She started the opposite way down the hall.

Aileen demanded, "Where do you think you're going, then?"

Merida said, "To eavesdrop, of course."

6

PASSAGES

ONE of the wonderful things about DunBroch was that it was full of secret passages. They were in the walls. The ceilings. The floors. Some you had to crawl through. Some you had to climb to. Some had obviously been put in during the original build, behind secret shelves, and others had obviously been opportunistically added when parts of the castle were expanded over the decades. Some of them were so haphazard or small that it was difficult to tell if they were intended to be secret passages or even passages at all, but regardless, if one was not afraid of either heights or tight spaces, one could do a credible job of getting nearly anywhere inside DunBroch without leaving the walls. When Merida had been no bigger than the triplets, she'd lost many an afternoon to getting pleasantly turned around in them, emerging only late in the day to get a good talking-to from her mother, who couldn't understand how she'd managed to make herself so filthy without leaving the castle. Merida wondered if the triplets had found any of them yet. Harris seemed like the secret-passage type, but Hamish was afraid of places where things could hide and jump out at him, and Hubert wouldn't know a door unless it opened into him.

Merida used one of these smelly, ratty corridors to sneak into the wall behind the common room and eventually pop out on the third-floor balcony of the Great Hall.

The Hall was the centerpiece of DunBroch Castle, a massive, soaring space to greet fellow royals and to host massive feasts. When Merida had passed through it on her way to the common room, she'd found it nearly ready for the public celebration. Each fireplace had been set to merry blaze, as had every candle in every massive chandelier. Each table held colorful centerpieces and bowls for discarded rinds and bones. Bread and meat were piled in artful arrangements, and servants stood watchfully by to keep the dogs from stealing any morsels. Elinor's harp had been brought down from the music room to crouch in the corner, waiting for other musicians to arrive. Everything had been hushed and anticipatory in the way of all late-night feasts. It had all made Merida quite wistful; she'd wanted to be hushed and anticipatory, too, but this year was spoiled by the Cailleach's moaning voice and Feradach's oxblood-stitched gloves.

And now the Great Hall looked very different. The tables were in disarray. Some of them were turned on their sides. Food was ground into the rugs and smeared across the stone floor. And instead of a room full of revelers, there was a tense standoff. On one side were her parents in their thrones and their royal guards still festooned in Christmas wreaths and sashes. And on the other were the six armed strangers from the Dásachtach, all impressively dressed in new armor and good boots.

The intruders' big, thick-skinned dogs loudly tore the fine Christmas boar to pieces in front of one of the fireplaces, which was burning a tapestry. Her mother's winter tapestry, actually, the one with the Cailleach stitched on it.

Merida knew nothing about these men, but she hated them already.

"These men have *terrible* energy," Leezie remarked.

"Leezie!" Merida twitched with shock as she realized she'd been so focused on the scene below that Leezie had managed to kneel close beside her. How many people were going to sneak up behind her this Christmas? "What are you doing here? How did you even get here?"

Leezie made a little crawling motion with her fingers across the floor to demonstrate her technique. This disrupted her headdress, which Merida couldn't help straightening for her. Ridiculous that even in moments like this Merida could not but feel like she ought to help her. Ridiculous that even in moments like this she also noticed that Leezie had managed to drench herself in some sort of perfume, so strong that it felt like the scent alone should be loud enough to give away their hiding place. Ridiculous that even in this moment, Merida was glad that Leezie hadn't gotten married and that they were together, looking over the edge of the balcony at these usurpers, shoulders pressed together.

"What terrible timing to come on Christmas," Leezie whispered.

But Merida knew this was intentional. These men had known the Clan DunBroch would be home feasting at Christmas. The destruction of the celebration was part of their weapon.

"We're not leaving until we have a show of loyalty to Lord mac Alpin," a voice growled from down below. Only one of the Dásachtach's henchmen spoke; the others simply watched him. This spokesman had an impressive cloak made entirely of wolf tails, which made him look nearly as broad as Merida's father, and almost as wild as the wolves killed for the cloak. His voice always sounded close to a snarl. "We don't want to make things unpleasant."

"*More* unpleasant," Elinor murmured. "Surely there was a more civilized way."

Elinor looked regal and self-contained, as if these men had been invited here rather than barging in. Merida's mother hadn't lost her temper since the incident with magic and bears years before, but it didn't stop Merida from longing for her to shout at these fellows. Tear the Christmas boar away from their dogs. Throw them all out. But she knew that was impossible. DunBroch wasn't at war, and they had no standing army. The guards here in the Great Hall were probably the most that could be mustered on short notice, and even these were halfway to drunk because of the feast day.

"Lord mac Alpin has been sending requests the civilized way for months," said Wolftail. "It's you who've forced his hand by not answering."

Merida whispered to Leezie, "Have you heard anything about this?"

Leezie pouted prettily. Her cheeks were flushed. She looked becoming dressed in disaster, as she looked becoming dressed in anything even a little messy. "I saw a couple of the letters when I was cleaning your mum's room. He doesn't sign them 'the Dásachtach.' He signs them with his real name, Domnall mac Alpin. Very fancy-like. Domnall is a pretty name, don't you think?"

"Leezie."

Leezie went on in a low voice, "All his letters were about something bad coming from the south, a threat, and he's all about, you know, stopping it. He went on and on about the army he's building and how he wants everybody, every clan, that is, to prove their loyalty by sending sons for it."

Merida felt a nervous squeeze in her stomach. "So, the triplets."

The triplets had received only a very little combat training, just for fun, but on her journeys, Merida had met families who had sent even smaller boys to be trained to fight. She'd run across fully trained soldiers younger than her; boys who had had their skin and bones already replaced with steel and flint. It was bad imagining that for Hubert or Harris, but imagining soft Hamish being so hollowed out turned her stomach even more.

"Right," Leezie said. "Or you. The letters said daughters,

too, I mean. Not for the army, but for marrying into other clans, to make sure all the clans are friendly-like, I guess? United against this bad thing from the south." Leezie covered her mouth as if it might make her quieter, but it just made her a little harder to understand. "So the letters were asking after the boys, and you, and asking why your mum and dad weren't answering."

The voices were still growling back and forth down below. Merida asked, "Is what he said true? That she didn't answer them?"

"I don't know. I put them back where I found them, but later I saw them all burnt up in the fireplace."

Merida had to reluctantly admit to herself that this avoidance-of-unpleasantness was something she already knew about both her parents. Not that they had always been this way. When she was younger, her mother had been sharper: quicker to judge, quicker to act. And her father had been more nuanced: slower to joke, slower to push hurts under the rug. There had been more arguments, but also more action. Back then, the classic DunBroch solution to everything had been to react as quickly and definitively as possible, no matter how many heads one had to crack or hearts one had to break.

But somewhere along the way, a DunBroch solution had shifted to making as little a fuss as possible and hoping the problem went away. In fact, Merida could see a classic DunBroch solution visible from where they were perched: an enormous chest, sat upon a threadbare rug for easier tugging, blockaded the doorway to the armory. There *had* been a proper door there once, but snowmelt and a roof leak had conspired to absolutely ruin both door and hinges. As it had been a busy planting season and there was no pressing reason for a new door aside from keeping the dogs in the armory overnight, the family DunBroch had simply blocked the doorway with the heavy chest until better timing came along. That had been years ago.

Now, it seemed that even powerful warlords received DunBroch solutions.

Merida was uneasily reminded of Feradach's accusations the night before.

"Wait," she said, a thought striking her. "How did you know what the letters said? And _you_ were *cleaning* Mum's room?"

"I had Harris read them," Leezie admitted. "After I sounded out some of the more exciting-looking parts. And I was looking for ink for my drawing."

So that was why Harris had looked unsurprised about the intruders. In the old days, before Merida left, he would have already told her. This was exactly the kind of thing they used to tackle in their long sibling conversations.

Down below, Fergus's voice was beginning to rise. "Six men against our kitchen and an already deceased Christmas boar might have been a fair match, but I don't think you'd care for the mess if you try to press your luck now."

"We aren't looking for a fight now," Wolftail said in his gravelly snarl. "If we leave without satisfaction, more than six of us will return, though."

"You'll be leaving without satisfaction, then," Fergus roared.

Wolftail's lip curled and now even his face looked like the wolves he wore on his back. "I canna believe that we come peddling peace and loyalty and safety, kinship and companionship with your neighbors, and you don't have so much as a how do you do for us."

"Your dogs are eating my Christmas boar and my people's feast is under your feet, for what? For peace? For ego!" Fergus said.

Elinor's voice cut through the noise, although she didn't seem to have raised it in volume. "How about you give us the season to discuss and when the weather is good, we'll send word with what we decide."

"Unacceptable," Wolftail hissed. "We leave with your sons tonight or proof of your daughter's marriage betrothal with another clan, or the next time you see us, it will be with the rest of the army. That brings us no pleasure to say."

Merida could see Elinor and Fergus exchange a look she knew well. Despite the ruined feast, her parents weren't taking this seriously; they assumed the men were blustering and would forget all about DunBroch on the long dangerous journey home through the snow.

A DunBroch solution.

This was all reminding her of the DunBroch solution that had convinced Merida to go off on her travels: Spain. Spain, a far-off country an ocean away, a place supposedly so warm and dry that all the trees and animals and people looked different, having changed their ways to live with the sun's fierce attention. Elinor had decided to visit. As a young queen, she'd organized the domestic trade routes that still supplied the kingdom with both cabbages and *the* Cabbage, and now, in her middle age, she had more worldly aspirations. She would travel all the way to Spain, she decided, and return back home with a collection of foster girls to learn about Scotland.

That's my ambitious queen! Fergus had roared.

Elinor drew up plans. She studied maps. She consulted merchants, career soldiers, and Fergus on the different configurations of travelers and ships and provisions required for such an undertaking. Merida got quite excited for the trip, because of course she would go along. What an adventure.

Then, weeks of planning stretched into months, until finally Merida realized: Elinor wasn't going. She was just going to talk about going. Merida's excitement had been for nothing.

It had been the last straw, after a few too many years of DunBroch solutions.

Now, as Merida saw her parents exchange that telltale look, she knew Feradach was right about her family. He was *right*. She couldn't believe how they kept proving it again and again, in only a day's time.

But he was still wrong about the way of fixing it.

Merida squeezed her hands into fists.

"Oh, Merida," sighed Leezie. She could tell Merida was going to do something even before Merida could tell, and she had learned to accept this Meridaness, just as Merida accepted Leezie's Leezieness.

Merida stood up.

She spoke loudly so that her voice could be heard all through the Great Hall. "I'd like to propose a plan."

All faces turned up to her. Elinor's face went immediately worried. Fergus simply looked like someone had stuffed bees in his cloak. The Dásachtach's men looked mystified, as if watching someone with bees stuffed in their cloak.

Wolftail shielded his eyes. "Who's up there?"

"I am Merida of DunBroch," she called down. She used her most royal, confident voice. "The princess you'd like to see married. I can tell you why my parents will not agree to marry me off, even though it would make their life easier. Many years ago, they agreed I could choose my own hand, and so they won't ask me to marry against my wishes. And the triplets are simply not prepared for battle, so that's right out, too. But if you're truly here about loyalty rather than coercion, then we're in agreement! DunBroch believes in kinship, as you can see."

She gestured to her parents, who arranged their faces to look less like taxidermied animals and more like royalty. They inclined their heads.

Wolftail now lowered his head and bunched his cloak on his shoulders in such a way that his hackles appeared to bristle. "Then do you have a counter proposition?"

"The goal is community, right? Family?" she said. "Well, I've been traveling all over DunBroch this year and I'm more than willing to travel further in the name of community! If it's acceptable to you, I'll go to three territories on diplomatic passages to improve relationships with our neighbors."

The same plan that she had decided on earlier that day. How wonderful it would be to use one solution to fulfill another. Cross the angry warlord off one list, cross the frightening gods off another.

Wolftail growled, "That will not satisfy Lord mac Alpin. Travel's not enough. *We* traveled here on a diplomatic passage, after all, and I think you'll find we're no more friendly with DunBroch than when we arrived, are we?"

Merida went on, "But that's not all. At the end of the journeys, I'll choose one of the kingdoms to join. Not as a wife, mind you, but as family. As kin."

Elinor's mouth dropped regally open in shock. Fergus went even redder. Leezie said, "Oh, Merida!" again. The Dásachtach's men murmured among themselves.

Eventually, Wolftail said, "Lord mac Alpin will never believe that is as tight a union as marriage."

Merida whispered, "Stand up, Leezie."

Leezie stood. The men blinked in surprise at the sudden appearance of another girl, and with even more surprise as Leezie waved at them. They were taken aback, as people always were, by her Leezieness. She was still in her festive headdress and she still looked as if she could use some help.

Merida put a firm arm around Leezie's waist. "This is Leezie Muireall, daughter of Jonet. She's been with us just four years, since her mum died, but she's my sister. Not by blood, but in every other way. My heart near to broke when

63

I found out she was getting married, because we're that close. I'd live and die for her same as any of my brothers."

"Really?" Leezie said. "Ah, thanks."

Merida went on. "Kin bonds have to be won, not just stitched, or they can be snipped just as easily. Give me a chance to go see which family might have me, and who I might have."

The men looked at Leezie and Merida. They looked at Fergus and Elinor. They looked at Wolftail. In the background, they could all hear the sounds of Harris's dog Brionn whining and barking his high youthful bark and scratching at the other side of the chest. Merida's cheeks burned with embarrassment over the shoddiness of the blockade in front of the door, but she hoped they just interpreted it as passion for her proposal.

"And how will we know of your progress?" Wolftail asked finally.

It was working. They were considering it. Merida said, "I'll send word from each territory, and your lord will have his proof."

Wolftail's hackles were lowering. He snarled, "This is a strange place."

"Merida's proposal is more than fair," Elinor said. She'd returned to her usual self-contained form, with no evidence that she'd ever been out of step with her daughter. "Do you accept it?"

"He'd be bloody mad to not," Fergus said. "Is this about peace or isn't it?"

Wolftail shrugged. "Yes. The bargain is made."

7

THE FAMILY DUNBROCH

AFTER Wolftail's men had taken their leave with their big ugly fighting dogs and the rest of the boar, Aileen's staff immediately scurried back into the Great Hall to begin cleaning the mess. Merida remained there on the balcony, her hands pressed into the railing, her heart thudding in a way it hadn't been during all of her speech. Leezie thoughtlessly rubbed her hands against her cheeks over and over as if she was trying to warm them, her big eyes vague but distressed. Across the Great Hall, Merida saw the triplets on the opposite balcony, looking down at the castle staff doing their work. Hamish looked pale. Hubert had a wooden sword in his hand and kept smacking it off balcony supports. Harris simply watched Merida.

So this was their Christmas. Merida felt hollowed out. She didn't think she could bear seeing her parents making light of this and sweeping it all under the rug. Not after the night and day she'd just had.

"Leave it!" Fergus roared suddenly.

Everyone in the Great Hall stopped. Merida's father stood in the middle of the disarray, his great big arms hung down by his great big sides.

"Fergus, what are you about?" Elinor asked.

Fergus mashed one big fist into one big palm. "I won't have it. It's Christmas. It's Christmas, and I won't have everyone's Christmas ruined by those pups. Is all the feast on the floor?"

"First courses, sir," Aileen said. "And half the meats. I held back some for the next courses."

Fergus stretched a hand to her as if revealing a magic trick. "She held back some for the next courses. There's still a feast. You see?"

"Yes, sir, but the villagers have all been driven away," Aileen said. "And what's left is a hodgepodge, not suited for tabling—"

But Elinor had brightened, all her confusion disappearing. She smoothed her hair around her veil and knocked invisible wrinkles from her dress. "Fergus, my love, of course you're right. Aileen, I know this isn't the feast you'd imagined. But please take the staff to the kitchen and pack up everything that's left for travel."

"Yes, ma'am."

"Gille Peter, ready the horses!" Fergus howled.

Merida and Leezie exchanged a look.

"Are we going to battle?" Leezie asked.

"With biscuits?" Merida said. Although as soon as she said it, she realized that going to battle with biscuits was the only way she could imagine DunBroch doing it.

"Girls!" Fergus shouted up. "Stop your havering! Get down here! Boys! Down! We're going out!"

And just a little while later, the family DunBroch were riding out into the frigid, windy winter night with much festivity, as if they hadn't just been tousling with a warlord's henchmen. The horses had been decked with all the bells and boughs that could be scavenged from the destroyed decorations in the castle, and with every step they took, they jingled and pealed. Pack ponies ambled behind them with laden baskets slung over their withers. The triplets sang carols as they rode on their matching geldings, for once using their energy to harmonize beautifully instead of cause chaos. Fergus had even allowed Leezie to quickly braid holly stalks with the pokiest bits trimmed off into his beard, and the berries gleamed red-red-red against his russet beard. ("The berries represent good fortune for the season," Leezie had told him. "Do they now?" Fergus asked. "Probably," she replied.) On all sides, Fergus's men-at-arms carried torches and lanterns that lit the night.

They were taking the Christmas feast to the blackhouse village. All the potential partygoers had fled from the potential trouble the Dásachtach's men represented, and now the king and the queen were going to reassure their subjects the danger had passed and make sure they still got the celebration they'd been looking forward to.

Merida couldn't believe how different the night felt from just an hour before; she couldn't believe how different it felt from the night twenty-four hours before. There was no wild fear or catastrophe threading this chilly blackness. Instead it was an intimate, convivial party bolstered against the cold.

As they rode, Elinor came alongside Merida and said, "My brave, hot-tempered Merida. What a wild plan. You will not have to go live in those places, though. Your father and I will come up with a solution for this bully before that."

Merida basked in her mother's words and wished she believed them.

"Ardbarrach," Fergus said, riding his big warhorse Sirist up alongside them both, the breastplate jingling merrily. "That's my suggestion. It's just a day's ride. Colban was trained there and he'd be happy to go back for a little visit. They run a tight ship, Ardbarrach does, and they'd be proud to show you how they do things. You can nip over there even before the weather turns if you're crafty about it, give you something to do in these dark months."

Good, Merida thought. The sooner this got underway, the better.

"I was thinking of taking a triplet along with me," she said. "You know, get one of them out of your hair for a bit."

Elinor glanced over at the triplets, who managed to jostle their horses against one another even as they sang in harmony. "A kind thought! Hubert would like Ardbarrach."

"Yes he would," boomed Fergus. "What about Caithness for the next?"

"Oh, no," Elinor said, "Caithness is so backward. What about Kinlochy?"

"Oh, Kinlochy!" Fergus sang the word. "Fair Kinlochy town, how I miss thee, many a month, it's been since I've seen—They have that handsome fella just about Merida's age. Would make a fine match!"

"Fergus," Elinor admonished.

"I'll pretend he didn't say that part," Merida said. "Is it far?"

"A few days, but this big father of yours would be glad to escort you on the journey to grand old Kinlochy to see old friends," Fergus said.

That was exactly what Merida wanted to hear. "And where for the third trip, then?"

Fergus and Elinor batted words back and forth. *Strathclyde? Carrick? Buchan? Fife? Lennox? Mull?*

Merida could tell they were getting into the fun of it, imagining the shape of all these possible trips. She knew better, too, than to expect them to follow through with their enthusiasm. That was all right, though. That was her job. All she needed at first was their cooperation.

"What about Eilean Glan?" asked Fergus.

Elinor went very still.

For a few strides, she was a carved statue of a queen, face unmoving. Merida stared at her, because it had been a very long time since she had seen her mother completely unable to put together a composed reply. Eilean Glan. *The clear island.* Merida had never heard of it before, but it clearly meant something to her mother.

"We don't have to decide tonight," Elinor said eventually, and then, after another long pause, found her gentle smile again. "Your quick thinking served us well, Merida. And yours too, my big bear." She patted Fergus's arm. "The Clan DunBroch! I am glad we are still sharing our good fortune and cheer."

Without another word, she steered her horse away to the triplets. Merida heard her voice rise to join their harmony, and they kept it up right as they rode into the blackhouse village. The horses towered in comparison to the low stone buildings hunkered against the hills. It seemed quite abandoned, every tiny window and door shuttered tightly against the wind, but Fergus laughed his huge laugh, full of the joy of riding out with his family and the holiday, despite everything, and bellowed into the cold air, "Come out for your gifts, come out for your gifts!"

The villagers slowly began to emerge. Initially they appeared with weapons in hand—so Wolftail had been here first, Merida thought—and then, as they realized it was the family DunBroch, with babies in arms instead.

"Sorry for the scare," Elinor gently told mothers as she handed out cakes and meat from the baskets.

"Thank you for your service," Fergus roared at fathers, handing out oats and salt and candles.

"These are my favorite," Merida added, giving the children some of Aileen's ginger biscuits. "They bite you back."

Through it all, the triplets kept singing lustily as they threw candies at other boys, and eventually the villagers joined in, too, with the familiar old songs. As the stars shone hard and cold above, Gille Peter and the others put out wood and set the big Christmas bonfire alight at the end of the main street. They'd brought enough timber to burn a bonfire straight through to the late winter dawn, and soon, dozens of people were gathered around it, singing and laughing, voices raised high and joyful, all of it a bulwark against the dark and cold and loneliness and violence.

Magic, magic, magic.

A very different type of magic than the Cailleach's or Feradach's. A magic that Merida liked an awful lot. The mundane, generous magic of her family.

She liked *them* an awful lot.

For all her complaining and frustration, they were still the marvelous family DunBroch, with all their messy and passionate affection for each other and the world. Three journeys to strange places? Merida would do three *hundred* journeys if that was what it took to save them.

As they gathered around the equitable Christmas bonfire as usual, the experience changed only by the location, she wondered at how, in the year to come, she would know the difference between stagnation and tradition. Was it possible to change the parts that were bad and keep the parts that weren't? Was she in danger of losing moments like this by putting her family on a different path?

But in truth, any fear she felt about the future was feeble before the roaring bonfire and roaring voices. Uncertainty was burned to bits, drowned out by harmony.

That was the point of this celebration, wasn't it?

Hope.

8

THE FIRST JOURNEY

"**I** THINK we should make the Ardbarrach trip a Hogmanay visit," Merida announced the following morning, over a breakfast of yet more canceled-wedding buns. Elinor was writing away in her little journal while the triplets threw sticks into the smoky fire to make it smoke even more. Merida hadn't slept a wink all night with the two bargains hanging over her and she was determined to get started on the plan as quickly as possible. "We can be mummers!"

She would have been annoyed to give up Hogmanay for anything less important than this. Hogmanay in DunBroch was a splendid time, a noisy end to the Yule season. Like Christmas, Hogmanay sometimes involved presents, but it also involved balls of things set on fire and mummers dressing in heavy masks or donning antlers and blowing bull horns and springing suddenly out at doorsteps singing songs and asking for money for the poor or food for their supper. Some people preferred Hogmanay to Christmas Day, especially the sort of people who liked other people jumping out at them and saying *oodley-oodley-oodley*.

"*Yes!*" said Hubert. He was often the person jumping out and saying *oodley-oodley-oodley*.

"No," said Elinor. "You are a *princess*, Merida. You will not be going in costume like a *jester*. Also, that's only four days from now, which isn't nearly enough time to get a letter out announcing your visit, explaining why you're there, telling them why they should take you on. It must be a lovely, cordial letter. There are ways these things are done. Boys, get out of here, you're driving me mad. Go find your father."

The triplets sprang from the room, shouting *oodley-oodley-oodley* (except for Harris, who never shouted if he could help it). Merida hadn't thought they were making much noise, but it was true that the common room felt absolutely silent in comparison to just a few seconds before.

"It's enough time if it goes out by pigeon," Merida insisted. "If we go now, it'll be more likely to be dry. You know it'll start to be wet and snowy again in a few weeks. And after that's the thaws. Sooner's better, surely."

"Ah, Merida, these trips don't come together quickly!" Elinor said, as Ila stole into the room and cleared away her plate. "Thank you, Ila."

"Of course, ma'am," Ila replied. "Your handwriting's beautiful, ma'am."

"Oh, this is just a little list," Elinor said, but she looked pleased with the compliment. "Just to put my thoughts together. I can help you practice sometime, if you like."

"Ma'am, I'd be very grateful, if it's not out of place."

Merida was feeling quite cross. She could tell that her mother was trying to get ahold of the plan. Elinor and a plan was like a dog discovering a well-seasoned carcass. Elinor picked it up and put it down and worried at its joints and dug a little hole and sort of nudged it in like she was going to bury it and then she picked it back up again because maybe she would toss it around in the sun for a little longer, no, Merida, don't touch it, it's *mine, mine*—

"Mum," Merida broke in. "I've been traveling all over. I know how long things take."

"Not as a royal! You're representing DunBroch. Which means you can't do things hastily! They should be done properly!"

Ila was still admiring Elinor's handwriting, which gave Merida an idea. She said cunningly, "You can make us one of your lists. Everything we need to do and bring before we set out. We'll make sure we do the whole thing, beginning to end. I'll be hasty, and you'll be proper, and together, we'll be proper hasty."

Elinor sighed. "Fine, Merida, you're impossible. But I'll need your father to dictate the letter for me—he's the one who knows the lord there. You'll have to have a hand-maiden if you're going out as a princess; Leezie will have to do. And you're *not* going as a mummer. And stop hovering. I'm finishing my breakfast before I do anything. If your mind needs something to keep it busy, perhaps you should go practice that embroidery you've left for the better part of a year."

Slim chance of that. Merida would sooner stitch her own fingers than the blasted embroidery up in the tapestry room. Instead, she took her bow and went out to the high field to shoot at targets. Her mind was wheeling. It was truly sinking in that these trips were happening, and moreover, that they weren't just adventures. Yes, her mother had said they'd find a solution to the Madman before it came to that, but Merida wasn't naive. She knew she had to expect the worst. Was she serious about moving to another kingdom? She had to be. *Some storms move no rooftops.*

Ugh. How was it that Feradach's words kept finding her long after he'd said them? She was moving rooftops. She was moving herself.

Partway through her shooting session, Fergus came out to shoot with her. He was far more hopeless at it than she was, because his strength was with the sword and the spear, but she was touched by his presence. For quite a while they practiced alongside each other in silence, as the short winter day hurried on toward night.

"So, Ardbarrach for Hogmanay," Fergus boomed finally, in a casual sort of way, like they were just talking about the weather.

"That's the plan," Merida answered back, just as casual. She wanted to ask why Elinor had gotten so quiet after he'd mentioned Eilean Glan, but she knew this would drive her father right back to the castle. She and her father didn't really have meaningful conversations these days; the closer they got to real feelings, the more uncomfortable both of them became. So instead, she said, "Did you send off the letter?"

75

"I dictated it to your mother," he said. "I asked them to take you because you were a handful and you were also eating us out of house and home."

"Dad."

"I said 'please,' too."

"That's better."

Merida felt quite desperate for him to say something else, although she didn't know what, exactly, that something else was. What she wanted was to talk with him about the intense combined weight of the bargain with gods and this new bargain with the Madman, but the first subject wasn't allowed because of magical rules, and the second one wasn't allowed because of father-daughter rules. So she just asked, "Will I like Ardbarrach?"

Fergus shot a few more arrows off into the darkening brush. None of them were anywhere near the target. Finally, instead of answering directly, he said, "It's no DunBroch. But what is, really? Hubert will be wild for it, I'm sure. This bow is useless. Look how it does whatever it wants. I think it's bent. It's broken in some way, obviously."

Merida reached for the bow and he handed it over with a rueful smile. It was a lovely bow, in much better shape than Merida's, because it was used less. Unlike hers, with all its carvings worn to smooth invisibility, his bow was still etched up and down with a beautiful stylized pattern of flowers and bears. It was sized for her tall father and not for her, so she stepped up on a stump so that its height had somewhere to go. Then she nocked an arrow.

"Would you like to place a wager where you think this arrow's gonna go, then, Dad?" she asked, with a wicked smile, testing the tension of the string.

"I'm no fool," Fergus said. "I know where it's gonna go."

"With this wind, you can't know anything for sure," Merida said. She nearly said *With this breath of the Cailleach* instead of *with this wind*, and then she realized that this casual phrase she'd said a hundred times before felt dangerously close to talking about the bargain.

Her smile had slipped. She put it back up again, but she knew Fergus had seen it.

"When it's you, I'm sure you hit your target," he said. "Wind or no wind. Poor target. I shed a tear."

Merida felt the breeze on her cheek and against the arrow's tip, watched the way it shook the empty branches at the end of the field, and waited until it stilled just a bit. Then she loosed the arrow.

Thwuck!

"Bull's-eye," Fergus observed. Then he paused. "It's a brave thing you're doing, Merida. All this."

Merida looked over at him, her heart pattering. It was what she wanted. Well, it was part of what she wanted. She wanted him to talk about how she was the one to stand up and make a counterproposal instead of him. She wanted him to talk about how Elinor had gone quiet at the mention of Eilean Glan. She wanted to hear him promise that she wouldn't have to move anywhere if she didn't want to. She wanted him to ask *Did you make a bargain with a death god?* so that even though she couldn't answer, she could just look at him heavily and he'd know all the things she had to bear for the year to come.

But Fergus just blustered, "Now give me back my bow before it forgets everything it just learned from you."

And just like that, their meaningful conversation was over. But Merida tucked away the tenderness of his expression in her memory for easy access later.

Just a few days later, only slightly behind schedule, they set out for Ardbarrach. Either way, it was a good, bright January day. The sky was beautiful and high above them, with thin, icy clouds that looked like interlacing fish scales. The landscape was frozen so that nothing moved. Ice coated every single branch so that it glimmered. Every time the horses put a hoof down, it made a delicious crunch through the thin snow.

The hope was to arrive before dark. This was not the most dangerous season for wolves, but it was the most dangerous season for going to sleep and waking up frozen to death. Traveling only when the weak winter sun was out and being tucked away from the weather before the wild winter night wind kicked up was important.

It felt glorious to be out of the castle. Merida couldn't tell if this was because it felt good to finally be doing something about the bargain, or if it was simply because she'd gotten so used to traveling that staying in one place had started to feel odd. Either way, it was startlingly satisfying to be on the road again.

Unfortunately, they were very slow.

On horseback were Merida (on the Midge, the bitey young mare she'd been gifted when she began her travels last spring) and Gille Peter, one of Fergus's oldest guards (on Angus, Merida's former horse, who had been pulled out of retirement as no other horse was tall enough for Gille Peter). Elinor's two ponies, Humor and Valor, pulled the Friendly Box (which was what the triplets called DunBroch's old pony cart), which carried Hubert, Leezie, and another of Fergus's guards, Colban. Following behind was Harris's terrible spoon-eating dog, Brionn, as he'd shot out after them and no amount of calling would bring him back into the courtyard.

The Midge was plenty fast. Too fast, really, getting her and Merida into and out of scrapes at high speed. Angus wasn't half bad either, even though he was quite ancient. His long legs covered a lot of ground when they needed to.

The problem was the Friendly Box. It was designed for dry roads, not snowy paths. They had to stop often to give it a good shove through snowy mud, or take a longer route to ford frozen creeks. But the cart was necessary because of Colban, who was so old and crispy that he had to be cradled to keep from shearing into old bits of Scottish bone. Of all the people to choose as escorts! "He knows the way," Fergus had said, "because he was trained there."

("Decades ago," Hubert had whispered.

"Centuries," Merida had corrected.)

Gille Peter was slightly younger than Colban, but he was still so old that his words had died long ago and now all that came out of his mouth were nonsense ghosts. He was not there for his oratory skills, however. Fergus had decided he was the best escort for protection.

("From *what*?" Hubert had asked.

"Frivolity," Merida had replied.)

Like most DunBroch solutions these days, they were solutions of either convenience or emotion, rather than practicality.

They were never going to make it there by nightfall at this rate. Merida had only recently nearly frozen to death herself and was not at all eager to do it again, but no one else seemed to share her urgency. Gille Peter moved with the ponderous grace of the extremely tall. Leezie was regaling Hubert with tales of some island saints and their daily rituals, and he was having a grand old time listening to stories about demons in milk pails and monks in barrels. Colban did not seem to notice the passage of time at all; he had to be shaken awake to ask for directions.

Only Merida and the Midge fretted as the journey used up the short day.

Eventually, Merida lost her patience, told the others she was scouting the road ahead, and let the Midge quicken her step.

She hadn't gotten very far away before she heard a voice from deep in the snowy trees:

"It won't work."

The Midge spooked mightily at the sound. Merida kept her seat with some effort and then looked over her shoulder.

Feradach.

Feradach stood among the trees, his cloak dark, his mane of hair bright. His gloves were firmly on his deadly hands. He did not look anywhere near as uncanny as he had by moonlight. His cheeks were reddened from the cold like any mortal's would be, and his breath puffed out in visible clouds just like Merida's. In this clear light, she saw that the broad furred shoulders of his cloak were dusted with powder, and that there were footprints through the snow behind him, as if he had arrived here by ordinary means. If Merida had not seen him at their first meeting in a very different context, she would have simply thought he was a young man on a journey, just like them.

And yet her heart was pounding dance steps against her ribs.

It seemed unfair that just the sight of him sent her body straight back to how it had felt the night of the bargain. Liquid terror and dread. Not magic. Just ordinary fear. Merida, annoyed by this unbidden response, told her body to calm down. It didn't, so instead, she told Feradach, "That's very rude! To just . . . appear!"

Feradach bowed his head apologetically. "I should have announced myself. Good afternoon."

"How long have you been following us?" Merida let the Midge sidestep uneasily away from him; it let her keep her eyes on him while still putting a little distance between them. "You told the Cailleach to not cheat; you can't cheat, either."

"I'm not here to cheat. I just wanted to see what you were doing."

"We're out for a nice walk." To demonstrate, Merida urged the Midge down the path back toward the others.

Feradach strolled alongside. "A nice walk with your brother and foster sister, far from home."

Merida had to think about it for a moment before realizing he meant Leezie. "How far is far, really. What do you mean it won't work, anyway?"

"Changing other people. You can only change yourself." Feradach watched the Midge stumble into some fallen branches; she spooked and had a bit of a temper tantrum until her legs were free. "And you should be. Working on yourself. Saving yourself."

Merida did her best to look regal as she maintained her balance on the shivering Midge. "You're always full of advice."

"Just the truth." Feradach tilted his head. "What's your plan?"

"Like I would tell you!"

"What could it hurt?" he asked. "I'm not going to stop you. I don't need to. I will win this bargain, and not by tricks; DunBroch is winning it for me just by continuing as it is."

Merida, who had previously felt quite annoyed by her family, now felt very defensive of them. "And yet who's in that cart up there? Two people who haven't traveled this far away from the castle in ages!"

"Change comes from the inside, not the out," Feradach reminded her, not unkindly.

"Hubert's never seen another kingdom," Merida said. "He's only ever been as far as the blackhouse village."

"What if he changes in a way you don't like?"

The Midge pranced some more; Merida had gotten so annoyed with Feradach that she'd tightened the reins, and now the mare felt persecuted. Merida loosened her grip on the bit. "Now you're just being contrary. Don't you have a village to ruin somewhere else?"

"Yes," Feradach said. "Actually. Are you going to Ardbarrach?"

"Please don't tell me that's where you're headed!"

"No, but neither are you," he said. "You're going the wrong way, did you know?"

Now Merida was completely flummoxed. She pulled the Midge to a complete halt. Both girl and horse stared angrily at Feradach. Merida demanded, "Why should I believe you?"

"Again, I have no need of tricks to win," Feradach said. "And it would bring me no valor to win just because you've frozen to death on this road only a few weeks in. Don't believe me. Ask your guardsman."

"Ho! Fanfarich tol de parsesh!"

Both Merida and Feradach turned to see Gille Peter and the horse Angus picking their way slowly through the brambles the Midge had dashed through helter-skelter. Gille Peter's words, as ever, were all squashed into some-thing else, everything in an old dialect lost to time. "Drownt mootin dar!"

"This is about to be odd," Feradach warned Merida in a low voice.

"How do you figure?"

"Everyone sees me as something different," Feradach

said. "I don't know how you see me, but he will see me as something else."

Merida frowned. "Like, as a bear or something?"

"No, just—"

"Whush dooyer mutter widish worm!" Gille Peter said, with some suspicion, as he finally rode right up to them on Angus. Merida noticed with some anxiety that their shadows, already long because Gille Peter and Angus were tall, were getting very, very long indeed as they lost even more daylight hours.

"I mean no harm," Feradach said respectfully.

"Whart bees nish haften?" Gille Peter demanded.

Feradach looked amused. "Your companion tells me you are going to Ardbarrach. Are you headed by way of the old oak copse?"

There was the briefest of pauses, and then Gille Peter's face went completely white, and Merida knew that Feradach had been telling the truth. Gille Peter *had* forgotten their way.

In a smaller voice, Gille Peter admitted, "Ah ahmosh toot me all quegg ittoo flop."

"Could have happened to anyone," Feradach said, with a glance at Merida. It was not quite a *told you so*, but it was very, very close.

"Kweet fannish!" Gille Peter replied. "Goch shave, yung wonk."

"I'm not as young as I look, but I appreciate the thought. Do you think you know your way from here?"

Gille Peter put on a brave face. "Narf enkerly . . ."

"If you'll allow me," Feradach said, looking at Gille Peter but clearly speaking to Merida, "I can describe a more direct route that might get you there before nightfall if you are quick about it."

He theatrically clasped his two gloved hands together, letting his cloak partially fall over them, displaying his intention to let them touch nothing but one another. Merida regarded his carefully contained hands and his earnest expression. She didn't want to be a fool and trust a god who was doing his best to win the right to kill them all in a year. But Gille Peter obviously could not be trusted to put them back on the right path in time.

"Fine," Merida said, in such a bratty tone that Gille Peter looked at her with surprise. She took a deep breath and said, in a more princess-like fashion, "That would be welcome."

Feradach and Gille Peter engaged in a brief descriptive conversation, which ended up with Feradach drawing several diagrams in the dirty snow and Gille Peter drawing several others in the air.

"Coweron, Merida!" said Gille Peter. "Lecket todders."

With brisk enthusiasm he set off back toward the others.

But Merida did not immediately follow. Instead she kept the Midge dancing in place long enough to narrow her eyes at Feradach, who once again stood quietly in the snow, hands folded inside each other, tucked away inside his cloak, looking for all the world just like an ordinary young man, albeit one deep in a vast forest in the middle of nowhere.

She said, "I would say thank you, but I'll believe it when I see Ardbarrach."

Feradach shrugged.

"And stop following us," Merida added. "It's off-putting."

Feradach shrugged again.

"And stop shrugging," Merida finished. "Say something."

"Enjoy Ardbarrach," he said.

9

THE ROAD TO ARDBARRACH

MERIDA had given quite a bit of thought to how the triplets might change. Before the bargain, she would have thought growing up was change enough. Merida felt as if her childhood had been one massive change after another. First her father had lost his leg to a bear—a bear! Then the triplets had come along after years of her being an only child. Then the fight with her mother over marriage, the tousle with a witch. Nursemaid Maudie moving off to the village. Leezie coming to stay with them. The trip to the shielings with her mother.

But she supposed the triplets had had a very different childhood than she. They were over a decade younger; Fergus and Elinor were different people. Plus there was the sameness of them, the threeness of them, the way they shared a life as "the triplets" instead of as Hubert, Hamish, and Harris. *Where are the babies,* Elinor would say, *someone should take them on a walk. The triplets need to get some writing practice in. Let's get the triplets their dinner and then we'll do our dinner after. Merida, show the triplets how to play Whips and Hounds.* The triplets' room, the triplets' hobbies, the triplets' schooling.

They were always being compared to each other. Always bouncing off each other. Always finishing each other's sentences, each other's pranks. If they had any specific traits, they were always expressed in relation to one of the other boys. Hubert was louder than Harris. Harris was cleverer than Hubert. Hamish was sweeter than Harris. So on, so forth. Maybe just spending some time being one boy instead of part of a three-headed monster would be enough.

Her father had suggested Hubert for this journey because he thought he'd like Ardbarrach, and Merida was glad, in retrospect, to have him as her first task. Hubert was the easiest of all the triplets. Not because he was the best behaved—that would have been Hamish—but because he was the most like her. Neither was good at focusing on a task for too long unless it was physical, like Merida shooting arrows or Hubert banging nails into boards. Neither minded if things were messy or loud; in fact, sometimes messy and loud made it easier to think. Both were happy to go wandering in the woods by themselves but also wanted to return home to fiddle music and good company.

It meant Merida could almost certainly predict how Hubert would feel about Ardbarrach because of how *she* felt about it.

And this was how they felt:

"Whoa," said Hubert and Merida in the same breath.

Merida thought she'd traveled quite a bit this year, but she hadn't seen anything that looked like Ardbarrach.

Feradach had been as good as his word, because even with the pony cart slowing them down, they arrived at the stronghold only about an hour after dark. The landscape had slowly transformed from DunBroch's rolling, snowing terrain into a snow-free, colorless landscape, empty of trees. The path had changed from an arduous single track to a wide, beaten road broad enough for three carts to travel wheel to wheel. When Merida had been with the mapmakers, they had come across only one road like this: the main trade road that led clear on down to Gowrie. It was the only one traveled by enough feet to keep it that bare and wide.

But this road was even more impressive. It had clearly been scraped and graded to perfection. Water did not pool on this road; it ran off to the edges, where channels wicked it away out of sight. This road had not been built. It had been engineered.

Ardbarrach stood at the end of it, and like the road, it did not seem built, but rather engineered. The fortress was as unlike Castle DunBroch's soft, ivy-covered form as one could imagine. DunBroch's eroded stones seemed to have been around for ages; Ardbarrach's sharp, clean walls had clearly been built in this generation. DunBroch's towers were round and organic; Ardbarrach's were sharp and geometric. DunBroch's green banners were tattered and worn; Ardbarrach's red and gold were crisp and certain.

Candles glowed welcomingly in DunBroch's mismatched windows. Ardbarrach's narrow arrow slits were dark and brusque.

"It looks ugly," Leezie said from the cart, her voice shivering with the rest of her.

"It looks strong," Hubert said.

"Es veffid so," confirmed Gille Peter.

Most importantly, it looked like not freezing to death. The temperature had dropped precipitously as soon as the light was gone, and the wind had doubled, tripled, quadrupled. There were no hills or trees to interrupt it, so it boxed Merida's ears without pause. Her cheeks actually hurt from her hair striking them with each gust. It was a deadly cold night.

Because of the lateness of the hour, Merida worried they wouldn't be able to get anyone's attention from outside the featureless wall, but the gate opened smoothly as soon as they approached, and behind it guards stood at the ready as if they had been waiting all along. Each guard was so identically uniformed and positioned that Merida couldn't tell a difference between them in the flickering torchlight. Beyond them, she saw an open courtyard so huge and bare that its walls were lost in the dark. Everything was as flat and even and perfect as the road that had led there. Not even a shadow could be misaligned in this place.

"Merida and Hubert of DunBroch?" said the closest guard, as Merida dismounted to approach.

"Yes," Merida said, surprised.

"Please wait a moment while we get an escort for you and your men. We apologize for the wait."

The guard pulled a cord, and in the wall above him, a bell chimed three times. From somewhere further inside the castle, a matching bell chimed with precisely the same rhythm. From even farther away, Merida heard the same sound echo once more. There might have been even more after that that she simply couldn't hear.

A moment later, more soldiers appeared, and a pack of page boys, and then some maidservants. Each class of person was neatly and identically dressed so that it seemed to be one soldier, copied many times; one page boy, copied many times; one maidservant, copied many times.

Hubert looked at Merida and simply mouthed *Wow.*

Wow indeed.

In just minutes, Merida and her party were entirely seen to. The Midge and Angus and the ponies were untacked and unhitched and taken away. Colban was tipped out of the Friendly Box, and he and Gille Peter and Hubert were bundled off to the men's barracks. A good effort was put into catching Brionn, although eventually they gave up. Merida and Leezie were whisked to a room with two narrow beds, an inch of candle, and a simple dinner of bread and meat; presumably Hubert and the men had a similar meal in the barracks. If this had been DunBroch, everyone would have still been trying to figure out what to do with their guests, even if they *had* been expecting them, and they probably would have all ended up eating a dinner of leftover sugared Christmas plums in front of a fire and telling stories until dawn.

Was this how most castles ran? So far, Ardbarrach was even more efficient than the nuns Merida had stayed with over the summer, which was saying something. The sisters liked a good schedule, but they also liked talking, so living with them had been less like a military drill and more like living with a flock of coordinated, noisy birds.

Three soft bells rang, and the maidservant who'd brought their dinner warned, "There is no unnecessary talking after the candles are out; ring a bell if there is an emergency."

And then they were alone.

In the last of the candlelight, Leezie's eyes were heavy-lidded. "This was the longest day somehow."

"We came a pretty long way," Merida replied. "I wonder what this place will look like in the morning. Do you think they all look the same when the sun's out?"

"I'm not in the mood for scary stories," Leezie said. She yawned messily, looking suspiciously like she would need help getting to bed, as she always needed help. "However did you do this all the time? You traveled for ages."

"I got lost less," Merida replied, but she didn't think that was it, exactly. She'd always seemed happier traveling than other people, and more frustrated sitting still. Even as Leezie crawled into bed gratefully, Merida thought about how she would have been happy to stay up talking after the hard day. In fact it might have improved her evening—it felt so odd to climb straight into bed now as the candle burned out and left them both in the dark.

Merida unbraided her hair so that it was finally free and used her veil as another layer on top of the blanket, which she'd already doubled over against the cold. Unlike back in DunBroch, this room didn't have a fireplace, and it was cold enough that she could feel her nose going numb.

But it felt good to be traveling again, she thought. She was eager to see what Ardbarrach was like in the morning, to learn its culture. She wasn't as tired as Leezie, she thought, because she was built to blow from place to place.

Some storms move no rooftops.

Blast it, she thought. Feradach was still in her head. She wanted to hate him properly, but the feeling was somewhat diluted that night. It was likely he'd saved their lives today on the road. She wondered if he really had gone to ruin a village after encountering them. Maybe at this very minute, he was creeping outside someone else's door right now, tugging off one of his gloves.

"Merida?" Leezie whispered.

"Shh," said Merida.

"I forgot to take my hair down." Leezie didn't care that they'd been told not to talk after the candle was out any more than she cared about being asked to tidy the common room. It had gone in and out of her head without even landing. "Do you think it's all right to sleep in the veil?"

"Probably be warmer." Merida thought about how Leezie had looked like she needed help getting to bed and had, in fact, actually needed help. It was all right. Leezie's veil would be very rumpled after sleeping in it, but Leezie always looked rumpled. "Now shh."

"Do you think Hubert's all right?"

"Hubert can sleep anywhere," Merida replied. "Now *shh.*"

"How many bells do you think they have here?"

"Lots. Now *shh*."

Leezie persisted. "Do you think I'll ever fall in love? And get married?"

Merida put her blanket over her eyes and pressed it hard enough that she saw little sparks of light. "Leezie, you were just *about* to get married."

"I'd really like to be married."

It was as if Merida hadn't said anything at all, which was one of the most Leezie-ish things that she did; she carried on the conversation she wanted to have no matter what anyone else said. This was an old conversation, too. Leezie had always been talking about getting married. Merida couldn't quite wrap her head around it; she herself had yet to meet a potential suitor she hadn't gotten frustrated or bored with after a few hours or days, and she'd stopped imagining she might find someone who'd please her for longer. The closest Merida could come to understanding the intensity of Leezie's devotion to the concept was remembering a brief stretch of time at the convent when Merida had been unreasonably infatuated with a wheelwright who came to mend things a few times a week. It embarrassed her hugely to remember how she had studied his movements, memorized his features, thought of him constantly. Her fixation on the wheelwright had been cured by the reality of the wheelwright, however. Every time he opened his mouth and actually spoke, the spell broke a little more, until eventually he was just a wheelwright and Merida was a princess trying to pretend she had never drawn the memorized line of his nose in the dust of the convent floor.

Opening her eyes, Merida stared sightlessly into the dark. "Why do you want to be married?"

" 'Ms. Leezie, good morning, are you ready for your cup of warm milk?' " Leezie said, her voice dreamy. "That's what he would say when we woke up. And I would call him Mr. whatever his name was. 'Yes, that would be very nice, Mr.—' "

"Cabbage," interrupted Merida. "Mr. Cabbage."

Leezie giggled in her messy, pretty way.

There was a warning drum of fingers on the outside of their door and both girls went still.

"Good night, Ms. Leezie," Merida whispered, after a few minutes.

"Good night, Ms. Merida," Leezie whispered back.

10

THE WOMEN OF THE BELLS

*B*RRRRONNNNG! *Brrrronnnng! Brrrronnnng!*
Another bell woke them in the morning.
The door opened, a maidservant set breakfast just inside, and, just as the door shut again, an authoritative voice from behind the maidservant said, "I'll be back shortly to take you through the day."

"Look at all these squares," murmured Leezie, standing at the window of their bare, bright room. Merida joined her there. The huge space they'd come through the night before looked completely different in the daylight. Unlike DunBroch's untidy, overgrown little courtyard, this one seemed to resemble the Roman arenas Merida had read of in stories. The vast castle walls framed an enormous courtyard paved in geometric stonework. But it wasn't the patterns in the stones Leezie was talking about—it was the people. The bright, shadeless courtyard was filled with soldiers drilling in perfectly straight lines, blocks upon blocks of men swinging arms, legs, swords. Boys practiced in smaller square formations, too, lifting weights and practicing feints in perfect unison. Merida tried to see if she could glimpse Hubert or even Colban or Gille Peter among them, but everyone looked identical from this vantage point.

There was something both thrilling and intimidating about the sight. It was exciting because it was nothing like DunBroch, reminding Merida that she was on an adventure again, but also intimidating because it reminded her of the soldiers she'd sometimes encountered on those adventures. Sometimes they were brash and boisterous, just men with swords, but other times there was a glinting intensity to them, a savage surety of purpose that Merida wasn't sure she agreed with or trusted.

Merida asked, "Where are the women?"

Leezie peered out at the courtyard again. There was not a woman to be seen. "Maybe we're the only ones?"

They soon found out.

At the ringing of another bell, the maidservant who'd brought breakfast returned with a woman dressed in a sharp, dark dress and sharp, dark wimple who introduced herself as Mistress mac Lagan. A handful of other young women stood behind her, quiet and demure, also dressed in sharp, dark dresses, their hair up and tidy and hidden away beneath veils. Leezie looked very rumpled in comparison and Merida suspected she did, too, despite her best efforts.

"Have you been fostered before?" Mistress mac Lagan

asked, in the same authoritative voice they'd heard from the hall before.

Fostered! Even though none of the DunBroch children had been fostered, Merida was familiar with the custom. Most noble families sent at least some of their children off to neighboring families to learn new skills, sometimes for a few months, sometimes for a few years. As a child, Merida had first dreaded the idea of fosterage, then begged for the adventure of it, then dreaded the idea of it again. She'd always been torn between staying in the nest of DunBroch or borrowing someone else's life for a little bit. She wouldn't have considered her current journeys searches for fosterage, though. Fosterage was for children, for dependents, and Merida wanted to be an equal.

"No," Merida said, and then, belatedly, "ma'am. My lady."

Neither felt particularly right for either her mouth or Mistress mac Lagan's face, but Mistress mac Lagan didn't remark on it. Instead, she just said, "You will walk through your typical day as a foster daughter with us. You will be well taken care of; your handmaid can join the others."

A second line of young women waited behind the first; these were dressed in matching gray dresses and white veils. Without waiting for Merida to answer, two of them stepped apart to make room for Leezie. Leezie waltzed over with her usual float and vague smile. She was wildly out of place in their orderly line, but if she noticed it, she didn't show it.

Brrrronnnng! Brrrronnnng! Brrrronnnng!

Mistress mac Lagan said, "Girls, let's go."

And then Merida was plunged into life at Ardbarrach.

For the next several hours, her movements were dictated by the clockwork ringing of bells.

Three chimes: she was led through the bedchambers she'd share with the sisters and daughters of the warriors who practiced out in the courtyard.

Three chimes: they knelt in the chapel to say prayers for the warriors as blocks of uniformed clerks moved in lockstep in the background.

Three chimes: they sat in the sewing room to embroider cloaks for the warriors to wear and banners to fly above the warriors and colors for the warriors' horses to wear.

Three chimes: they memorized war poetry in the dining hall, where they would sing or recite the lengthy ballads and poems about the warriors' feats.

Three chimes: they took instruction on foreign languages, reason, and beautiful speaking in the library.

Three chimes: they paused to pray again in the common area, where they'd listen to visiting musicians and speakers tell tales of what was happening on foreign shores.

Three chimes!

Everywhere was order.

Three chimes!

Every person in Ardbarrach moved like a piece of a massive war machine.

Three chimes!

Every moment of every day was accounted for. It didn't seem possible that anything was missing in this machine, but there must have been, because Mistress mac Lagan demonstrated the perfect, Merida-sized hole that she would fit into if she came there.

Three chimes! Three chimes! Three chimes!

"Is every day like this?" Merida asked the girl next to her. The bells had rung to order them to take their evening exercise strolling through the winter gardens. There were no flowers, of course, but it was still handsome in the waning sun. Like the rest of Ardbarrach, the garden was symmetrical and geometric, evergreen yew and holly trimmed into unforgiving knots beside neatly kept paths. Mistress mac Lagan had informed her that each of the girls was meant to walk at a slow, even pace, hands folded, meditating on their roles at Ardbarrach.

"Of course," the girl replied in a low voice. She slipped on ahead.

It was a very chilly walk. The sun was very nearly gone and the garden was lit by a few torches in protected alcoves. The wind that had battered Merida on her initial approach to Ardbarrach now battered the young women as they strolled; Merida found herself meditating less on her role here and more on how she couldn't feel her toes.

Merida dawdled until the girl behind her caught up. In her veil and wimple, this girl looked nearly exactly like the girl Merida had already spoken to, and Merida had to study her nose and mouth shape hard to make sure she wasn't actually talking to the same girl. She asked, conversationally, "So, where are you from?"

"Why?" asked the girl.

Merida wasn't sure how to reply to that. "Curiosity?"

"This isn't a time for talking," the girl replied, giving Merida a look like she might be stupid. "This is a time for meditating."

"I was meditating on where you might be from," Merida said, with a light smile. She glanced toward Mistress mac Lagan to be sure they weren't about to get in trouble.

The girl stared at her with confusion. "What's wrong with you? Please don't be disruptive. I've been looking forward to this since library."

Her voice was quite earnest. Maybe there *was* something wrong with Merida.

"Merida, please step out of line," Mistress mac Lagan said. "Girls, continue and I will catch up." As the other young women stepped off in unison, she asked Merida, "Is there a problem?"

Merida wasn't exactly sure how to answer. She'd encountered plenty of hardship while traveling, and she was used to being places that weren't exactly to her liking. She liked to think she could put up with quite a bit of discomfort for quite a bit of time, but this had been only a single day and she already felt very out of sorts. She asked, "When is there time to ourselves? Free time, I mean?"

With a gesture, Mistress mac Lagan directed the rest of the girls to file inside the castle, and then touched Merida's elbow so that Merida walked with her down a separate hallway. There were no tapestries to soften the sound, so her clipped words echoed off the bare, stark walls at Merida. "You just had free time. Did you not enjoy it?"

"I meant free time to do what we'd like. If I wanted to ride, or practice archery, or read."

"There is a time for riding in three days," Mistress mac Lagan replied. "Twice a week we strengthen our legs that way. And we already did our reading today, and there will be more reading and reciting tomorrow. And of course there is no archery. You are not a child anymore." Whatever she saw in Merida's face made her clarify further. "I understand you are coming from DunBroch; you have been raised differently—children stay children longer in places like that, where it doesn't matter as much."

"Doesn't . . . matter as much?"

"Yes, in little kingdoms like DunBroch, it is not so important how well you know the customs and how society behaves, because it's not really a kingdom, it's just a field with a castle in it. The stakes are different when the castle doesn't have any power outside of that field. It's all right, don't look like that, you'll catch up here soon enough. Here in Ardbarrach you will put that away and join society as a woman. Do you have any other questions?"

Merida's cheeks burned, though she couldn't pinpoint exactly why. Fury. Embarrassment. Was this how everyone saw DunBroch from the outside? She wondered if Hubert was getting a speech like this over in the barracks, too. She wondered if he believed it. "Can I see my brother?"

Brrrronnnng! Brrrronnnng! Brrrronnnng!

"No, that's the bell for lights out," Mistress mac Lagan said. She put her head on one side, then, studying Merida, and seemed to decide something. She directed Merida to a narrow window in the middle of the hall. It was just wide enough for an arrow or a fiendishly cold night to fit through. "Look."

Merida put her cheek to the cold stone of the window's side and looked out. Outside, a line of page boys filed neatly across the courtyard toward the barracks, silhouettes in the deep blue light. One of them was unmistakably Hubert; she saw the outline of his wild hair.

Merida called, "Hubert!"

The Hubert-silhouette stopped just long enough to peer in her direction. It waved cheerily at her and gave her a thumbs-up, barely visible in the dim space. Then he caught up with the other pages and disappeared into the shadow by the wall.

"Now I trust there will be no further disruption to the schedule tonight," Mistress mac Lagan said. She didn't say that shouting out of windows had been allowed only because of the special circumstances, but it was heavily implied. She patted Merida's shoulder twice. Pat. Pat. Merida understood this was meant to be taken as compassion; she was meant to be grateful.

Merida didn't feel grateful, but as Mistress mac Lagan brought her back to the room she'd shared with Leezie the night before, she said, "Thank you."

Mistress mac Lagan looked embarrassed. She said brusquely, "You will grow to like this schedule."

Leezie hurried up just then, out of breath, holding a stub of candle in one hand and a plate of their dinner in the other. Merida noticed that Leezie's ridiculous embroidered dress was gone, and instead she was dressed in the neat gray dress of the rest of the servant girls.

"Do you have the princess's dress?" asked Mistress mac Lagan.

Leezie lifted one of her arms, making the dinner plate tilt dangerously, demonstrating that she had a dark dress draped over it. Then she wordlessly moused into the room in front of Merida.

"No talking once the candle is out," Mistress mac Lagan said.

The door shut.

Stuffing the bread into her mouth, Leezie collapsed into a relieved heap on her bed; Merida rescued the bit of candle just in time to keep her from setting the blanket afire. She lifted the dress from where it had fallen on the floor by the bed. It was a sharp, dark dress and crisp light veil that matched Mistress mac Lagan's.

"Am I meant to wear this?" Merida asked.

"Mm."

"What was your day like?"

"Mm?"

"Are you all right? Did you get enough to eat? Were they mean? Where is your dress?"

But Merida could tell Leezie was already properly asleep. She had begun producing a fluttery snore. With a sigh, Merida took off her dress and took her time to remove the personal effects she'd sewn into hems and tucked into pockets. A handful of coins. A brooch of her mother's to prove her identity if needed. A hand-sized stuffed bear she'd brought for Hubert in case he lost courage during any part of the journey. She folded all of it up and tucked it away underneath her straw mattress. After a moment, she added her bow and quiver of arrows. She didn't want to risk her things getting spirited away like Leezie's dress.

Then she pulled on the dress Leezie had brought. She didn't need a mirror to know that she now looked like all the other girls in the winter garden.

"Michty me," she whispered softly.

A moment after that, the candle went out. The first Ardbarrach day had come to a close.

That was how it went for what seemed like innumerable days. At first, Merida didn't think to tally them, and then, by the time she decided to, she couldn't tell them apart. Every day felt like the same day:

Brrrronnnng! Brrrronnnng! Brrrronnnng!

The routine. The bells. Every day, the clockwork moving from task to task. Every evening, getting back just in time to scurry to the window in the hall in time to see Hubert's wave and thumbs-up. Every night, Leezie falling asleep nearly before getting into bed.

Brrrronnnng! Brrrronnnng! Brrrronnnng!

"Can I talk to Hubert?" *The pages are caring for the yearlings right now.* "Can I talk to Hubert?" *The pages have guard duty now.* "Can I talk to Hubert?" *The pages are scrubbing shields right now.* "Can I talk to Hubert?"

She thought about asking Mistress mac Lagan if she would take the little bear to Hubert even if she herself wasn't allowed the time to go see him, but she could just imagine Mistress mac Lagan saying that it was a backward, childish toy and destroying it "for their own good." So it stayed hidden under the mattress like the rest of Merida's DunBroch artifacts.

Brrrronnnng! Brrrronnnng! Brrrronnnng!

What had she expected to happen? She supposed she had expected to meet the lord of Ardbarrach. She had expected to picture herself here as a potential family member. But she supposed that was because she had been imagining other places would be more like DunBroch, who had folded Leezie in as one of their own. It was clear that was never going to be an option here. Her parents had been worried about writing a letter persuasive enough to encourage Ardbarrach to accept Merida, but it was obvious now that Ardbarrach would have never rejected her or any other newcomer. They had infinite places for new bodies, each slotted into their roles just as she and Hubert had been, but not for family.

Worst of all, she assumed Hubert was probably bored out of his mind but otherwise unchanged. He had to be. Nothing here changed. That was the Ardbarrach way; they were proud of it. Everything was the same, week in, week out. She wondered why Feradach hadn't already razed this place to the ground.

Brrrronnnng! Brrrronnnng! Brrrronnnng!

Over and over, Merida made up reasons in her head for why they should just go back to DunBroch. Time was passing. Spring was coming. She had other brothers to change. Other journeys to make to satisfy the Dásachtach. They should go. They should go! But she kept hearing Feradach's observation that some storms didn't move roofs. Why, of all the things she'd forgotten in her life, was that phrase not one of them? She refused to let him be right about her. She wasn't going to just give up because she was set in her ways and hated this place.

But then came the night she didn't see Hubert in the line of pages.

Another mind-numbing day, another set of bells, another dashing down the hallway to peer out the window to catch a glimpse of him. But that night, Merida couldn't see him. There was no silhouette of bushy red hair, just the other boys with their identical close-shaven haircuts.

Brrrronnnng! Brrrronnnng! Brrrronnnng!

Where was Hubert?

"No talking once the candle is out," Mistress mac Lagan reminded Merida as she trudged back to her room. Then, as always, "You will grow to like this schedule."

She didn't seem to care that she had said it the night before, and the night before that.

No more, thought Merida.

This time, as a heavy-eyed Leezie stumbled toward her bed a few minutes later, Merida snatched her sleeve to stop her. She stood with her in the middle of the room, listening to the shuffling of the footsteps in the hall and all the doors closing. The candle in Leezie's hand died down to nearly a wick.

Finally, when Ardbarrach had fallen quiet, Merida said, "I hate it here."

"*Yes,*" Leezie whispered back, relieved. "I feel like I'm

a cow. A cow in a line. Not a nice cow life. One of those cows that—"

There were footsteps outside the door; both girls went still until they'd passed.

Merida whispered, "I think I will go mad if I hear that bell one more time."

"I haven't been dreaming and I haven't had any time to set up a shrine or anything," Leezie said, then added thoughtfully, "I haven't even had time to cry. It's been ages since I've had a good long one."

Merida saw about as much appeal in this as daydreaming about marriage, but that was *just Leezie* for you. And this was *just Merida*: "We're leaving."

"Tonight?"

"No, we'd freeze. And we need Hubert and the others." Just saying it out loud was a relief. Tomorrow would be different. Finally. By tomorrow night, they would all be back in DunBroch. And maybe, just maybe, the difference between this place and home would already have been enough to permanently set Hubert on a new path.

Leezie whispered dubiously, "Will they let us leave?"

Merida said, "We're not prisoners. Tomorrow morning, we get Hubert and we go."

11

WAR GAMES

IT SEEMED very important to stay ahead of the bells.

This was a diplomatic mission, so Merida couldn't leave under bad circumstances. She had arrived as princess of DunBroch and she had to leave as princess of DunBroch, even if Mistress mac Lagan didn't think that meant anything. This could not be a bitter escape; it had to be a polite farewell. Courtly. Intentional.

Merida woke even before the first gray light began to illuminate the room. She woke Leezie, knowing she'd have to wake her again, and then tipped up her mattress to retrieve the things she'd hidden there after the first day. She gratefully replaced the dark Ardbarrach dress with her DunBroch green one and tucked the little bear up into her sleeve. Her mother had always insisted she travel with a threaded needle stabbed through the hem of her dress, and even though Merida had scoffed at the time (*who needs to do emergency embroidery!*) she used it now to quickly restitch the coins and brooch into her skirt. The bow and quiver she strung over her shoulder. Mistress mac Lagan wouldn't have approved of it as a ladylike accessory, but some things Merida wouldn't compromise on.

Then she woke Leezie again. "Leezie, get up. We have to do our hair before the bells."

The hair, the hair! Most noble households thought it appropriate for a woman to simply cover her head with a veil or wimple when out in public, but in Ardbarrach they took the most severe view, identical to the convent Merida had stayed in. Not a single lock of hair was meant to be visible beside a lady's face. It had to all be braided neatly and hidden away under austere pinned layers of cloth.

Be royal, be royal, Merida thought.

"Ow," Leezie complained.

"Have you been storing mice in your hair?" Merida muttered, leaning in close to finish tucking the last of Leezie's hair beneath the veil. It was tricky to see how well she'd done the job in the weak gray light, but surely it was sufficient. In any case, she didn't dare invest any more time, lest the bells ring and the two of them had to explain themselves to Mistress mac Lagan. "It's done. Finally. Let's go."

At the door, Merida turned to find Leezie at the window rather than at her heels. "*Leezie!*"

"Wait!" Leezie said. She had saved a bit of bread from last night's dinner, and now she threw it out the window. When she saw Merida's bewildered expression, she explained, "An offering for Lugh, for good favor!"

That was *just Leezie*, too. A ritual or god or religion for all occasions. Merida wasn't sure what or who Lugh was, but she supposed she'd take all the good favor they could get.

They crept out of their room.

The bells had not yet rung.

It was barely light enough to see their way down the still corridor; the circular stair down to the courtyard level was pitch black. Merida ran her palms along the stone wall as they circled down, and Leezie held a handful of Merida's dress in order to follow close behind. Merida was reminded of sneaking through DunBroch's secret passages in her youth. She suddenly thought it seemed like an incredible omission to have never shown them to Leezie, to have kept them to herself. But Leezie was too old for such things now, surely, and so was Merida. She and Merida weren't children anymore; they were turning into women, and the existence of secret passages meant something different, something having to do with hiding during shocking visits from people like Wolftail, not spending long rainy spring mornings playing hide-and-seek.

Children stay children longer in places like that, Mistress mac Lagan had told Merida, and perhaps she was right, because just then, thinking about how she had run out of years to show Leezie the secret passages felt awful.

But then the dark was over and Merida and Leezie were into the light: they emerged from the passage into the garden, and just as they did—

Brrrronnnng! Brrrronnnng! Brrrronnnng!

Merida and Leezie exchanged a triumphant look. They'd made it. Mistress mac Lagan's handmaiden would open their door and be quite unable to fold them into the unending routine.

Moreover, in this first cold light of dawn, they could see they hadn't done a half-bad job on their wimples and hair.

"Now we have to find Hubert," Merida said. "It's not going to be easy in a place like this."

"I know where he is," Leezie replied confidently.

Merida stared at her. Leezie preened, delighted to be the expert for once. "His group passed ours in the court-yard every morning when we were on our way to do the privies. This way."

Quite smug, Leezie led them from shadow to shadow, avoiding knots of various Ardbarrach citizens all locked in their precise bell-driven schedules, and, sure enough, right to a group of page boys in a side courtyard. The boys were gracefully moving as one, like a dance, or like a school of fish, their breath puffing out in white clouds around them as they did arm lifts and jumps and dangled from bars set up in the courtyard. It seemed likely they'd been up since before dawn doing these war games. Because Merida knew that was what they were. She hadn't seen them at this scale before, but she knew the techniques. It looked like dance or exercise, but it was all just play practice for when they'd be told to kill other people. They'd need those muscles and those moves in real battle.

It was difficult to see how this was any different from what the Dásachtach wanted out of the triplets. Trained up for war, knowing nothing else, turned into tiny soldiers, no childhood, no frivolity; just like Gille Peter, but much shorter.

"Oh, *his* hair," Leezie said.

Merida followed her gaze. There was Hubert! His wild red hair had been shorn as short as the other boys' hair. Probably he had been among the boys last night, too, and she just hadn't been able to tell, because he looked just like the others. Merida had a shivering memory of the first night they'd arrived, all the guards looking like the same person many times over. How strange that she'd never had a problem telling Hubert apart from Hamish and Harris, but now she could barely pick him out from all these strangers.

Regret stung her again, just as fiercely as it had as she thought about Leezie and secret passages. She'd waited too long to lose her patience with this place. Poor Hubert, smushed into this mold.

Hair will grow back, she told herself. *Let's just get out of here.*

But there was only one problem.

Hubert didn't want to go.

The guardsman in charge of his group looked bemused as they asked to pull Hubert from the exercises to speak to him, but he allowed it. Hubert wore a matching bemused expression, which turned absolutely cross when Merida informed him they were leaving at once.

"I don't want to," he said.

"What do you mean?" Merida asked in a low voice. "Are you just saying that? No one can hear you. Whisper in my ear."

"We've only been here twelve days," he said, glancing back at the rest of the boys and their exercises.

"Is that all," Leezie murmured.

Twelve days, but hundreds of bells. Thousands of bells. Merida said, "I thought you'd be dying to go."

"What? Why? It's great! Look at it! Whoa! Wow! Yes!" He made some muscles and grinned at one of the other kids behind Merida's back. "What don't you like about it?"

Brrrronnnng! Brrrronnnng! Brrrronnnng!

Merida winced. *Everything.* "What do you *like* about it?"

Hubert's attention was pulled once more to his group as they moved to another part of the courtyard, letting a second group take their place at the bars. "Everything!"

"Every single moment is scheduled," Merida said.

"I know," he said, but in a pleased way.

"Every single thing is training for war."

"I know," he said, but in a pleased way.

"They have your entire life planned out for you."

"I know," he said, but in a pleased way.

He looked so different with his short hair. Was that the only thing different about him? He seemed utterly unlike the boy who'd arrived just twelve days before. She felt stupid for having brought that little bear in case he needed comfort. Hubert had not been the little boy who needed that for a long time, and he was even further away from it now. She didn't know what to say. Finally, she just exclaimed, "Your bum's out the window! I wouldn't have thought you would have liked someplace like this."

"Me neither," he confessed. "If you hadn't brought me, I would've never known someplace like this existed, even."

The two DunBroch siblings were identical in their bewilderment . . . that, for once, they weren't exactly the same. Merida felt for just an instant, very unhappily, that she might cry, but then she didn't.

"I don't have to go, though, do I?" Hubert asked anxiously. "They said I could stay on as long as I liked. I thought we could stay till it was warmer, then we could have Dad come visit and see how well I was doing."

No, he didn't have to go. That was the worst of it. Of course he didn't have to. Ardbarrach was all too delighted to fit him into the Hubert-sized hole in the game board. And Merida—Merida had to let him stay. It was clear he was changing, and that was what she wanted, wasn't it? At least, it was what she needed. Surely it was better to lose him temporarily to this warlike place than to lose all of them to death by Feradach.

"I can't stay, though," Merida said finally. "I have to visit two other places still."

"I know."

"You aren't going to miss home?"

Brrrronnnng! Brrrronnnng! Brrrronnnng!

The bell rang more insistently. Hubert looked up, and it was clear he wanted to go join his group again. "They're calling me. Please, Merida? *Please?*"

Merida couldn't quite believe that she'd come here for a quick journey, to see about maybe staying here herself, to perhaps open Hubert's eyes to another way of living, and now was leaving without him. She felt like he'd managed to grow up too fast, too, just like Leezie, just like Merida herself.

"You better write," Merida said, hating every bit of this.

She hugged him. He was disgusting and sweaty, even in the cold. He grinned at her, visibly relieved that her face was no longer so serious, and then scampered off to join the others. He was just a boy, after all.

And because he was just a boy, Merida could not leave him entirely alone, even in a place like this, where she was sure they would watch his every move closely. Instead, she and Leezie wandered until they found Gille Peter in the barracks and asked if he'd be willing to stay with Hubert. He seemed enthusiastic about the prospect—or at least that was what Merida thought he was trying to say. He even helped them shovel Colban's old bones into the back of the Friendly Box and capture Brionn, who'd been driving the stable boys mad with his chewing.

"Merida! Are you leaving us?"

Mistress mac Lagan's voice came to them just as Leezie was doing her best to steer the Friendly Box back through the gate; she was letting the ponies boss her. Merida tilted her head back to see Mistress mac Lagan and the other young women on their way from the chapel via the walkway on the castle wall. They peered down at Merida and Leezie.

"I have two other kingdoms to visit this year," Merida said.

Mistress mac Lagan's expression pinched with disappointment.

The woman had done nothing but make Merida's life difficult, but Merida nonetheless felt strange about letting her down. She had a thought, and she added, "Have to stay on schedule, you know?"

Mistress mac Lagan's face cleared at once. "Oh, yes. I didn't know, or I would have been happy to assist you with the timing. Well, I hope you'll be back. You have promise. You could be a fine woman one day, with work."

Merida managed to stretch her face into what she hoped looked like a grateful smile.

Behind them they heard the three chimes of the bells one more time.

Brrrronnnng! Brrrronnnng! Brrrronnnng!

When Merida thought of the journey back to DunBroch, it felt longer this direction than the other.

It hadn't occurred to Merida she might not like her family changing.

PART II

SPRING

12

Three Visitors

THE weather turned wretched for several weeks after they got back to DunBroch, which was fine; it matched Merida's mood. As the flat white sky pressed down low and ice layered over icicles outside and the wind howled like a betrayed lover, she moped around the castle. Ardbarrach, one of the least enchanting places she had ever been, nonetheless seemed to have extended an enchantment over her, because when she got back, she couldn't stop seeing DunBroch through Mistress mac Lagan's eyes. A little backwater kingdom; just a well-read family playing pretend with crowns and fake titles. For all that Merida had hated her time at Ardbarrach, she could see all the royal things Ardbarrach did that DunBroch didn't. They trained an army to protect their people. They trained their dutiful women in scholarship about their history. They hosted visitors for trade and diplomacy. They fit into the world and exerted change upon it and themselves.

DunBroch had gotten so small. And the family DunBroch had shrunk to fit it.

How Merida despised that Feradach had made her see her home differently.

How Merida despised that Feradach had made her lose one of her triplets to Ardbarrach.

How Merida despised Feradach.

"You should sleep more," Elinor told Merida. "You look like the mice have had their way with you. Come into the common room; I had Aileen make us a lovely cake with the last of the drowsy Christmas pears."

Elinor and Fergus's reaction to Hubert's decision to stay in Ardbarrach had only worsened Merida's poor mood. She wanted them to be horrified, like she was. But instead—

"I expect Hubert's too busy to be homesick—thank you, Ila," Elinor said, accepting a slice of the pear cake from the young girl, who was just as catlike and graceful as Merida remembered. "He *has* been saying for ages that he wanted to do more training."

"He *has*?" demanded Merida. This felt like information that she could have used. "I don't want any cake, thank you."

"She's just in a poor mood, Ila," Elinor told Ila. "Give her some anyway."

Ila did, pouring extra syrup from the drowsy pears over the slice while Elinor nodded approvingly. Merida just stared crossly at the Brandubh board. It was dusty. Hubert was usually the one who played with Harris. Everything felt dusty.

"I know you miss Hubert," Elinor said. "I do, too. But

it's not for long, and heaven knows I've tried to teach him discipline, so more power to their arm."

"Personally, I'm proud of the wee crumb taking some initiative!" Fergus declared. He appeared in the doorway, bracing his hands on either side of him so it appeared he was holding the entire castle up himself. "I heard there was cake!"

This broad, cheery acceptance was how Merida's parents always were about change they couldn't control—they talked themselves into thinking it was for the best, no matter if it was or not. The thing was, Merida used to appreciate this plucky, can-do attitude. It meant they were never knocked down for long, because they always turned everything into a positive in the end. But now she could see how this way of thinking could also be used to talk yourself into not pushing back.

"You have a knack for hearing a cake getting sliced," Elinor told the king of DunBroch. "This is turning into quite a little ceilidh. Where's Leezie at, then?"

"She was peeling apples in the kitchen," Fergus said. "Make it as drowsy as you like, Ila, if you will."

"Peeling apples?" Merida demanded with disbelief. "*Leezie* was?"

"Peel, peeling away," Fergus said, easing himself into a chair and stretching his wooden leg out. "She's using the peels for one of her things. Throwing 'em over her shoulder and seeing if they'll spell out the initials of the young man she'll marry. Leezie magic."

"Ah, that makes more sense," Elinor said complacently.

"Already looking for her next wedding and the Cabbage barely done leading his cows out of the castle!"

"That's just Leezie," agreed Fergus. To Ila, who was still pouring copious amounts of drowsy pear sauce over his cake, he said, "That's enough there. Save the last bit of that for yourself, now."

"Oh, thank you, sir," murmured Ila, although it was hard to imagine her smacking her lips over drowsy pears or, really, doing anything remotely gluttonous. "Also, sir, you told me to remind you to speak to the queen. About Kinlochy."

"I did?" boomed Fergus.

"Sounds like you," Elinor murmured. "I don't want any talk of going there until the spring rains are over, though. Do you remember that washed-out bridge near there? What a time that was."

Kinlochy. Ordinarily, Merida would have been quite happy to plan a future adventure, but not in her current stormy mood. Who was to say that the trip to Kinlochy wouldn't somehow go awry just like her trip to Ardbarrach?

"It's going to be glorious." Fergus spoke through a mouthful of cake. "Merida, you're going to love it. The times your mother and I had there when we were young! The stories we have of Kinlochy! The stories Kinlochy has of *us*! Perhaps with your mapmaking know-how, Merida, you can help us find the best route."

Merida knew her father was just trying to improve her temper with a bit of flattery, but it only made her feel contrary and more likely to be sour.

She stood. "I'm going to go."

"Don't go shoot your bow in the rain," Elinor said mildly. "You know it will take ages for your dress to dry and you'll be miserable. Why don't you go work on your new dress so you'll have a spare?"

Merida's new dress, a project Elinor had suggested, had been languishing in the tapestry room for ages. It was exactly the kind of sewing project Elinor liked (intricate, technical, time-consuming) and exactly the kind of sewing project Merida hated (intricate, technical, time-consuming).

"I'm not going shooting," Merida snapped, although it was exactly what she had intended to do. Instead she went to the triplets' bedroom, where she found Harris squinting into a book.

"Harris," she said.

"What," he replied. It was not a question.

His tone didn't make Merida feel kindly toward him, but she forced herself to be the bigger person. "Get up. I'm going to show you the castle's secret passages."

He didn't look up from his book. "I've already seen them."

"I don't believe you. Tell me where the closest one is."

Harris blinked up long enough to give her a condescending look. He didn't bother to even answer. Merida fought the urge to give him an old-fashioned sibling pummeling, but before she did, Leezie floofed in.

"Merida," she said, pinching Merida's elbow. "Have you seen Ila?"

"Ow. She's in the common room with the cake," Merida said. "Also, ow."

Leezie continued absently pinching, unconcerned. "Did you know Ila has the Sight? She's been teaching me Signs and Portents."

Unlike Hubert, Leezie seemed unchanged by the trip to Ardbarrach; it had only made her even more Leezie-like. She was leaning into yet another new religion. Now she kept track of how many cows she'd seen huddled out her window and if she saw a dead bird on the snow when she emptied the chamber pots and what shape she found her fireplace embers in after they'd died down in the morning. And apparently used apple peels to find her next husband. She seemed as untroubled by the disastrous trip to Ardbarrach as she had about the canceled wedding. Merida once again wished she could just toss off mixed feelings as effortlessly.

"Ila has the Sight?" Merida echoed. She didn't know why this seemed so surprising. Possibly because magic felt wild and unpredictable, and every time she saw Ila, she seemed just as she had when Merida had first seen her on Christmas Day: tidy, diligent, put together. She seemed quite unlikely to find herself following will o' the wisps into the woods and getting herself into trouble. It would be like imagining Elinor having the Sight. "How do you know?"

"I sensed it deep within her and asked her," Leezie said rapturously. "It was the first Sign. I think I'm learning."

"Learning to be gullible," Harris said. His tone had

reached new levels of condescending judgment. "Only children believe in the Sight, and you're old, Leezie. *Old.* Old enough to be married. *Old.* Do they have a religion for old people? That's the one you're after."

Without any further warning, Leezie burst into tears. She fled the room. Her wails were audible as she proceeded down the hall.

Merida allowed this to be the excuse she needed to throttle Harris.

"You jam-handed scab!" she roared, and threw herself at him.

Really, she'd been wanting to throttle him for days. His attitude had already been terrible by the time she returned for the wedding, but now it was simply unbearable. Neither Harris nor Hamish had said anything about Hubert's absence, but they'd been quarreling constantly. The triplets had fought before, but with Hubert involved, it usually ultimately exploded back into hilarity. But without him, it just went on and on. Hamish got more fraught. And Harris got more superior.

"Merida, that's not princess-like!" Elinor called from deeper in the castle, managing, as she often did, to somehow sense that Merida was doing something she found disagreeable.

It was for naught, anyway. Even though Harris sounded snotty as a middle-aged lord, in the end, he was still a younger brother, and he had that secret talent of younger brothers to scramble and skitter away after only a few seconds of ear twisting.

After the commotion died down, she noticed that Hamish had been snuggled in his bed all along, his blanket around his shoulders as he drew on some already marked-up parchment.

"He had an ear-twisting coming," she told Hamish.

"Yes," Hamish agreed.

"Do *you* want to go see the passages?" she asked.

He shuddered. "No, they sound dark."

Merida sighed noisily.

The gray frigid weather dragged on, the wind ceaseless and irritable against the walls. Hamish and Harris kept fighting. Leezie kept weeping. Elinor and Fergus kept not talking about Kinlochy because the time wasn't right.

I've ruined things, Merida thought miserably. *I changed one thing and now it's all gone wrong.*

But then the weather broke, quite beautifully, in the way it did sometimes at DunBroch, and just like that, it was spring. It was still frigid overnight, but the daylight sky became blue and deep instead of white and the trees got that warm color to them that meant buds were coming, and birds suddenly became brilliant and enthused in the mornings, which started coming earlier and earlier.

With the good weather came visitors, and DunBroch found itself hosting three in quick succession.

The first visitor was the pigeon Elinor had sent off to Ardbarrach at the beginning of the year. It returned to the dovecote with a letter from Hubert attached to its leg, for which it was given a grand treat of a buttered bun and some new young lettuce. Aileen had just made custards with the very earliest of spring berries, so the entire family gathered in the common room to hear the letter while puckering their lips over the barely ripe fruit, a tantalizing promise of what spring was to bring.

" 'Dear Mother and Father and Merida and Hamish and Hubert and Leezie, I recommend me to you,' " Elinor read from her chair in the common room, blinking through the smoke.

"That doesn't sound like him," Hamish protested.

"This is how you open a letter, my love," Elinor said. "Look, it's his handwriting."

She turned the letter around for Hamish and Harris to see it for themselves, but the triplets waved their hands for her to simply go on reading. At Elinor's insistence, all the family knew how to read and write (except Leezie, who said it was too hard because the "letters moved round" when she wasn't watching them), but Elinor remained the most proficient. She had come from an educated family and had been taught quite young by good tutors in France; she could read and write in a half dozen languages. She was proficient enough that she could read aloud at normal speaking speed, as she did now, or she could write her Pasch letter to the villagers and hold a conversation at the same time, or play any of the word games they had in the cabinets that no one else was really good at. Fergus was very proud of her ability and sometimes had her read to him in the evenings, although he usually fell asleep during these tales.

She read on: " 'I am doing very well. You would not

believe how strong I am or how well I can use the long sword.' "

"Ardbarrach is a place for sheep," Harris sniffed from his seat on the floor cushion. "Hubert always did like being told what to do."

"Shhh," Hamish said.

"Shhh yourself."

"I said shhh first."

"And I said it second."

Merida, annoyed that Elinor had not yelled at her brothers, took the liberty of doing it herself. "Would you two stop being such right scunners!"

"Merida, hush!" Elinor said (which Merida found exceptionally unfair), before shaking out the letter to continue. " 'Hamish would not like it here at all, but I think Harris would do quite well. He is smarter than anyone here and could fool them all quite easily.' "

"You happy now?" Hamish hissed.

Harris preened. "Are *you*, wet blanket?"

Without taking her eyes from Elinor, and still perched delicately on the arm of one of the chairs, Leezie silently reached out and twisted Harris's ear right round until he howled.

"Harris!" Elinor said (which Merida found exceptionally fair). Merida and Hamish wordlessly looked to Leezie with appreciation. " 'Please tell Merida we do not only do war things. They are also working on my writing and reading and I am even supposed to be writing this letter for practice—' There are a lot of mistakes in here, poor thing," Elinor interrupted herself, but she seemed proud and happy. " 'I hope you will come visit when the weather is good, miss you all, with great regards, yours, Hubert of DunBroch. Oh also I think Gille Peter wanted to send his regards, too, but I could not tell what he was saying. And Angus is doing well, too, though I can't understand him either.' "

"Aww, there's his old humor!" Fergus said in his big voice. "We should head down there to see him now that the weather's broken."

"Yes," Elinor said.

So that was the first visitor.

The second visitor came to DunBroch a few days later. This visitor was less welcome, and, unlike the pigeon, received no bread and butter for his arrival: Wolftail.

He arrived during one of those spring rains that arrives on a nice day, makes itself at home, and doesn't leave for a week. The air drowned. The ground was awash. Everything was turning green and sodden beneath the rain's exhaustive attention, including Wolftail and his group of men and horses and dogs, who had been intercepted in the courtyard this time.

The Dásachtach's horses stood with their hooves half submerged in mud. The Dásachtach's men sat astride with rain dripping from the ends of their beards, looking as if they'd been dredged from the loch. Wolftail's wolf tails were colorless and bedraggled on his shoulders. Their big dogs huddled miserably in an alcove, looking much less terrifying than before.

King Fergus of DunBroch stood in front of his castle's big door, arms crossed over his barrel chest. He was just as wet as the rest of them, but he looked no smaller. Water does not shrink a mountain, after all.

Merida and Leezie eavesdropped from a dry but precarious spot; they both balanced on a single stair in the tower above in order to hear out the narrow window.

"To what do we owe the pleasure of your return?" bellowed Fergus.

"I'll make this short," Wolftail said in his usual snarl. "We were told DunBroch would send a diplomatic group to three territories."

"We've honored that word," Fergus replied, "and I'm down one son to prove it, so why darken our door before the year's up? Is it the weather you and your men are enjoying?"

Wolftail discreetly wiped rainwater from the end of his nose. "We know all about your trip to Ardbarrach and the son you left there; we came to DunBroch by way of Ardbarrach. I was told you'd send word from each territory and we got no satisfaction in that department."

Embarrassment burned Merida's cheeks. Of course. She had been so completely scheduled among the bells that it hadn't even crossed her mind to send word from Ardbarrach. But that didn't change the fact that it had been her responsibility.

"I didn't remember either," Leezie whispered, to make her feel better. She put the back of her hand against Merida's hot cheek, underlining Merida's suspicion that she'd gone completely red.

Wolftail growled, "You should be glad we were at Ardbarrach to see that you had begun to keep your word, or else this might have been a different sort of visit."

It was a threat, but Fergus's expression remained broad and good-humored. "That's a funny way of saying you're glad to see we're reaching out to neighbors. But I hear your complaint and I agree, we did promise to send word. We won't forget it next time. Now is that all you've got to say, or can I get back to my fire now?"

Wolftail gazed around the courtyard, which winter had left in an untended shambles. The pitted ground. The broken shingles that had come free from the roof. The split rain barrels on their sides. He took long enough looking that Merida realized he was doing it to make a point: to let Fergus feel his judgment. To make Fergus feel like Merida had when Mistress mac Lagan talked about castles in fields.

Merida didn't know if it worked on Fergus, but it worked on her. Her red cheeks got redder.

Finally, Wolftail just stroked the rainwater from his eyebrows and, without another word, rode from the courtyard, taking his soaking wet companions and his pack of dogs with him.

"Five dogs," Leezie remarked.

"What?" Merida asked.

"I was counting them for their meaning. Five dogs. Their four, plus Brionn under the wagon, that makes five. You're still really red."

"Thanks. What does five dogs mean?"

"Usually it means rain, I think."

They both looked at the weeping sky.

"See?" Leezie said. Then she ducked out of the window and back into the castle.

Merida stayed where she was at, watching her father, who also stayed where he was at in the rain, watching the departing company. It was hard to tell what he was thinking. She saw his head turn to look at the split rain barrel and then at some of the roof tiles. Then he spit and retreated indoors.

Maybe, Merida thought, he was feeling a little bit like her. Which was to say: bad.

She spit out the window like her father. Ugh, Wolftail.

So that was the second visitor.

And the third visitor, who arrived on a much nicer day, with much less fanfare, was Feradach.

13

THE GOD OF MANY FACES

FERADACH had arrived at the castle while Merida was practicing her archery in the game fields, although she didn't realize it right away. She knocked the mud from her boots just outside the door, tramped inside, leaned her bow against the wall, and headed toward the kitchen to find something to snack on. She had that free and cheerful feeling one has after a good practice session, and all things seemed possible. She thought after she got something in her belly, she would get out the maps and see about firming up the route to Kinlochy.

To her surprise, as she approached the kitchen, she could hear Aileen speaking musically. This was unusual. If one met Aileen anywhere besides the kitchen, she was perfectly civil, but try to talk to her in front of the stove or next to a bowl—she became a screaming gamecock. But on this particular day, Merida could hear her describing how to make a certain sort of vegetable stew in great and pleasant detail.

And when Merida got to the threshold, she realized she recognized the voice murmuring in reply.

"You!" she said.

Because *of course* it was Feradach—Feradach in his gloves with their oxblood stitching, with his tree brooch and his light mane of hair, looking very real and close in the low-ceilinged kitchen beside Aileen and her cut-up vegetables on the board before her. Both of them were lit by the newly warm light through the wee window that looked out just a few inches above the ground, and in that gentle light, one would have been hard pressed to say that one seemed any more uncanny than the other.

Merida stood askance in the doorway. "What are *you* doing here?"

Feradach regarded her without malice. He was holding a turnip.

"Why, Merida, that's very rude," Aileen said.

Merida didn't care if it was rude or not. She cared that she had only so many more months to sort this out and she did not like having Feradach here among her family, talking to Aileen as if he were just an ordinary man, holding one of *their* turnips.

"I know this man—" started Merida.

"Who knows a man who knows me," Feradach interrupted smoothly. "Thank you for the recipe, Aileen. I'll try it now that spring onions will be coming in."

"I'd be so pleased to hear how it turned out, madam!" Aileen said. "Is your business with Merida, then?"

Madam?

"Yes," Feradach said. "She's the one I was told to see."

Aileen turned to Merida, still looking far more pleasant than she would have ordinarily. "Will you be seeing the lady in the Great Hall or the common room, Merida? I will have Ila send a tray."

The lady?

Feradach was looking at Merida quite intently, waiting for her to put it together. Finally she remembered what he had told her: everyone saw him as someone different. This magic had seemed like a strange but unimportant wrinkle when it was just him and her and Gille Peter out in the middle of nowhere. But the castle was full of people in close proximity.

This could get messy very quickly.

Merida told Aileen, "No tray is necessary. I won't be seeing the *lady* for long."

She ushered Feradach into the dim back hallway. Strangely, it still smelled of wedding buns and Christmas, even though much time had passed. She and Feradach were as close as they had ever been, and this close, it seemed impossible that other people might see him as anything other than what she was seeing. The details seemed too precise. His eyes were dark gray with a darker gray ring. His mane of hair was dark at the roots, faded to nearly white at the ends. He had a small pock scar underneath his chin; every time he pursed his lips, his mouth looked suddenly youthful and boyish; two of his bottom teeth were slightly crowded together so they had to turn sideways to both fit. And those gloves, of course, with their bright red stitching, wondrously formed to his hands so that the shape of them was quite clear beneath. Such thorough details for an illusion. But illusion it was nonetheless, as obviously Aileen had been thoroughly convinced by whatever *she* saw, too.

"I told you to stop following me," Merida hissed.

"I cannot stop doing that," he said, "because you still smell of rot." Merida's mouth came open right away to protest *this* and so he went on, "But that's not why I came today. Have you already forgotten the Cailleach requires you to show me your work, and vice versa?"

"No," lied Merida. How embarrassing that she'd forgotten both the message-sending part of the bargain with the Dásachtach *and* this part of the bargain with the gods. She'd never been marvelous with the more fiddly, boring details of a project. In her loftiest voice, she added, "I was just hoping *you* had. I was not overeager to see you again."

"Mmm," he murmured. "I would have thought you would be pleased to gloat about your brother Hubert's change."

Her heart lurched. It was a multipurpose lurch. It lurched because this was acknowledgment that Hubert truly had changed, which meant this entire game *was* winnable. But it also lurched because—again—this was acknowledgment that Hubert truly had changed, which meant he would never again be the brother he had been when she took him to Ardbarrach in the first place.

Elinor's voice rose. "Merida, who is this visitor?"

Both Merida and Feradach turned abruptly to see

Elinor standing at the end of the hall. Even in silhouette, she managed to look both very royal and very suspicious, the line of her spine straight and proper, the tilt of her head wary and imperious.

There was no way of telling what her mother saw Feradach as, so Merida considered several answers before landing on a neutral one. "Aileen chased us from the kitchen."

"Why is he being greeted here of all places? It is hardly . . . appropriate."

There was no way of telling if it was inappropriate because Feradach appeared too highborn to be greeted in a hallway, too lowborn to be allowed into the castle, or too eligibly bachelor-ish to be standing so close to Merida alone. And Feradach was no help in solving the puzzle of how Elinor saw him, either. He simply stood there, his gloved hands clasped together, looking from mother to daughter.

Merida applied cunning to the situation. "Where do you think would be more appropriate?"

Elinor's silhouette managed to look aggravated. "Merida, don't be saucy. Both you and this young man must know that anywhere is more appropriate than a dark hallway, no matter the discussion."

Understanding crystallized. Merida said, "He's not a *suitor*."

"And yet you're still a young woman and he's still a young man," Elinor said, stepping close enough that Merida was now able to interpret her expression as distrust. It was hard to tell if this meant she didn't trust Merida, or didn't trust whomever Feradach looked like. Since their giant argument about marriage years ago, she and her mother had simply avoided the topic of matchmaking altogether, so neither knew the other's opinions on it. "Now please take this conversation to the Great Hall; it's terribly dingy back here. Don't judge us by this, sir. Lovely hat, by the way. Have you been to France?"

Hat?

Feradach replied, "It was a gift."

"A lovely one." Elinor turned. "I haven't seen one since—Fergus! There you are."

Fergus had just appeared at the bottom of the stairs with a breastplate of armor in each hand. "I've not been hiding, my love!" Catching sight of Feradach, he nodded his approval. "Looking fine, grandpa, but it's late for mumming, isn't it? Elinor, those ailettes are still missing and I canna find them anywhere."

Grandpa? Mumming?

Elinor's arched eyebrows became puzzled eyebrows as she processed Fergus's words.

Michty me, Merida thought. Whatever Fergus saw Feradach as was obviously quite at odds with Elinor's version. Merida really did need to get Feradach away before things got more tangled. The moment anyone guessed there was magic involved, it would get very difficult to avoid talking about the bargain.

"Great Hall," Merida ordered Feradach, and he obeyed.

"So, Lady Madam Grandpa," Merida said, as soon as

they were out of her mother's earshot. She kept her voice low, because even though the Great Hall was empty, the high walls wanted to take her words and throw them around. "A domestic woman to Aileen and a suitor to my mother and a mummer to my father, and who knows what you'll be next."

"I told you I look different to each person who sees me," Feradach said. "What do I look like to you?"

"You don't know?" When he shook his head, she asked in disbelief, "Your magic changes your face but doesn't tell you what it looks like?"

He peered up at the flags hanging from the ceiling of the Great Hall. It was difficult to tell if he was interested in them or deciding if they were rotting and required his ruinous attention. "I only know what I look like if the person looking tells me something about what they are seeing. Your mother mentioned a French hat. Your father mentioned my age, my costume. These are clues."

A melodic plink drew Merida's attention.

"Hamish!" she said, horrified. The smallest of the triplets was tucked away in the corner of the Great Hall, nearly hidden by one of the tables. In his hands was a lap harp Merida had definitely heard their mother say was not to be touched. When he saw Merida, he immediately tried to stuff it behind his back, but she wagged a finger at him. "What did you hear?"

"What?" Hamish whispered shyly.

"Did you hear us talking?"

He shook his head. He was still trying to slowly move

the lap harp behind himself, as if Merida might forget she'd seen it at all if he got it out of sight. Merida knew the feeling exactly. Behind her back, she pointed aggressively at the door to the outside and hoped Feradach obeyed.

"I won't tell," Merida said. "But don't break it. We're going outside."

But Feradach hadn't moved toward the door as she'd indicated. This was because Hamish had stopped trying to squirrel the lap harp away and was instead staring at Feradach. It was so thorough a stare that it was like a string connected Hamish and Feradach, a string that would be unkind for Feradach to break. So Feradach stood there, letting Hamish stare at him, the triplet looking like a rabbit frozen in place.

Finally, not taking his eyes from Feradach, Hamish lifted one of his long spider fingers to touch his own cheek, almost like he didn't realize he was doing it. Merida realized he must be seeing some kind of wound or mark on Feradach's face, something major enough that he was completely transfixed. Elinor would have told him it was appallingly rude to stare and make a fuss over anything odd he might have seen, and Merida might have too, if she had any idea of what he was looking at.

"You can ask," Feradach told him. "It won't offend me."

Hamish glanced at Merida, as if for permission. She shrugged. In his small voice, Hamish asked, "Does it hurt?"

Feradach's fingers hovered over his own cheek, not quite touching. "What does it look like?"

"Like it hurts," Hamish said in a low, reverent voice. His eyes were absolutely enormous. "Did a wolf get you?"

"A wolf . . ." Feradach gently ran fingers across his own cheek, tracing a shape Merida didn't see, flinching and probing. Ultimately his fingers rested exactly where Hamish's fingers had indicated on his own cheek. His eyes tightened, as if something had just occurred to him, and then he said, "Fighting dogs, not wolves. But it doesn't hurt anymore. It's only a memory now, and you know what, the other eye sees just fine. Try not to let your memories hurt more than the wound, friend."

Hamish twisted his fingers round each other nervously. It was the longest conversation Merida had seen him have with a stranger; normally she would have been delighted to see him being so brave, but not with a god who intended to kill them all later.

"Put that harp back," Merida ordered Hamish. She could see Ila moving around deeper in the Great Hall, and she was determined to get out before this happened again. "Don't tell Mum we had this conversation, or I'll tell her you were staring at people. Feradach, *out*."

She practically vaulted across the room, pushing open not the Hall's big doors, but rather the little door that was disguised within one of them. Outside, she hurried him through the bright overgrown spring courtyard, past the raised vegetable beds and the kennels and the chicken house.

Finally they were on the other side of the gate and on the outside of DunBroch's wall. It was cool here in the shadows, but it was beautiful with its view down to the shimmering loch. And at least there were only the tall pine trees to see and hear them; they could speak freely.

The needles beneath Merida's feet threw up their sharp scent as she turned on her heel to point at Feradach. "You just said you only knew what you looked like if people told you what you looked like."

Feradach hovered his hand over the geometric bark of the closest pine tree but didn't touch it. "That's true."

"But Hamish didn't tell you what you looked like. He just said—what did he say? He just asked if you'd been bitten by wolves. Obviously you didn't look like that to any of the others. Obviously you don't look like that now. So what is the truth?"

Feradach touched his own face, ran his fingers over that blond mane, but it seemed as if he didn't quite know the shapes beneath; he was guessing and missing. "It was enough for me to remember."

"Remember?" she echoed.

He said, "I wear the faces of those I've brought ruin to."

The beauty went straight out of the day, replaced by a bone-deep chill as thorough as the first day she met him. So the specifics of the face she saw now were simply a dead man's portrait, worn by the god that killed him.

Merida refused to let Feradach see that she was bothered, though. She just made her voice very brash and careless and said, "So one day you might look like me."

Feradach flinched. Or rather, the body he borrowed flinched. Merida wouldn't let herself be fooled again. There was a monster inside that suit.

144

He said, "I thought you might be interested that I don't forget any of them. Since you seem certain I delight in this task."

"I'm not interested," Merida said, "in what you feel at all. I'm only interested in winning this bargain."

Feradach's voice was cooler than before. "Well then, the sooner we fulfill the Cailleach's requirements, the sooner I can be on my way."

If he had been human—if he had been any of those humans whose faces he wore today—Merida would have felt bad for obviously offending him. But he wasn't, so she just said, "Then let's go see what you've ruined."

14

KEITHNEIL

RAT and *blast* being a princess!

Merida only made it just out of the shadow of the castle wall before Elinor's voice reached her and called her back into the courtyard. She had the nerve to sound suspicious—she thought Merida had been creeping off with the man she'd believed a suitor. When Merida said she was going for a long walk, Elinor demanded Merida take Leezie.

"I'm going *alone*, Mum," Merida insisted.

"All the more reason to take Leezie," Elinor said, adding ominously, "A princess should not travel alone."

As a princess who *had* been traveling alone for much of the year, Merida resented this sentiment. Not only would Leezie not offer much in the way of protection if danger came about, but she certainly wouldn't provide an obstacle to Merida's amorously entertaining a suitor, either, since she was easily distracted. Surely Elinor was well aware of both of these facts. Moreover, the last thing she wanted to do was take Leezie along on a trip to bear witness to destruction. She would have to invent an excuse for visiting a ruined place without mentioning the bargain, and she was already tired of lying.

But Merida understood the true nature of Elinor's request immediately after her mother pushed Leezie into the courtyard. Leezie's lovely face was tear-streaked and puffy, and she looked, as ever, like she needed help. It was clear she'd been crying for a good long time. She had made herself a wreath of fragrant leafy bog myrtle and bright pink campion, and two branches were drooping on either side of her face, like the wreath was crying, too.

"Have a good time," Elinor said, and closed the door behind her, leaving the two girls alone in the sunshine.

"Leezie, why are you crying now?" Merida asked, tucking the loose branches back into the wreath.

"That would spoil it. As soon as you say why you're crying, you always stop," Leezie replied, but she sounded cheerful about it. She wiped her nose on her sleeve. "Oh, hello, Brother, are you coming inside?"

This was directed at Feradach, who had stepped into view the moment Elinor had shut the door. His fingers strayed over his head and face, subtly feeling for his own appearance. He said in a very clear voice, for Merida's benefit, "This particular monk is accompanying the princess on a walk."

"Oh, good," Leezie said. "Three is a much luckier number. Are we going far?"

147

Feradach looked at her curiously. This was a common effect Leezie had on people. Merida wondered if he'd ever seen anyone like Leezie Muireall in his long, strange existence. She wondered if he'd killed anyone like her.

Feradach said, "Not far at all."

She didn't ask where they were going, which was good, because Merida didn't know. Somewhere Feradach had ruined.

The only thing was: it didn't seem very ruined, once they got there.

Keithneil was a perfectly lovely little village arrayed on the banks of an idyllic wide river. Modest timber homes with neat new thatch roofs lined a center street busy with chickens and children. Long-horned, hairy cattle chewed early spring grass. Kittens swatted new spring flowers. The clouds were high and airy and white in the deep blue; the river reflected them beautifully. It was within several hours' easy walking distance of DunBroch, but Merida had never been there. There was no reason for her to have visited. It was just an ordinary, peaceful little village. If there was anything remarkable about it, it was that it was so unremarkable, with no overt signs of hardship or illness.

"Are you sure this is the right place?" Merida asked dubiously.

"This is the right place," Feradach replied.

"It's so pretty; I could just *eat* it," Leezie said, snuffling and wiping her nose with her sleeve again. It was a habit that would've gotten Merida chastised, but Elinor let

Leezie get away with it because, she said, *Some habits are hard to break.* "Is that the town name? What's it say?"

Leezie gestured to a stone that rested at the edge of the village; it had a word carved into it. Her mouth sounded the letters out, but she didn't attempt it aloud.

"Keithneil," Merida read, knowing even as she did that she was doing what everyone did: seeing Leezie being helpless and helping her. "You know what, Leezie, you really should let Mum teach you to read. You could probably catch a better fish than the Cabbage if you knew how."

Leezie's eyes and nose immediately turned red at the mention of the Cabbage, but her voice was completely cheerful as she remarked, "Ila's been teaching me to read . . . the clouds! Those stringy clouds there that point at the trees mean that luck is coming for fishermen. Or for fish. I can't remember if they . . ." She turned her head sideways to look quite suddenly and alertly at Feradach. "Your gloves are very elegant with their red stitches! But they don't match your robes at all—they aren't very monkish."

"The gloves were a gift," Feradach said, same as he had said to Elinor about the hat Merida hadn't been able to see.

Leezie smiled at him. Her tears-to-cheer ratio was improving. "I fancy them a lot."

"Thank you," Feradach replied gravely.

Feradach had avoided conversation with them during the walk to Keithneil, which suited Merida at first. But as they walked together on the worn track through the hills and fields, the silence eventually grew so deep that it became like a fourth party on the trip. Merida, Leezie,

Feradach, the Odious Silence, four walking companions. If the silence had been radiating from one of the triplets or her parents, Merida would have assumed it meant their feelings were very hurt indeed and a sulk was in progress. But that was such a mortal, small reaction that Merida thought she had to be mistaken. Surely a god could not be that deeply wounded by a single human's distaste for him.

She saw that he was glancing at her now, however, and as she tried to interpret the meaning of this look, it occurred to her that Leezie was talking about the same gloves that *she* could see. Even though he wore a different face for her, the gloves stayed the same. Choosing her words carefully to avoid mentioning magic, she asked, "Do you always wear those gloves, no matter whose company you're in?"

Feradach seemed to have been waiting for her to speak to him, because he replied nearly before she was done asking the question. "Yes. No matter what, they are always there."

"They must be very precious to you," Leezie said. Merida could tell she liked the idea of this; she sensed a romantic story for this monk. "Who gave them to you?"

"I'm afraid the name would mean nothing to you," Feradach replied. "I'm sorry."

"She doesn't want information," Merida told him. "She just wants the juicy story."

Leezie smiled breezily, looking pretty and helpless and appealing against the roses that grew around Keithneil's marker stone. Merida wasn't sure if this effect would work as well on a god as on mere mortals, but it must have, because Feradach said, "The story is a simple one, I'm afraid. I wanted something to cover my hands always, no matter the season, but there were no gloves that could do the job. A long time ago I met a man who had a special skill, and he said he thought he could manage the task. He made them for me and they have covered my hands ever since."

He did not tell her why he wanted to have his hands always covered, and Leezie, to Merida's great relief, didn't ask. But Leezie did ask, "Does he still make them?"

Feradach folded his gloves tightly in each other. "He died shortly after he made them for me."

There was a silence after the end of the sentence and Merida filled in the blank in her head: Feradach had killed the glove maker. It seemed obvious from the weight of the silence. From the way Feradach just stepped off and ended the story without any further niceties.

"I spoiled the story," Leezie told Merida, "by asking for the end that came after the end. Never ask the minstrel what happened after the song ends, that's what I've learned." She looked suspiciously watery-eyed again.

"Is all this crying because you've changed your mind about the Cabbage?" Merida asked.

"Oh, no," Leezie said. "It's because I'm so sad I almost married him."

"But you didn't."

"But I nearly did."

"But you *didn't*."

Leezie sadly removed her wreath and put it on top of

the Keithneil marker. She absently traced a mysterious little shape in the center of it and then burst out, "I wish I was like you, Merida. Your mum is always telling you what to do. I wish someone would just tell me what I was supposed to be doing and how to act and then just hand me the right man and tell me the right way to go instead of making me decide everything for myself."

Merida was agog. Leezie had very succinctly summed up the source of every argument she'd ever had with her parents in the last decade. She would have traded for Leezie's breezy, unfettered life in a moment. "Leezie, you don't do what people tell you to do anyway."

Both girls stared at each other for half a moment, and then they both burst out laughing. Then Leezie sang a little nonsense song as she sprang off to prance through the village.

"Well, go after her," Feradach said. "Go look around. That's why we're here."

"Ugh. I have looked around," Merida said. "What am I looking for?"

"For what this place is like."

Merida could not see how that would take much time at all, but rules were rules, she supposed. The Cailleach had told her she had to see his work, and even if she couldn't understand it just yet, this was his work.

And Merida and Leezie actually had a brilliant time.

Even though the village was not far from DunBroch, the villagers had only the vaguest understanding of Merida's being their princess, which made it better, since they didn't bother with all the bowing and ma'aming; they just treated Merida and Leezie as two visiting young women with means. The girls got to see new lambs and new kids. Merida bought a scarf for Leezie, and in return, the weavers taught them a new weaving song. Merida made a bet with some of the older boys about who could shoot an arrow farther and truer and she won a carved wooden frog for her efforts, which she then lost almost at once betting on a game of nine-men's morris. Leezie conspired to learn a flower language from some of the older girls and wrote coded poetry with assorted bouquets that made them all giggle.

At one point the villagers took Leezie and Merida out to see the old pointy-roofed structure on the crannog, an artificial island built into rivers. For all her traveling, Merida had never seen one in person, and she and Leezie took their time exploring it. Leezie, clumsy and vague, slipped off the edge and right into an empty boat floating alongside. She flailed prettily in the boat, gently moving downstream, until villagers—moved by the universal urge to help her—plunged into the river to retrieve her. Then they went a step further, everyone taking to the other boats to join her and teach her how to steer. This pleased everyone. Leezie loved to be helped; people loved to help her.

Feradach and Merida stood on the shore, watching this spectacle, and it occurred to Merida then as he stood there, the strong spring breeze lifting his mane of hair and crinkling his eyes, that he liked Leezie, that he liked *people*. He had brought Merida and Leezie here to admire this place, because he found it admirable.

But this didn't make sense to Merida. His entire purpose was to destroy.

She asked, "Am I the only person who sees you the same every time I see you?"

"Yes," he said.

"Because of the bargain?"

"I assume so."

"No wonder you don't understand family," she said. "How can you, if no one sees you as the same more than once? Apart from the Cailleach, I suppose, but does she count? You can't ever have a conversation that lasts more than one day. You can't fight with anyone for longer than a single encounter. You can't ever be in love. No one can miss you. You don't know what it is to miss someone, either. You don't know anything about being human."

"I watch them, though," Feradach said, and she noticed that, as he did, he unconsciously fisted his destructive hands in their gloves against his body as she had seen him do before.

"Is that enough?"

"I watch them a lot. And I have a very good memory. I remember almost everything I see." He fell silent. Then: "Will you tell me what I look like to you now?"

She glanced over at him, thinking to herself that what she was seeing was not quite a lie, but not quite true, either. It *was* technically his appearance, because it was the appearance he always had for her. But it was also *not* his appearance, because he had not had to live with the consequences or benefits of it. He had not worked for those muscles; he had never had the pain of whatever pocked that small scar on his jaw; he had not chosen to wear his hair like that; he did not know what effect his handsomeness had as he grew from boy to man. He had not earned that face. He had not lived in it. He had not been formed by it in any way.

So really it was not his appearance at all.

She shook her head.

He didn't seem to have expected her to, because he said, "Then let us get on with showing you my work here before we lose daylight for the journey back."

"What else is there for me to see?" She glanced at Leezie, who was still well occupied in the middle of the river with the villagers.

"Magic," Feradach said. "Leezie'll be all right; this will not take long."

He led Merida back to the big old stone carved with the village's name. The sun had progressed through the spring sky and, along with it, so had the shadow behind the stone. Now it left the opposite side of the stone clearly visible instead. In the middle of it was was a handprint, sunk deep into the rock as easily as into potter's clay.

Feradach pointed to the handprint.

If it were anyone but Feradach standing beside Merida, she would have assumed that the handprint had been carved from the rock with tools, just the same as the name on the other side.

"I suppose that is yours," she said.

"Aye."

A hand that could sink straight into stone. Impossible. But so was a hand that could summon a winter storm to immediately kill a tree. Merida tried to sound light. "I would ask you to put your hand in there to prove it fits, but I assume it was a different hand you had back then?"

Feradach inclined his head. "It's your hand that will go in there now, in any case. Put your palm flat against it."

Merida hesitated.

"It will not hurt you," he said. "Aside from being the truth, which can sometimes be more painful than we expect."

Merida still hesitated.

"It is only magic," he said.

That didn't make her hesitate any less.

"Merida of DunBroch," Feradach said, "of all the things I have seen you be since I have begun to watch you, a coward is not one of them."

Merida put her hand into the print. It was not that much larger than her fingers after all. Somehow that seemed more daunting.

"Stone," Feradach ordered, "show her what you've seen."

15

THE STOLEN VILLAGE

ALMOST immediately Merida felt she was somewhere else.

Some *when* else.

She was looking at this stone, this river, this landscape, but there were no buildings.

The trees were vaster. The animals were stranger. The river was wilder.

Nights became days became nights again; time was moving fast before her eyes.

People moved in. First they had rudimentary camps, sleeping alongside the cattle they drove. Then they built little round bothies from rocks. They planted, fished, built more houses. Barns to save their livestock from the weather. Places to worship gods Merida didn't recognize. Crannogs out into the river to fish from. It was a hard place to get a foothold, but they did it; they built a community.

For quite a few days and nights and days and nights this went on, and the community thrived.

Then it changed: men who looked very like the men who drilled in Ardbarrach arrived in neat rows, with impeccable weapons. Fire raged through the village, and the things the men did to the villagers were so terrible that Merida had to close her eyes. When she opened them again, the village looked quite different.

The houses were more prosperous, decorated with things from far away. There were more of them. More people altogether. A more prosperous living was being pulled from the land by many more hands, because it was obvious now that the women and children who had not been killed in the attack on the village had been pressed into slavery instead.

The land gave up more and more.

The days and the nights continued to go by. Now the ground was ugly and stubbled, bitten to nothing by too many cattle in too close quarters. Slaves grew hay and carried it on their backs to keep the cattle alive. The village didn't even need all that they had; pails of milk spoiled in the street even as children who had never been free carried in yet more pails on their shoulders from the fields.

Every so often there was a rebellion; every so often there was a public killing in the streets and blood mingled with the spilt milk.

It turned Merida's stomach.

Then in the night came a figure. He did not look exactly as he did now, but Merida knew who it was anyway.

She recognized those gloves with their oxblood stitching, gifted to him by someone who knew how to make them stick to a god of many faces, many hands.

Feradach strode through the streets, looking this way and that.

He took off his glove. He put his hand onto the stone. Merida watched it sink right down into it, just as she'd pictured it, soft as clay under his touch. Then he walked a few feet and, without flinching, put his hand where the blood and the milk ran together in the street. He walked a few more feet to where the body of the latest rebellion's leader still lay on her face. He stood there for a bit longer than he'd stood by the stone and the pools of blood, just looking at the corpse, and then he put his hand on the back of her head.

Merida *felt* the ruin.

The night turned into day and Feradach was no longer there, but the ruin his hand had triggered was. Merida could feel the village's doom. She heard the first cow cough and knew it was fatal. She saw the days and nights flip by and, with each, more death. First the cows, then the calves, then the bulls, then the weakest humans in the village, then the strongest.

And then the village fell into empty ruin for a very long time. Grass and roots tore down the houses, slow but steady. The rain and the river carried away the corpses. The seasons passed and the sickness that had begun with a cough slowly passed with it.

Slowly the people whose village it had been in the first

place returned from the hidden burrows they'd made for themselves alongside the badgers and foxes. They cautiously rebuilt the first crannog, and waited for invaders. But the invaders were all dead. So they built up the main street again, and they fetched even more of their people from the hills, and slowly, as the days and the nights went by, they thrived again and became the village Merida and Leezie had just walked through. Keithneil.

The days and nights continued to cycle until it came to the day Merida was living and she saw herself standing there with her hand upon the rock. Her red hair curled down her back. The elbows of her dress were worn from her pulling arrows back and the right shoulder was worn from her carrying her quiver over it. She could see from here that she had grown up to have her mother's mouth and her father's eyes.

And then she was no longer in the vision. She was simply standing there with Feradach, looking at the stolen village that had returned to its builders.

She felt out of sorts. The breeze on her skin felt slower, somehow. Minutes went on forever now in comparison to what she had just experienced.

"Couldn't it have been changed my way?" she asked. "Couldn't it have been a leader who made the people see the error of their ways?"

"Don't you think I waited for that?" Feradach asked. "Surely you see now how patient I am. Do you understand the value in what I do?"

"No," Merida replied, even though she wasn't exactly

sure *what* she understood anymore. She felt like she wanted to cry, but she wouldn't let herself in front of him. "But I at least see why you think you have to do it."

Feradach said, "For now, that's good enough."

16

MOTHER AND DAUGHTER

MERIDA studied DunBroch in a different light after returning from Keithneil. She had seen the entire progression of a village from birth to death to rebirth in just a few minutes, and once she got back to the castle, she couldn't stop trying to decide at which stage of its life span DunBroch was. Clearly Feradach thought it was ready for ruination, so he must look at it and see it in the same way she had seen that overcrowded stolen village.

But that village had been overrun with wickedness and selfishness. DunBroch's supposed crimes seemed gentler. Yes, the courtyard was no longer as neatly planted with spring herbs as it had been at one time. The Great Hall had not hosted a festival for some time. The smoky common room had not been repaired nor its contents swapped to the music room. But these were faults of omission, surely. Plus, there were plenty of run-down things in Keithneil, too, and Feradach hadn't seemed wild to tear through it now.

His desire to destroy DunBroch felt, to Merida, capricious.

Still, it was hard not to see Feradach in a different light, too. She wanted to see him as cruel and villainous, but he never behaved quite as she imagined him. She'd thought he would force her to look upon death and destruction and admire it, but instead, he'd shown her a perfectly lovely, living place. Before he put his hand on it, he'd stood over that dead rebel's body with something that seemed very much like regret. In the end, maybe they *did* want the same thing.

Merida was finally ready to take the trip to Kinlochy.

Now that the weather had at last decided to stay spring, plans had begun in earnest. Merida had proposed they leave as soon as it was clear roads would stop being regularly washed out by snowmelt; Fergus had counterproposed a day just after Pasch, so that "everyone would be feeling more hospitable." It was true that everything got very austere and churchy in the forty days leading up to Pasch (essentially the opposite of Hogmanay in every way), and everything was looser and more celebratory after, so Merida saw his point.

She was growing excited.

She knew the real reason for the trip was inciting change in her family, but her heart was just happy to be traveling again. The only part she wasn't looking forward to was having to banter with her father about this prince there, the one he thought would make a good match. Otherwise, she couldn't wait to get back on the road and adventuring again.

"Merida, you're making me nervous with your pacing," Elinor told her, rising from her chair in the common room. "Is it warm out? Shall we take some air? Yes, we should. Ila, you should come, too."

Ila had been carefully and thoroughly wiping the soot out of the carvings around the fireplace, a process that took forever and only had to be repeated the moment the fire was set again, but she put her duster down and said, "Thank you, ma'am."

Elinor gave the room a *look*.

This happened every time Ila was polite, which was always. It was as if Elinor would have very much liked to have said, *See, children, this is how polite you could be,* but knew how insufferable it would sound, so instead, she just did the *look*.

Harris rolled his eyes and went back to writing something in small letters at his place before the fire.

Hamish's mouth made a very upside-down smile shape and he sulked off toward the music room, where petulant harp noises began to sound.

Merida let out a breath so that her lips went *phbbbbbbbt*.

Elinor pretended none of this had happened. She just said, "Leezie, are you taking some air with us as well? We're going to the wall."

Leezie was lying on her stomach in a slovenly way, dress dangerously close to the hearth, slowly turning the pages in a book Elinor had pressed flowers in and studying each page. Her hair was curled prettily all around her face from where she'd splashed water on it. Every so often she reached to take a honey-covered almond from a tray beside her, licking her fingertips after each one. Merida had never seen someone who looked less likely to go on a walk.

Leezie said, "Take my spirit with you; she's all that has energy. Tell me how many doves you see between you and the moon, though. I need it for my records."

They did not take Leezie's spirit, but they did take some warm spiced bread from the kitchen on their way out. Merida held hers to her cheek as they headed out. Ila cupped hers in her hands. Elinor tore hers into small pieces and ate it on their way to the guard tower that offered access to the top of the wall.

"Spring is finally here after all," Elinor said, gazing out as they emerged at the top of the stairs. This was less a remark on the chill, which was still quite present, and more on the light, which remained even this late in the day. The brief winter days were slowly stretching into the lovely eternal, elastic things they'd become by midsummer, and it felt nice, like being given more time overall. "I always manage to forget how good the view is from up here."

The wall, which partially surrounded the accessible side of DunBroch, had been built by long-ago defenders to repel long-ago invaders, and all along it was a high protected walkway meant to be patrolled by guards. Now it was more often patrolled by red squirrels and stoats. And Elinor. When the weather was kind (meaning the wind was not so vigorous that one would be knocked askew), Elinor walked the wall to "take some air." Elinor's mother had died of some illness that had come about from *not* taking air, apparently, and so Elinor took literal steps to avoid the same fate.

She used to insist the triplets come as well, but they groaned so much about the length of the walk that she eventually gave in. It was true that once you began, you were somewhat of a prisoner of the walkway. There were guard towers every hundred yards or so, but they had not been cleaned out in decades, so the stairs inside them were masses of brambles and bracken and the creatures that lived in brambles and bracken. Only one tower at each end was kept tidy enough for human passage.

"This weather will be very good for journeying," Ila said. She was still holding her bread, uneaten. Merida squished hers into different shapes. Aileen would have been annoyed that she wasn't enjoying how light and airy she'd managed to make the buns, but Merida preferred these spiced ones when they were gummy and dense.

"Yes, you will have a good time, I think," Elinor said.

Merida walked on for several yards before the phrasing of this struck her. "I'll have a good time?"

Elinor inhaled deeply, taking in the earthy scent of the wall, which was all moss and soaked ivy. "Yes, I think so."

Merida repeated, tone a little more dangerous, "*I'll* have a good time? You're going, too."

Elinor's tone was precisely the same as she continued strolling. "I know you heard us discussing this. Your father and I decided that one of us needs to stay behind to run all the affairs of the kingdom; it's just too busy a season to delegate to someone else for that amount of time."

This was a trick, Merida knew, just as clever as one of the Cailleach's. "I definitely did not. You knew it was going to be this season when you agreed!"

"I was hopeful," Elinor said. "Optimistic, really. But then reality set in."

"Perhaps, ma'am, you could go and the king could stay," Ila said. "I would watch your things for you."

Elinor laughed gently and hooked her elbow in Ila's as they walked. "That's very kind of you, Ila. But the king loves Kinlochy and I wouldn't take this trip from him."

This was what Elinor always did. She always made it sound inevitable. Merida should have remembered what happened with the Spain trip. Instead she'd been thinking of the last trip she'd taken with her mother, to the shielings.

The trip had happened quite a while ago, when she was about the same age as the triplets were now. Merida had spent plenty of time riding in the countryside, but none living in it. She didn't know anything about the subjects her parents ruled: the crofters, the fishermen, the dairymen, and the weavers. Back then, Merida had thought perhaps everyone lived in a castle. She'd never seen anything else, and for all she knew, everyone who worked in and around the castle went back to their *own* castles.

But one spring, Elinor had told Merida it was time for her to see what a queen's job was. She packed for an extended journey, and then they went on the first trip Merida had ever been on. It was wonderful.

The shielings were seasonal. Every fall, the crofters moved their cattle to the richer lowland pastures near the village, and over the winter, the cattle nibbled them to nubbins. In spring, the crofters drove the skinny cows up to the shielings, the sloping mountain pastures, so that the lowland pastures could recover.

It wasn't just a place. It was a way of living. All through the warmer months, families lived in simple summer bothies with just bundles of heather as beds, and they ate oatmeal and cheese and butter and milk from the cows they watched, and they sang songs and traded stories under the stars. It was the very best of a simple life, and it was very different from the very best of castle life.

Merida flourished. Her hair never had to be tied away under wimple and veil. Every day was different. She was never asked to perform or pretend to be someone she wasn't.

But, even more astonishingly, *Elinor* flourished. Elinor—delicate, cultured Elinor, so suited to all things royal—was a force of nature there among the bothies. Merida had never seen her so powerful as she was that summer, even in her plainest tunic and her hair knotted messily to keep it away from the butter she churned alongside the other women. All day long, no matter where she was, people came to Elinor for advice, and for plans, and to settle arguments. She never gave orders, but because she was so clever and fair, she ended up ruling the bothies anyway—not because she was their queen by name, but because she always knew how to set things right.

Merida had never thought she was much like her mother, but that summer, she'd never wanted to be like her so badly.

And part of Merida had hoped the trip to Kinlochy might feel the same.

But, walking along the wall with her mother, she realized she'd forgotten how *just Elinor* had come to mean never leaving DunBroch. She wheedled, "Mum! *Please* come!"

Ila spoke up in her dainty tone, "You said I did a very good job, ma'am. You said I made it easy to imagine being able to nip away, don't you remember?"

Exchanging a look with Ila, Merida saw that her expression was conspiratorial. She was on Merida's side. She added, "It's only a few weeks!"

"If Aileen's not cooking for the whole family, she'll have time to help with the rest of the castle, too," Ila pitched in.

Elinor gazed out over the darkening landscape. From here there was a good view of the loch, and it was golden and illuminated in the low light. There were a few swans still left, and they glided like dark dragons across the glinting water. Somewhere close by a fox barked. "This just isn't the right time, girls."

Merida burst out, "You always do this! You always wiggle out of it!"

"Don't be mercurial," Elinor replied, not raising her voice. They hadn't fought for years and she wasn't about to start now. "Look, there, two doves for Leezie. Don't forget to tell her."

"I don't care about the doves! All this time you let me think you were going to go and now you just pretend like all along I was supposed to think you weren't! It's always excuses!"

Elinor's voice got a tiny little edge to it. "Being a queen is not an excuse. It's a duty."

It was like a white rage came down over Merida. Her ears hissed with it. Her mind was full of Mistress mac Lagan telling her how Ardbarrach thought of DunBroch, and her cheeks went just as hot as they had been that day. "And what is a queen's duty, Mum? What is it you do all day? Who are you writing letters to at your desk? What would happen if you stopped?"

"Merida!" Elinor said, sharply. Then, with obvious effort, she repeated in calmer tones, "Merida. That is inappropriate."

"When is the truth inappropriate? You don't *do* anything anymore! You just pretend to be a queen! Dad just pretends to be a king! The world is laughing at us! We're not—" Merida pulled herself back from saying *changing*, because she didn't want to violate the terms of the bargain. Instead she said, "Get mad, will you! Get angry! Shout! Do something!"

But Elinor didn't lose her temper.

Elinor just looked at Merida, her expression sad and sweet. "I'm not mad, my darling. I'm disappointed that's how you see me, is all."

In the old days, this would've become an enormous row, and then mother and daughter would have made up and come to a compromise, and things would have been different on the other side. Now it was as though Elinor was just simply giving in.

The hiss in Merida's ears was a roar. "I'm disappointed this is how you *are*!"

She spun and stormed away.

It was hard to believe she'd ever want to be like her mother again.

PART III

SUMMER

17

THE WOLVES OF SUMMER

"WHAT a comely season!" Fergus roared.

They were on the journey to Kinlochy. Finally, finally. It was weeks later than they'd originally agreed upon; the plan had gotten worried to death, back and forth, dogs with bones, dogs with carved spoons. In the end, it was only Fergus, Hamish, Merida, and Brionn the spoon-eating puppy. Harris had been slated to come but was in trouble for biting Hamish; he'd been assigned a month's worth of scribe work as punishment. And Elinor continued to be Elinor. Merida was still not speaking with her.

"I'll go on the next one," Elinor had said, right before they left.

Of all of the things she could have said, this one stung Merida the most. She wouldn't go, of course. She was never going to go. Why did she keep *saying* it, if she didn't mean it? And if she meant it, why didn't she *do* it?

Merida had left without answering.

"What a glorious country, what a noble land!" Fergus continued.

"It is gorgeous," Merida admitted.

She was annoyed at the delay in their departure, but it was true that they were now riding through the most tender version of Scotland. These long northern summer days stretched out forever and ever, turning into a short gray night for just a few hours before rolling right back into another bright day. The trees were every color of green: the warm ashes, the blue pines. Birds were everywhere. Since they'd left the castle, they'd encountered dramatic capercaillies with their high-spread tails, V-tailed kites, long-legged corncrakes, dire-faced rooks, and cheery little swallows.

Unlike the trip to Ardbarrach, this time they moved swiftly, with no pony cart to slow them down. They didn't even have any attendants or guards. Traveling with her father, Merida required no maid for propriety, and Fergus didn't need a guide to tell him how to get to Kinlochy. He had left his soldiers guarding DunBroch and urged Merida and Hamish to dress austerely on the road, not as royals. He didn't want to draw any more attention than was required to the fact that the king was away from his castle and his queen.

So they rode swiftly, unadorned with royal trappings, through the best days Scotland had to offer, toward an exciting city Fergus loved.

Merida could not complain, really.

An enormous shadow fell across the Midge's neck.

"Look!" Merida cried, and pointed overhead. An enormous white-tailed eagle, big as one of the triplets, swooped low. It got close enough that the Midge, always eager for an excuse to spook, skittered sideways, and that Merida could pick out every one of its brown wing feathers and see its great yellow beak, which was parted opportunistically.

"What a champion. Fellow king. King of the air. You have the sky, fellow, and I'll keep this down here, right? Hold on to the saddle, Hamish!" Fergus laughed. "You'd be a tasty snack."

Hamish squeaked in fear.

"It's a joke," Merida told him. "Hamish. It's a joke."

This was one thing Merida probably could complain about. Just a bit. Hamish had already been frightened once that day by Brionn leaping out of the brush suddenly. He'd been riding Humor, a pony who generally couldn't be bothered to be frightened, but Hamish had screamed with such convincing fear that Humor had thoroughly believed him and taken off galloping. Merida had had to fetch him back. Now Hamish rode in front of Fergus on Sirist while Merida led Humor behind the Midge, which was part of why they could move so quickly. There was no pausing to make sure Hamish was keeping his seat or steering his pony; Humor was just an unburdened pack pony at this point. There had been a time in the past when Fergus would have gotten quite cross over all this, but now Hamish had been this way long enough that Fergus had accepted that this was *just Hamish*.

The short list of what Hamish was afraid of: everything.

Hamish was afraid of the dark. He was afraid of loud noises. He was afraid of weasels and wolves. He was afraid of insects with stingers. He was afraid of earwigs, which didn't have stingers, but looked like they might. He was afraid of getting thorns stuck in his skin. He was afraid of getting food stuck in his throat. He was afraid of heights. He was afraid of depths. He was afraid of thunder. He was afraid of lightning. He was afraid of large groups of people. He was afraid of small groups of people. He was afraid of Harris.

These were all things Merida could mostly understand. These were all things that could possibly hurt or startle. She could try to comfort him about all of these fears. But Hamish was also afraid of things that she couldn't understand: concepts and situations that didn't seem to have any particular terror to them. He was afraid of the third stair that led up to the music room, so he always skipped it. He was afraid of the suit of armor displayed on the second-floor balcony over the Great Hall, so he always cried quietly if asked to fetch something from the second floor. He was afraid of how the swans left the loch every summer to spend the year elsewhere, and hid in his room for days after the last one had gone. He was afraid of turning the last page of a book, and so never knew how any text ended unless it was read to him.

Merida didn't know how to comfort someone with these fears.

The strange thing was that she didn't think he'd always been afraid; he'd just *gotten* afraid. And even stranger was that she couldn't think of anything that had happened to make him afraid. It felt like he should be less afraid, not more, because his life was so safe.

Instead, he was afraid of eagles.

He had never been carried away by an eagle.

"Dad," Merida asked pensively, as they rode along the well-worn path to the east. "When did Mum stop going places?"

"What," blustered Fergus. "She goes places."

Merida did not dignify this with a response.

"Your mother likes the finer things in life," Fergus said eventually. "Traveling doesn't always offer those."

"She took me to the shielings," Merida protested. "There's no creature comforts there."

Fergus didn't say anything for a bit. The thing about Merida's father was that if he couldn't say something loudly, he often didn't say anything at all. He fidgeted a bit instead. He adjusted Hamish on the saddle in front of him. He scratched his wooden leg before his fingers remembered he'd lost it years ago, and then he scratched the other. He stroked his beard. Finally he said, "I reckon maybe she's forgotten how good she used to be at it. You get stuck one way, don't you, sometimes."

"Is that what's happened to you, Hame?" Merida asked. "Did you get stuck scared of eagles?"

Hamish just blinked at her from the safe circle of Fergus's arms. He couldn't be goaded into bravery, and he was too used to being scared to be ashamed of it. It was simply who he was.

She thought about pressing him further, but then

Merida noticed the Midge's ears were turning this way and that. Not in her usual surly way, but in an urgent, wary way. Glancing behind her, Merida saw that Humor, too, was starting to prance a bit, his tail held high as if he was thinking of bolting. Humor was not a pony who thought of much but a good mouthful of grass, so for him to be considering a jog so soon after his last was remarkable.

In the woods, Merida heard a shudder as some birds took flight, squawking in warning at each other.

Brionn's wiry hair stood straight all up along his wiry spine. His little bright eyes, so rarely pointed in the same direction, were both pointed toward the woods.

"Dad," she said.

"I hear it," he replied.

"What?" Hamish asked nervously.

"I think we should—"

"Yes," Fergus said. "Let Humor go if you must, he'll follow!"

He clapped his big legs round Sirist's deep chestnut sides, and Merida did the same to the Midge. They burst into a gallop.

The wolf pack emerged from the trees.

There's a misconception that the spare winter times are the worst for wolf attacks. The reasoning goes that there's not much food to be had, so they turn to humans. But the truth is that it's far worse to be out on a fine summer's day when the pack's had a good year. Because then there are lots of new mouths to feed and the she-wolves are starving from feeding up their growing broods, and they're all wanting to be educational in any case. What better to teach a young wolf to hunt than some travelers?

That was what happened to the priest and that lad who'd brought that one board game to DunBroch. Wolves. That lady from France, too, had gotten eaten, and her escort had only barely gotten away and now, according to Elinor, had joined a monastery after what he'd seen. It was experience, not fear, that had made Hamish guess that the injuries he'd spotted on Feradach's face were from wolves. For quite some time, Fergus and the neighboring kings had an open call for wolf hunters, and the hunters would come at the end of the summer with a bag full of tails and get paid for each.

Merida had found the entire thing barbarous until the first time she'd gotten cornered by a pack. Wolves and humans were in a centuries-long battle where some years the humans won, and some years the wolves did.

So Merida and Fergus and Hamish galloped.

The wolves were silent as they hunted the family, unlike the silly-eyed hound dogs Fergus hunted with. The wolves were clever, too, trying to separate and trick the horses off the path and into traps, just as Merida had done with Feradach all those weeks ago. And the wolves were fast. The horses were, too, but they'd already been ridden all day after a lazy spring.

"I'm going to stop and fight them, Merida!" Fergus shouted. "You take Hamish!"

"I'm not leaving you, Dad!" Merida said.

Hamish's eyes were wide with fear. Brionn darted in and out of Humor's legs in a way that threatened to trip both of them. The wiry dog couldn't decide if he was valorous enough to face the wolves or terrified enough that he needed to take cover. Merida understood entirely.

She reached for her bow.

But before she could decide which wolf to aim at first, a wild, pure horn sounded.

The wolves faltered.

The horn sounded again.

Merida and Fergus wheeled their mounts in circles, searching for the source of the horn.

It sounded a third time.

Suddenly, a massive creature with spines all over its body barreled out of the woods and between the horses. It was roaring. Arrows sprayed around it; one of the wolves let out a squall and bolted. Again, that horn sounded wildly. The Midge reared; Sirist spun. It was chaos.

"We've got you!" someone shouted. "You're all right now!"

The commotion turned out to belong to a group of people dressed in leather armor and rough tunics. The creature with spines was a massive dog of the same breed the Dásachtach's men had brought to DunBroch, only wearing clever leather armor with spines made of antler stitched all over it. And the horn was a substantial, rough instrument that both commanded the dog and terrified the wolves, who clearly understood what it meant. They were all led by a man with very black hair and enormous black eyebrows. The back of his leather armor was similiarly covered with spines, just like the dog, who returned to him with its tongue lolling happily.

This man was the first one to notice whom they had just rescued. His enormous black eyebrows shot up, and then he dropped down to one knee in immediate fealty.

"I'm sorry, my king," the man said, head still bowed. He had the broad accent of the countryfolk. "I didn't recognize you in that plain getup."

The rest of the men dropped at once.

Merida and Hamish blinked at the line of kneeling men; it was an unusual sight, and not entirely comfortable. These men had just saved them, and now they were nearly flat before them in apology.

"Get up, get up, lads. I'll come down to you instead." Fergus laughed his mighty laugh and slid down from the side of Sirist, plopping Hamish down beside him, much to Hamish's visible distress. He addressed the man with the spiny armor. "What is your name and how can we thank you?"

The man stood. He rubbed the armored dog's scarred ears as he said, "I am Maldouen, the earl of Strathmannon's right-hand man. And there's no need to thank us. We're happy to escort you on your way to wherever you are headed."

"We're headed quite far east," Fergus said. "Kinlochy. We wouldn't expect you to escort us so far from your home. But we'll take a meal with you, if you'll have us."

"Sir," Maldouen said, "whatever you wish."

The men took them back to their small village, which turned out to be completely composed of beehive houses. Beehive houses were peculiar round structures built of flat pieces of rock, a method that made them look like the beehives that gave them their name, or perhaps like pine cones. They had tiny square doors and sometimes tiny square windows, and altogether they seemed like buildings a child would draw if you asked them to try. Merida had heard of them but never seen them and was delighted. She tried to get Hamish's excitement up, too.

"Look at them," Merida said, putting an arm over his thin shoulders. She could feel that he was still quivering every so often with his fear. "Have you ever seen anything like them?"

Hamish didn't answer. Instead he stood pressed against her, staring at the beehive houses with a hollow expression. She dug out the little bear that she'd first brought to Ardbarrach for Hubert and handed it over to Hamish, who silently accepted it. Brother and sister stood side by side like that, Hamish worrying his fingers over the bear's worn ears and Merida worrying her hand over the top of Hamish's head, as Fergus received an introduction to Maldouen's boss, the head of the village. Earl Godfrey of Strathmannon. It was a very big name for a very small village, and Merida was uncomfortably reminded of Mistress mac Lagan talking about rural kingdoms playing pretend. The earl's subjects were a few dozen scrawny villagers with not a lot of meat on their bones and not a single luxury to be seen, apart from smiles. There were plenty of those.

A royal visit would have been thrilling on its own. But a royal visit after a daring wolf chase? The village was in high spirits; the stories tonight would be good.

Godfrey trundled over to Hamish and Merida. He looked no more earl-like than any of the men he led, and he had the same broad accent as Maldouen. "You must be the princess."

"That's me," Merida said.

"And this the prince," Godfrey said. He squinted at Hamish, who was still visibly quivering. Instantly his face melted into sympathy. This was how it always went with little Hamish. Just as Leezie usually inspired people to offer her help, Hamish inspired people to offer him comfort. "Oh, wee prince, you're safe now. The wolves are bad this year, but Maldouen and Ol' Flower here keep them well away. Look. Ol' Flower, come on over to this boy."

Godfrey encouraged the dog with the spiny armor to approach Hamish.

Hamish, already small, somehow managed to shrink further. What Godfrey didn't know was that there was nothing he could say to improve Hamish's mood and that, moreover, the act of talking to him would make Hamish feel worse. He was still afraid of the wolves, and now he was also afraid of the armored dog, and also of being talked to directly by Godfrey.

Fergus saw this and said, "Merida, why don't you put up the horses, and check the bags after that gallop—you know what to do. Bring Hamish so he can see to Humor. And do something with that cockeyed dog of Harris's."

"I thought you said he was of good stock," Merida said. She and her father eyed Brionn, who was running in loopy circles around Ol' Flower, barking strange half-barks that just came out as nasal whines.

"Don't tell Harris I called him cockeyed," Fergus said. "But that dog was born under a broken star for sure."

The villagers offered to do the job for the princess, of course, but Merida waved them away. She knew what her father wanted her to do, and it was not simply take care of the tired horses.

"Have you ever seen Dad do this before?" Merida asked Hamish, who stood obediently beside her in the lean-to, eyes still terrified, fingers still trembling. It would have been easy to be impatient with him if he had been crying, but instead he just tried to quietly do whatever she asked despite his fear. She looked to see if he still had the little bear—he did—and kept up a cheery prattle she hoped would distract him. "Oh, of course you wouldn't have. You've never traveled with him. This village doesn't have any trade routes, and they don't have anything to trade, anyway. They just live off the land. They might have a few goats and maybe a pony or two. They gather food and store it for when it gets cold. So we're going to give them what we have, these things we brought for our treats. That's what Dad meant for us to do."

Hamish watched with serious eyes as she loaded his arms up with sugared fruits and preserved meats and spiced baked goods, all the royal luxuries they'd brought for the journey.

"But don't make a fuss—act like we don't know if they already have these things, okay?" Merida added. "Let them have their pride."

Later they sat around a big, roughly hewn table outside, enjoying a meal in the still-bright light. (Merida suspected the insides of the beehive houses were too small and dark for comfortable dining, and those living in them might not want to spare the rushes and animal fat to light them.) It seemed like it might be late, but it was hard to say what time it was. These summer days went on forever, and it would be bright until midnight or later. Fergus sat at the head of the table and the earl at its foot, and villagers packed the benches on either side and spilled into the grass as well. The tale of the wolves had already been told several times over. Every time it was told, Ol' Flower got thrown another bit of meat. She moved quickly despite her great size, and no matter how quickly Brionn tried to intercept the flying food, Ol' Flower always got to it first, to everyone's great delight. Well, everyone but Hamish, who was still terrified of her.

Hamish had calmed down a little, at least. With his big eyes he now watched the villagers savoring all the foods he took for granted. He also stared at the lute leaning against the bench a few feet away.

The woman beside it caught him looking at it but was smart enough to not bring it up directly. Instead, she said, "Thank you for these treats, little man."

He blinked up at her. The woman glanced at Merida, who shrugged a little.

"But what's nicest is your company," the woman added. She took the lute up into her lap. "A new audience to play for!"

As she began to play, voices whooped around the table. Some of the villagers banged cups against the wood in time with the tune. Merida watched Hamish's spidery, cold fingers subconsciously move along with the tune. How he loved music. He only had to hear a melody once or twice to be able to play it back.

"Does the prince play?" asked the lute player.

"Hamish is a wee beast with all stringed things," Fergus said. "Pity those wolves didn't have strings."

Immediately, the woman passed the lute to Hamish. He didn't move his arms in time to take it, so she simply plopped it down in his lap. "I'll trade you a tune for your dish of pears."

Hamish sat there, a frozen little creature with big eyes. Pinned to the bench by fear and by the lute.

How badly Merida wanted him to be able to play fearlessly for this group. Not for their benefit, but for his. How was it that his sense of fun had been replaced by a sense of fear? She whispered to him, "You could play 'Crosses and Squares.'"

Still he was frozen.

Maldouen said, "Don't you think you owe Ol' Flower a tune for saving your life?"

Maldouen was being playful, but he had, without realizing, hit upon the only way to make Hamish perform: obligation. Hamish let fear rule him, but not at the expense of other people.

Hamish whispered, "All right," and then added, to the dog, "Ma'am," which made the entire table laugh uproariously.

Hamish began to play.

The villagers began to clap in time with him. Hamish played faster. They clapped faster. Hamish played little riffs and twirls, and the villagers got up and danced along with the well-known tune. With the lute in his hand and the tune ringing out strongly, it was almost possible to believe Hamish wasn't afraid, but Merida knew better. This was how it always went. When Hamish played for other people, he always looked liked a different person. Straighter, surer. More like Hubert or Harris. This was part of a good show, after all, and he felt obligated to give Ol' Flower a good show.

Merida thought to herself that Hamish was actually much braver than she was. She did wild things all the time, but she wasn't afraid before she did them. Hamish was terrified to do almost everything, and he did a lot of things anyway.

She wished she could believe that playing for these people would change him. Convince him to not be afraid on the other side of it, since nothing bad happened to him during it. But then the tune came to an end and it was as if the music itself had propped him up. Hamish shrank back down into his usual shy self and handed the lute back. His eyes dropped away from everyone and he did his very, very best to disappear.

Merida had no idea what it would take to change him.

18

THE SLEEPING PLACE

I T WAS funny for Merida to see Fergus get excited as they grew close to Kinlochy. He began to point out landmarks and wave his arms and tell fragments of memories that trailed off as he realized the group he was traveling with hadn't been there for them and that it would require rather a lot of work to put them in context. He seemed rather like Hubert when he was like this, scattered and enthusiastic, too happy to focus. Well, rather like the *old* Hubert, pre-Ardbarrach, the Hubert she used to think would grow up to be like Fergus, big as a house, with his big Norseman hair and big Norseman beard. She had no idea what he would turn into now, with his hair shorn short and his blue beads abandoned beside his bed.

"Kin*lochy*!" shouted Fergus with enthusiasm as they rode into the town.

They arrived at the outskirts of Kinlochy just as the long, long day was coming to a close. The brief night seemed even less convincing here than it was at DunBroch, however, because Kinlochy was a kingdom on the sea and the sun lasted forever out there over the ocean. "Night" was simply a gray-brown version of day. Even though Merida couldn't see the ocean, she could smell it, that clean, fishy scent, and she could see it in the sky. Skies right by the ocean always had that strange, open look to them, as if the light was coming from all directions and the clouds couldn't be bothered to remember which way was down.

Merida was relieved to find that the town of Kinlochy was nothing like Ardbarrach. It had an altogether less strict look to it. Its partial wall was in fine shape but was clearly from an era long ago, from when the Romans had pressed as far north as they could before receding, leaving behind only odd names. The buildings inside the wall looked modern and productive to Merida's eye: shops and factories, places to buy things and places to make things, places to put things into carts and take them to other towns and places to unload carts from other towns. Signs and banners hung from all the gray stone buildings, showing and describing the jobs each did. An elegant, expensive tower dominated the town; the winding main street led to its silhouette by the seaside. The amount of prosperous trade that must have happened to build a town of this size dazzled Merida's imagination.

It all was quite lovely. Peaceful.

As they rode toward the tower, Merida tried to imagine herself living in a place like this. What were the people like? So far, they hadn't encountered anyone.

"The mead they have here," Fergus roared to his children. "There's a thing called Kinlochy ale, but it's mostly eggs. It'll put hair on your chest. Well, hair on your heads."

Their horses' hooves clopped across the cobblestones, echoing against the buildings assembled close to the road. Brionn ran busily up and back in front of them, sniffing away, tail high.

They still hadn't seen a single person. Was it because it was late? At DunBroch, when the summer sun stayed up late, so did the people. Perhaps here they kept to a better schedule and slept when they ought to, instead. The houses they passed did have their shutters closed, after all.

Fergus's voice bounced back at them in the empty streets, but he kept talking louder and louder, as if he could drown out the echo. "And Hamish, you'll love the music here. We once had a Kinlochy group out to DunBroch. You wouldn't remember it because you were just a little midge when we had them, but—"

"A harpist," Hamish said, without hesitation, "with a long pointy beard. And those three pipers. That musician with the lute with two necks that he played at the same time."

"By the Cailleach, however do you remember that? You would've been just an egg!"

Hamish never forgot something that had to do with music.

Where was the Kinlochy music now? There was no sound at all, apart from the cry of seabirds as they finally rode right up to the tower. It was an impressive shape against the ocean-shimmery sky above it, gulls white and buoyant around it. The tower seemed to be silently watching them approach.

"This is quite something," Fergus said, as soft as he ever said anything, his bluster quieted by the hush of the streets they'd come through.

The door to the tower hung open a little. Not propped, just hanging.

Fergus slid off Sirist and walked up to it. He called out and then, after a moment, pushed the door further open.

Merida caught her breath, wondering what was on the other side.

But it was just a man and a woman, half asleep in chairs just inside the door. They were dressed in the luxurious apparel Merida would have expected for a place like this. The man had little gold threads woven through his beard. The woman had a web of pearls netted over her hair. But they were both sitting quite lazily, and they didn't straighten when they saw they were observed.

"Who's there?" the woman asked in a sleepy way.

"Fergus of DunBroch, here to see his old friend Ronald of Kinlochy! Bang some pans and wake him up if you must!"

The woman just blinked at them. Without a lot of enthusiasm, she asked the man with the gold-threaded beard, "Do you know what he's talking about?"

The man shook his head. He yawned, more uninterested in the chore of greeting people than even Leezie was in any of hers.

"On your feet, man!" Fergus bellowed. "Can't you see we've come from DunBroch? Now, I'm not a boor, but I know what you're meant to do, and you're meant to tell your king when another king has arrived with half his progeny! Off you go!"

He said it all in his big voice with his big humor and it was the kind of thing that would ordinarily have made people laugh along with him and do what he asked. Another king would have been well within his rights to shout at these two for their insolence.

And maybe he should have, Merida thought. Because the man and the woman just regarded each other in a shrugging sort of way before eventually shambling deeper into the dim interior. They did it with so little urgency that it was hard to tell if they were going to do as Fergus had asked, or if they were merely leaving so he would stop asking them.

After they had gone, Merida said, "How rude!" even though rude wasn't exactly the right word for it. "Was it . . . like this before?"

"The discipline was never very rigorous!" Fergus said, but he looked disgruntled. When he saw Hamish leaning his cheek drowsily against Humor's mane, he added, "Don't sleep yet. There'll be celebration once we get to Ronald. That man can throw a feast like no one's business. Every night is ridiculous with him and Caitrina. Swimming in mead. Singing until dawn. Sword fights on the tables. Performers from Spain."

Time passed.

The town around them stayed quiet. The castle before them stayed quiet.

The horses began to fidget. Merida peered into the tower's dim interior for any evidence that the man and woman were returning.

"Any sign of them, bear-maiden?" asked Fergus.

Merida shook her head.

As the gray-brown night crept around them and the silence only deepened, Merida and Hamish at last dismounted. Fergus took Hamish onto his shoulders.

Then they cautiously led the horses right into the castle.

19

THE HOPELESS PRINCE

THE tower's entry hall was dim. The only light came from the ambient glow through the decorative windows, so it was difficult to tell how big the space was. The reflected sound, however, suggested it was massive. The hooves clopped loud as anything, and Merida couldn't believe that no one had come out to tell them off. Horses! Inside a tower like this.

Perhaps there was no one *to* come out and tell them off.

"Maybe that man and woman were ghosts," Merida said in a low voice. She didn't really believe in ghosts, but then again, she was in a pact with two gods. Anything was possible. "How would we know?"

"You wouldn't be asking me that if you'd smelled them," Fergus said, as they pressed deeper in. "Spirits don't have odiferous armpits."

Merida believed him, but nonetheless, she found the lightless tower eerie. Intimidating. She'd spent many

nights in empty landscapes, but darkness in the vast out-
doors felt like just a consequence of night. Darkness in a
tower like this felt hollow. There were candles and lamps
on tables and fixed to the walls, but none of them were lit.
The people who lived here had the option of light, but no
one had chosen it.

"Ladies!" Fergus said broadly.

They had finally come across some women. Handmaidens, perhaps. Courtiers. Like the others, the women were
dressed in feast-ready finery, but they were not celebrating.
They simply stood against the wall as if they were waiting
for something.

"Where is your mistress?" Fergus continued, his voice
still jocular. His good humor was his DunBroch solution
to this peculiar situation; he would be jolly even if no one
else would be. "Where are the stable boys? You see we have
to lead our horses through your halls for want of welcome!"

The handmaidens looked at him with an expression
Merida thought first was contempt and then realized was
apathy. Some of the women even turned away, posture
bored.

Merida and her father exchanged a look. Hamish
hugged the top of Fergus's head from his position on his
shoulders and looked worried. (Other things he was afraid
of: handmaidens who didn't answer direct questions.)
Humor nudged the back of Merida's hand, reminding her
of the absurdity of the situation. Ponies in a castle. Handmaidens paying visiting nobility no mind. An empty town
on a beautiful summer night.

After a long pause, Merida thought about it very hard and then asked the handmaidens where the king was. In French. Her French wasn't very good, but Elinor had insisted she learn enough to speak to the nobles who preferred it as their courtly language.

And to her surprise, she was rewarded with a vague response: one of the handmaidens gestured limply deeper into the castle.

Fergus gave Merida a subtle, approving nod. Merida was strangely moved by the smallness of the communication, as opposed to his usual bluster. She'd never been unsure of her father's love for her, but for once, she felt like he was seeing her in a way that he never had back at DunBroch: like an adult, not a child. Like an equal.

Deeper in, they found one flickering candle and, around it, a handful of soldiers. Like the others, they were dressed in absolute luxury, and also singularly uninterested in the family DunBroch. Eventually one of the soldiers directed them further into the castle, but no one offered even an escort.

"This is not the Kinlochy I remember," Fergus said.

Finally they came to a great hall with a few torches lit along the walls. Now there was enough light for Merida to see how wealth had shaped this place. Fantastically carved tables had marble inlays. Floor torches had great gold feet in the shape of bird claws and fish tails and animal paws. Tapestries and banners hung from the high ceiling, each intricately designed and threaded through with gold. Musical instruments both domestic and exotic gathered dust on an elevated stage (Hamish stared at these).

There were humans there, too, but they seemed nearly as lifeless as the instruments. They curled next to the harps or leaned on the tables, dressed in the same jeweled finery as everyone else. Like the others, they also did not react much to the presence of foreign royals and horses right in their great hall.

Merida wanted to shout, *What is wrong with you?* but somehow felt it would be rude, awfully rude, more rude than they were being by not responding. It felt like there *was* something deeply wrong here, but to point it out would be unkind, as the people they encountered already knew it themselves. Their faces were so bleak and detached.

"Can we go, Dad?" whispered Hamish. "Can we just go?"

"Is it enchantment?" Merida asked. She thought about what she had seen at the rock at Keithneil. "Are they sick?"

Fergus said, "We need to find Ronald. That's all that matters right now."

In a library farther down the hall, they found a young man about Merida's age, his chin on his hand, a book in front of him. The book had been open long enough to the same page that the ink had faded beyond reading, but he stared at it as if it would make sense.

"Rory!" Fergus said, his voice shocked. But he quickly became just as jolly as before. As her parents always did when faced with an unpleasant situation, he tried to turn it into something positive. He lifted Hamish from his shoulders and set him beside the desk. "Look at the height on you since last we met. Look at your beard. Where is your father, Ronald the king?"

This was the young man Merida been thinking she'd have to avoid? This was no potential suitor. This was a living statue.

Slowly, Rory lifted his gaze. Probably he had been handsome at one point, but it was hard to tell now, since his hair and beard hung limply around him and his skin was gray.

"We're looking at the books," he said. His voice had a recited, monotonous quality to it, as if instead of holding a conversation, he were repeating a poem or hymn he had heard many times before, one he was bored of. "We're looking for those funds. We'll get back to you. Take a table or a chair or sculpture if you need satisfaction before then. I'll find you in the ledger. I'll find you."

"Rory, I'm not here about business!" Fergus said, slamming his big hands on the desk on either side of the book. "We're here to have a royal visit of revelry and catching up! Don't you remember me from that summer of fireworks? Where is your mother? Where are your kinsmen? Why is there no music, why is there no light?"

"There's no light?" echoed Rory. He looked puzzled, and then he said in a dull tone, "We can't afford it. We've had to give it away. Made a mistake in the ledger. Must have. Something marked down wrong. We owe everyone everything. Just take what you think you deserve."

Coming round the desk, Fergus lifted Rory to his feet. "Get up, man. I don't know what's happened to you, but this is no way to handle it. Lead us to your father."

Without even a whisper at this physical treatment, Rory

just did as Fergus asked, his body stiff and unpracticed with movement. As they headed back into the hall, his eyes glanced off Merida and she shivered at what she saw. There was something flat and reflective about them, like an animal's eyes seen by torchlight, and when the light passed, nothing remained but that dull apathy. He didn't seem at all surprised that they were leading horses through his father's halls. Instead he just trudged ahead of them without looking over his shoulder to ensure they were following.

Merida put her free arm around Hamish as they walked. She could feel his fast little heartbeat where her hand was against his neck, and it matched hers. Her mind wasn't properly afraid, but her body was nevertheless prepping for an unseen battle.

They walked and walked, following Rory down vast hallways with soaring roofs. This castle! The tower they had seen was only one corner of it. The rest continued in great sweeping levels down toward the sea, which Merida could see out the windows. This dark maze must have been very grand indeed when Fergus was here, filled with hundreds of soldiers and traders and craftspeople and courtiers. They passed a room where children dozed with a nursemaid, and a room with a few elderly businesspeople slumped over ledgers, and yet more rooms of courtiers leaned against cushions and dusty chairs.

None of them lifted their gaze to the DunBroch party as they passed.

Eventually, they found themselves outside on a great

stone patio that overlooked the sea far below. It was nearly as large as the entire village of beehive houses, and was paved with beautifully painted tiles. An arching stone handrail protected occupants from the steep drop of the rocky cliffs. At the end of the patio, hundreds of precarious carved steps led down to a white shoreline. There, half-sunk merchant ships were visible in the sand, as well as a handful of old rowboats. Over all of it was the smell of the sea. Not the clean, saline smell Merida had picked up when they'd first approached the ocean, but the rotten, mouth-puckering odor of spoiled fish.

Hamish took in a sharp, uneven breath. He'd never seen the ocean before today.

Rory had stopped. He passed a hand slowly over his temple, eyes confused and vague. "I'm sorry, I misremembered where . . ."

"Boy," Fergus said, his voice worried. He put his hand on Rory's arm. "Don't lose hope."

There was something so touching in the way Fergus spoke that both Hamish and Merida stared at him. It had been so long since Merida had heard her father not being blustery and loud and big and overtly cheery that she had convinced herself that he had always been that way. But now she remembered that there used to be more to him. Not a softer side, exactly, but a more complex side, like what had been slowly unfolding as they took this journey.

Hamish made his way over to him as he continued to try to break through Rory's stupor. He was so clearly fascinated by the change in his father that Merida tried to remember if Hamish was old enough to ever remember the Fergus of her youth.

But before she could ponder it too deeply, she realized they were no longer alone on the patio.

A figure had just climbed up the last step of the precarious staircase from the shore far below. The ocean wind tore at his cloak, his tunic, and his mane of light hair.

On his hands he wore gloves with oxblood-red stitching.

As Merida watched, he took one off and pressed his bare palm flat onto the stone railing.

20

I Am Nature

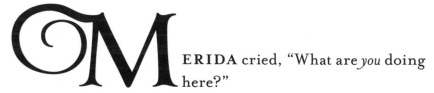ERIDA cried, "What are *you* doing here?"

Feradach's face was shocked.

He tore his hand away from the stone railing as if it were burning hot, but they both could see that his work was done: there was a deep handprint in the stone. In a voice completely unlike any she'd heard him use before, he snarled, *"Get out now!"*

And then things started to go very wrong.

This was nothing like the destruction of Keithneil that Merida had seen when she pressed her hand against the stone there. The disease and famine had taken weeks to ruin the villagers.

This was immediate.

From somewhere deep in the castle, there was a scream. A fresh odor of smoke had already reached Merida. It smelled deeply *wrong*. It was not the appealing, cozy scent of firewood burning, but the acrid, strange odor of shingles and tapestries alight.

It smelled like violence.

Feradach hissed, "This place is doomed. Save yourself."

"Quiet, merciless boggart!" Merida said as she leaned over the edge of the patio to see if there would be an escape by way of the sea. "Oh!"

Far below, the dark ocean was churned to madness and somehow, impossibly, the shore had disappeared. The ocean swirled right up to the cliffs, eating hungrily at the bottom of the steep staircase. A few hundred yards out, a strange circular tide had risen, a whirlpool that she could hear all the way up here. It was already devouring the half-submerged wrecks and the old rowboats, destroying all chance of leaving by sea.

"A rock shelf has collapsed just offshore, beneath the water," Feradach said in a flat voice. She knew he was offended that she'd called him a merciless boggart; but wasn't that just what he was? A feelingless god wearing a stolen human face. "Opening a cavern that had air in it, creating a whirlpool as it sucks water in. A rare occurrence; most men will not see it again in their lifetime."

"We won't be able to leave by sea, Merida!" Fergus called from farther down the patio; he had been doing the same calculations as Merida. "No one can get out that way."

A great crash echoed across the patio as a tower roof collapsed. Flames torrented through the tower and its neighbor; the great ocean wind was spreading the flames quickly.

Merida shouted, "Can we go back through the inside?"

"I don't know!" Fergus was still searching the shoreline for possibilities as the sound of chaos rose from the building.

Feradach continued, "A torch was left lit too close to a window tapestry and the wind turned. No one has refilled the bathing water in any of the towers. Laundry has been left hanging for weeks and is dry enough to catch. The queen had a penchant for potted palm trees from their southern trade routes and had hundreds inside the castle, but they were not taken care of, so they have died and dried. The walls are full of dry tinder of bird and rat nests."

"What a perfect confluence of events," Merida snarled.

Feradach said, "They glutted themselves with riches without asking where they came from and have been falling asleep after the drunken feast for years. You don't know who has died for this luxury you stand on. They earned this fate."

"And you didn't hesitate to give it to them! I saw you take off your glove!"

"You know what I do," Feradach said. "You know who I am. I told you."

Merida whirled away from him.

"Dad, we have to go!" wailed Hamish.

"I know. Rory," Fergus said, turning his attention to the prince who'd brought them to the patio in the first place. "You know this castle, you'll have to lead us. Take Hamish's pony."

Rory looked slightly more vital, but only because the light from the flaming tower was putting color in his cheeks. He said, "I can't remember how to ride."

Merida couldn't believe how passive he could remain in the face of this flickering disaster. She said, "Then lead us on foot!"

Rory said, "This isn't real, though."

"Boy," Fergus said, "now is not the time for your mind to flit."

For a brief moment, they went back and forth, Fergus trying to convey the urgency to Rory, and Rory failing to satisfy with his response. Then, with a mighty grunt, Fergus turned his attention from Rory. He raised his voice to be heard over the whirlpool, the wind, the crackling fire. "Father, take the horse, then, and come with us."

It took Merida half a beat to understand he was talking to Feradach, who stood several yards off beside the patio railing, unmoving. *Father?* A priest, then.

Merida sneered at Feradach, daring him to accept her father's kindness

Feradach remained where he was. His voice was polite. "Thank you, but I will chance the sea."

"Is everyone here mad? Your god might save you from many things," Fergus said, "but he won't save you from stupidity. I've no time to talk you out of it with my children here with me. Merida, on your horse!"

The horses were going mad where they were tied to the railing. As Merida untied the Midge, Fergus muttered, "Oh, I can't just—" And he dismounted long enough to grapple Rory onto Humor. He situated himself on Sirist, keeping a good grasp of Humor's reins as he did. Then he dragged Hamish up onto the saddle in front of him before springing off with a clatter of hooves on flagstone.

Merida pulled herself onto the Midge, and paused just long enough to level a dark look at Feradach.

"Go while you still can," he told her. "This is not how I wish to win our bargain."

The Midge whinnied, high and frightened; it mingled with the sound of human terror inside the castle.

Merida demanded, "How can you be so cruel?"

Feradach had no expression at all. "I am not cruel, Merida. I am nature."

The ruin was thorough.

Fire seared through the castle. At every turn, everything seemed to go wrong that could go wrong. Ceilings collapsed at just the angle to block a door so that the businessmen could not clamber out. Sudden breezes lifted tapestries to wick fire along the halls just so. Rooms that seemed like they should be too stony and vast to become death traps were dense with the queen's dried palm trees, which went up in infernos.

Again and again, Fergus and Merida arrived to a corridor just too late to either pass through it or stop the destruction. Doors dissolved into glowing embers inches from their fingers. Roof beams splintered and collapsed just behind them.

"This place is a blasted maze!" shouted Fergus. "Girl, why are you stopping?"

"The nursery!" Merida shouted back, sliding from the Midge.

What she thought was the nursery door was blocked by a pile of broken stone. She tested her strength against a few of the smaller pieces to no avail. There was no sound from within. Or if there was, it was drowned out by the other sounds of destruction. This was awful.

"Merida!" Fergus shouted.

His tone didn't say why to act, but it did say how to: Merida rolled and ducked away.

Just in time.

A wall heaved to bits behind her. Embers rose in the air. The air was alight. Suddenly the corridor they stood in was foreign and unrecognizable. The sky was open wide above them. Were they outside? Was the roof gone?

Humor scrambled past Merida, riderless; the Midge took off after him. Merida spun until she caught sight of Sirist. To her relief, Hamish was still hunched over on the massive warhorse. Her father stood a ways off.

"Where's Rory?" Merida shouted.

"Dead," Fergus shouted back, strained. He had a nasty burn on his arm where the sleeve of his tunic and his cloak had been burned right off in his efforts to help. "He came off and just stood there as it all came down. He just stood there!"

"Dad, please come on!" Hamish called out, frightened. His face blanched and glistened with tears. He was surrounded with his worst fears. They all were.

They might die here, Merida thought.

Suddenly it seemed very terrible that she hadn't made up with her mother before they left.

And then the ground collapsed around Fergus.

"*Dad!*" howled Merida and Hamish in unison.

Because of the fire and rubble, it was hard to tell exactly what was happening. It seemed like the walkway was simply vanishing. There was a father and ground beneath him and then, abruptly, these things were no longer true.

Despair was opening in Merida like the chasm in the floor.

Without hesitation, Hamish kicked Sirist into motion. The huge chestnut horse reached the edge of the collapse in one, two, three massive strides. Hamish urged him right up to the edge where it was crumbling still.

Merida's breath hadn't even had time to leave her chest.

Fergus's huge hand lunged from the chasm. It seized Sirist's leather breastplate.

"Back," Hamish shouted to the warhorse, his voice quavering, "back up, back up!"

He was little, so he threw his entire weight against the reins until Sirist began to obey, dragging Fergus from the hole.

The ground kept collapsing, but Sirist kept backing, and then Hamish kicked, kicked, until Sirist twisted and leapt clear. Fergus was dragged several more yards, his flesh leg sort of hopping on the stone, his wooden leg skipping after it, and then he managed to pull himself onto the horse behind Hamish. Fergus turned long enough to meet his daughter's eyes, to make sure she was coming.

She was.

There was a gap in the destruction ahead; Merida could see Humor, Brionn, and the Midge through it. She scrambled to it and finally emerged with her family through the ruined tower archway to stand on firm cobblestone street.

They faced Kinlochy proper.

The entire town was ablaze. Every roof that could burn, every wall that could burn. Smoke hid the sky.

Fergus suddenly hugged Hamish, fiercely. "You've saved me, boy."

But it was no time to celebrate. Feradach's work here wasn't done. It wouldn't be done until this place was completely razed. The Midge refused to be caught; Merida grabbed Humor instead. Coughing smoke from her lungs, she said, "We're sure Rory's dead?"

"They're all dead," Fergus said grimly.

As the fire continued to blaze, they galloped back down the unrecognizable cobblestone paths. A few minutes later, Fergus and Hamish plunged through the gate they'd entered earlier that evening, followed by the Midge and Brionn.

The moment Merida leapt after them, she felt as if the air was different. Cooler. Less marked by embers. An ordinary summer night instead of the hell inside Kinlochy's walls.

Then she heard something that made her draw up short.

She looked over her shoulder. Terribly, she realized the sound she heard was screaming. Just inside the castle wall, one of the most impressive of the stone buildings had partially collapsed, and fire was beginning to rip through it. The gaps in the collapsed rubble were just wide enough for desperate arms to stick out here or there. There would be no digging them out; the wall had crumbled into massive, cow-sized chunks of stone. And unknown to the victims inside, the gate's massive watch tower burned viciously just above, too, and it swayed, ready to fall on the rest of the rubble and finish them.

The ruin would be complete. Total. Unavoidable.

She didn't know what she could do. It felt wrong to just go, knowing they were still alive in this minute.

"Merida, there's nothing for it!" Fergus shouted from farther down the road. "Come away, girl. Shield your heart since that's all that you can do!"

Inside the castle wall, Merida saw a figure standing, watching, just yards away from the inferno. Feradach. Unharmed, unburned. *I am not a thing you can fight.*

Merida couldn't lift that rubble, but Feradach—he was immortal; he was magic. His hand could leave a print in stone. He could've saved them, all the people of Kinlochy, if he'd wanted to.

But he just looked at the outstretched hands of the dying people, the fire brightening and dimming his skin as it feasted.

One day, his face might be one of theirs instead.

21

THE HOLY WELL

THINGS were different at DunBroch after that.

Really, *Fergus* was different after that, and he was so big, such a huge part of DunBroch, that everything else had to be different to conform to the new shape of him. Normally he would have blustered and storied about what had happened at Kinlochy. Ballads and songs, epics and folklore, dramatic rescues and tragic escapes.

But he didn't bluster this time. He wasn't loud at all. Instead he simply went straight to work upon their return. He tore down all the tattered banners they'd been meaning to mend and rolled up all the tapestries that hadn't been cleaned in ages. He brought in men from the fields to help him move all the furniture from the smoky common room to the music room, and then got yet more men to climb up into the chimney to find out what the source of the blockage was in the first place, and then he put yet more men to work on replacing the old roof shingles.

For weeks he barely said anything at all. But all the noise he would've normally made was replaced by the noise of industry. Everyone else complained of the soot and the hammering and the commotion, but he was relentless. The stables were to be cleaned and decluttered from peg to peg, he ordered. The wall guard towers were to be weeded and scrubbed down and opened up. The trough system that brought water from the loch to the castle was to be unclogged and made workable once more.

He never said it out loud, but the message was clear: DunBroch was never going to meet the fate he had seen at Kinlochy.

But as DunBroch looked better and better, Merida felt worse and worse.

She spent as much time as she could out in the games meadow—which admittedly looked splendid now that Fergus had had all the targets repaired and repainted— shooting arrow after arrow. But her mind never got still.

"You should ask the Ladies of Peace how to improve your sadness," Leezie said, coming out with a dinner for her at one point (a touching gesture, even if she had snacked on it a bit during the walk there).

"I'm not sad," Merida said. "I'm cranky! There's so much noise. I haven't had a second's quiet to think over this year since coming back."

She was a refugee from the noise, which had spread now even to Merida's tower. Fergus had decided he didn't care at all for the look of the wooden handrailing on the stairs to her room, and it was all being ripped out and reconstructed. At the same time, he'd gotten a craftsman to come from Keithneil to build Merida a new bed. Carved, like all the spoons on her mantel.

Merida knew she should feel grateful, but she felt haunted and off-kilter. She hid herself away from the sound as best she could and wrote a letter to the Dásachtach explaining that she had visited Kinlochy but it was for naught, because Kinlochy was gone. She walked the letter down to the blackhouse village to Comyn the messenger, and then she returned to the noisy castle. She went back out to shoot some more arrows. She tossed restlessly at night.

It felt like everything was changing so fast, which was what she wanted, but at the same time, she felt like she had never left that collapsing Kinlochy corridor. She couldn't find solid ground to stand on. She'd returned home and home was gone.

"Ah, but it's nice to see your father with his purpose again, isn't?" Elinor remarked. She'd persuaded Merida to come with her, Leezie, and Ila to "take some air" down to the holy well, which was a longish walk from the castle, far enough to be out of the earshot of construction.

It was a lovely day. Generally it rained every day in DunBroch, but not *all* day, and it had already gotten its misting out of the way that morning. Everything looked bright and blown out in the way things get in late summer. All the grass had gone to seed, all the flowers were tall and weedy, all the tree leaves stretched as far as they could go toward the high, high sky, everything was as green as it could manage before the weather would begin to turn to plunge the world back into the winter dark. As they walked, pheasants flushed from the grass and deer bounded into the woods. It was all very idyllic. Good air to take.

"Can't he find a quieter purpose?" Merida said. "Or do just one room or tower at a time? It's madness! He's bitten off too much! It'll never be done by the bad weather."

The harrowing trip had been enough to get Merida speaking to her mother again, but because there had been no proper making up and sorting out, she still felt sour, and all her words came out petulant, no matter how she meant them to sound.

"You've not seen your father when he's got the bit between his teeth," Elinor said warmly, as if Merida had been pleasant. "When he gets it in his head to motivate people, he can move mountains."

"And he has," Leezie said. "Did you *see* they started paving the courtyard? First stones down today. I'm going to chalk runes on it."

"Whatever will we do without all that mud tracked in?" Elinor murmured, and Merida could tell that she was happy.

Why couldn't Merida be happy? Fergus had surely changed. Hamish, too. Merida would have expected the confirmation of his worst fears to make him more afraid, but instead, it was as if now that he'd seen how bad it could be, the shadows of the upstairs halls no longer had the same bite. He stood a little straighter. He crept a little less. He was braver every day, and she knew Feradach would see it when he came to check her work.

She dreaded seeing Feradach again.

She couldn't stop picturing the image of those arms reaching for freedom as the fire raged, and Feradach doing nothing. The kindness and humanity she thought she'd seen in Keithneil had clearly been just a sham, her projecting what she wanted to see upon him. He might not have chosen his godly duty of meting out ruin, but he didn't flinch from it, either. He had executed all of Kinlochy without pity or mercy, making sure there was no escape for anyone there.

I am nature.

She had to remember that he would not flinch to do the same to DunBroch. There would be no survivors.

"There's three rooks for you, Leezie," Elinor said.

Leezie had been twirling and making a daisy chain, but she gave off twirling at this and looked troubled. "I'm not counting signs anymore. It's too depressing. I've taken up with the Ladies of Peace instead. I've been trying to get Merida down there, too."

Elinor frowned. "Are those the ones down at the village with the cakes?"

"Yes, though they meet at the well sometimes, too, for moaning," Leezie said.

"I'm glad you've found a new interest," Elinor said. "That reminds me. Did you and your father meet a harper on your trip, Merida?"

"Why?" Merida's voice came out combative without any effort on her part whatsoever.

"Little Bear asked me today if I thought he could be a harper when he grew up. I asked him why such a thought came into his head and he said the trip had done it, but he didn't say what on the trip did it."

217

Merida said irritably, "I suppose you're going to say he can't be a harper."

Elinor's voice was thoughtful. "It's not a very royal profession."

"But he is the youngest of the three, isn't he, ma'am?" asked Ila.

"Ha, I suppose so," Elinor replied. "By a whisker."

"That means he can do what he likes, right?" asked Ila. She added swiftly and politely, "Ma'am. He won't be king?"

Once again, Merida suspected Ila was on her side.

"Not as long as luck holds; Hubert and Harris come before him," said Elinor. "Usually the youngest becomes a priest or a scholar or a soldier, but I suppose a harper . . . Fergus would probably pitch a table. Och, there's no one really to teach him, though. Before this, I would've said to send him to Kinlochy for apprenticeship, but it doesn't sound like that's possible now, is it?"

Merida couldn't bring herself to answer. Maybe she *should* see about doing some moaning with Leezie's Ladies of Peace.

Elinor quickly tidied up the mood by saying, "Look how pretty this looks in this light."

The holy well was before them. If it hadn't been marked as special, the place where the water came to the surface, fresh and clean and clear, would have been easily missed. But long ago, someone had built a stone border around it and added a vertical font with a woman's worn face on it. Water poured from her open mouth into the pool below. Little white moss flowers grew all around it.

A few yards away was a craggy standing stone. The stone was twice as tall as Merida and covered all over with carved spirals. On the first day of spring solstice, the sun lit up a perfect trail of light along the stone as it rose; quite magical. Merida used to ride Angus to the stone when she was first learning all the wilds of DunBroch; it was so impressive that it had taken her several visits to realize that the holy well, not the stone, was the reason this path was kept clear.

Leezie danced around it. She'd brought ribbons, because she was Leezie, and she spun them around her head in a complex pattern. It was hard to say if it was a real ritual or a Leezie-ritual. She said, "The Ladies of Peace talked about the well during the last meeting!"

Elinor looked privately amused. "What did they say?"

"It's a woman's well! Holy for all, but suited for affairs of women the most! Women's minds! Women's hearts! Put in an offering, food, coin, or your best flower from your garden, and pray to the lady in the well, and she will give you what you ask!"

Ila asked in a sort of sharp voice, "Who do the Ladies of Peace say the lady of the well is, ma'am?"

"Bridget," said Leezie. "I think. Or Mary."

"Mm," said Elinor.

Ila swiveled at this *mm*. "Whom do *you* say it belongs to, ma'am?"

"I was once told it was the Cailleach's well," Elinor said.

Merida had been looking at the surface of the well, but at this, her head jerked up. The Cailleach! Merida had never heard of her association with the well before, although her mother had told her the usual bedtime stories of the Cailleach. She supposed she'd never asked her why the well was considered holy; that was really more Leezie's domain.

"I was told that if you gave her something precious, in return she would give you a wish. That's why people throw things in here," Elinor said. She looked a little sheepish. "I made a wish here once, and it did come true."

Leezie was absolutely enthralled. "What was it?"

"Oh, you can't tell your own wish out loud," Elinor said. "It's bad luck."

Merida asked, "What about the stone, Leezie? Do the Ladies of Peace talk about that as well?"

"It's a stone," Leezie said carelessly. "I like that ring of them north of DunBroch better. There's loads of bog myrtle there that keeps the midges away."

"This is Feradach's stone," Ila said. "That's its name."

Merida instantly felt her hands go hot with anxiety.

Leezie asked, "Who is Feradach?"

"Can you tell with your Sight?" Ila asked.

"I don't think the Sight can tell me that," Leezie replied. She shrugged in an exaggerated way, emphasizing just how much she cared in her attempt to show how little she did. "It's just a silly thing, anyway."

"Maybe he was a chieftain," Elinor said. "Someone's son who died, someone who deserved a solstice stone in memorial."

As the others leaned over the well, Merida studied the stone anew. It was covered with little worn interconnected spirals all over, just as she remembered, but now that she was right next to it, studying it carefully, she saw an additional shape, right near its base.

A handprint, sunk deep into the stone, nearly worn away with age.

Feradach.

She wondered how old the print was. What terrible fate had this place endured because of him?

And what fate would it endure again, if Merida couldn't find a way to change Elinor, Harris, and Leezie still?

She hovered her hand over the handprint, thinking of how Feradach had shown her Keithneil's past. Then, because she also remembered him saying that he didn't think she was a coward, she put her hand right into it.

But the stone stayed just a stone, cold and worn under her palm, and she didn't travel through time and memory.

"I wish to fall in love," Leezie said, crouched by the edge of the well. "Oh, bother, I said it out loud, do I have to do another one?"

"I think so," Elinor said.

Sighing, Leezie dropped the other half of a sweet biscuit into the well and closed her eyes. Her cheeks pinked slightly, which made Merida think her revised wish was probably not too much different from her first.

"Are you going to make a wish, Merida?" Ila asked as Merida joined them at the well's edge again.

Merida would have liked to wish for her family's safety, but she knew that wouldn't satisfy the bargain's need for balance. The Cailleach had already given as much as she could. It was up to Merida to do the rest. Gazing at the water, she once more imagined the rubble of Kinlochy, the hands stretching out hopelessly. Only now the rubble was DunBroch, and the hands belonged to her family.

It was so hard to carry this entirely by herself, the weight of this knowledge—

Don't cry, she thought furiously.

But she did.

Just one tear dripped into the water. Her mother did not see the tear, but she saw the ripple stretch out from it, and she said sharply, "Merida, what's wrong?"

She wanted to say she was afraid that if Elinor didn't travel again, Elinor would die. They all would. She wanted to say that she had just seen a lot of people die and it was too easy to imagine it happening to DunBroch. She wanted to say that she was so scared that she would fail.

"Mum, please," started Merida. "Please, please. Come with me on the last trip? Don't just say yes. Please really do it. I'm sorry I was awful. Please just come."

To her embarrassment, more tears fell in the well. Not just a few. A lot. All the tears she'd wanted to cry for Kinlochy and hadn't been able to until now.

Ila dropped a flower on top of them, hiding the ripples away.

"Oh, Merida," Elinor said. She wiped away Merida's tears and brought her into a hug. For a long moment, she just held Merida, smelling, as she always did, of roses and the gentle smoke of the common room. "All right. I really mean it. I will come with you. I'll take you to Eilean Glan."

This time, Merida believed it.

22

NO ONE KNOWS YOU EXIST

THERE was one of Fergus's renovations that Merida liked at once. He had set quite a few hands on restoring DunBroch's wall, and now one could get to the wall walk from many points along it, as all the guard towers had been made accessible. Entire sections of wall that had been unpleasant to roam were now truly pleasurable, lifted many yards above the biting midges down below.

As Elinor threw herself into the planning of the long journey to Eilean Glan, which was apparently a distant island off the coast, Merida threw herself into walking the wall. She needed something to keep her from the anxiety of wondering if this was going to be just another Spain or Kinlochy trip, and Elinor had completely taken over the game fields at the moment, ordering a contingent of Fergus's soldiers to work on their archery and otherwise sharpen their skills.

Merida didn't think she could bear it if Elinor backed out again.

Luckily for her, walking the wall worked almost as well as archery to clear her mind, particularly at the golden hour of this golden season. The long warm light that came just before the night shimmered like water. As fall approached, the sounds of bellowing red stags punctuated the wood, fierce as bears. The leaves were not yet changing, but there was something substantial and weighty to them, a fullness that could be heard when the breeze lifted them. Summer was building, building, until it had to collapse into fall, and the effort was breathtaking to watch.

She stood on the wall on one of these evenings and listened to the sounds of DunBroch both natural and unnatural. In addition to the birdcalls and stag growls, there was also the rippling sound of Hamish playing Elinor's harp with the window open and Leezie practicing her moaning down by the vegetable garden and Fergus's ever-present workmen hammering away at some project in the kitchen. Merida couldn't hear her father, but she heard Elinor laugh, and she knew that Fergus had to be close, because her mother only laughed like that for her father.

She wondered what Hubert was doing. He had sent several more letters about how he intended to return home with Gille Peter and Angus for Christmas, which was bittersweet for Merida. If she didn't succeed, that would mean he'd arrive home just in time for destruction. She supposed Feradach would find it easier to do his job that way.

Merida pressed the heels of her hands into her eyes.

She had been traveling all year again, and yet she felt like she still needed to go somewhere and do something. This standing and waiting felt terrible. She didn't know what was wrong with her, or what she wanted. She wanted to feel like she was doing something. But this *was* something. This was living, surely. Why couldn't she just settle down and enjoy the few weeks she had here at beautiful DunBroch before the third journey? Why did she need to move again?

From her vantage point, she realized she could see Harris. He was a small figure down below, outside the wall, picking his way between the trees along the loch. A few yards behind him, Brionn tagged along, tail high, weaving back and forth in an aimless way.

Merida wondered what he was doing. Harris had somehow become even more irascible as the castle was being rebuilt. He always had a cutting or scathing remark about how he would have done this project differently or how that project didn't make any substantial difference to their lives, so why bother. When he wasn't sniping about the renovations, he was picking at Hamish or burying himself in a book. Merida couldn't remember the last time she'd had any conversation with just him, let alone one of a meaningful variety.

He would have to come along to Eilean Glan. She knew it would be a fight. Why? Because everything was a fight with him now.

As if he could feel her eyes on him, Harris suddenly turned to look back up at the castle. The tiny little silhouette of him shielded its eyes as it scanned up the wall.

But as he stood there, posture erect and suspicious, she realized he wasn't looking at her. Instead, he was gazing a little bit down the wall, and even from here, she saw him shake his head at whatever he saw before continuing through the woods.

Merida turned her head to see what he had been looking at on the wall, if anything.

What she saw, several yards down the wall, at the top of the next guard tower, was Feradach.

Her stomach twisted.

He was a dark, still figure in that long twilight, and it was easy to remember how he looked in Kinlochy, the embers lifting around him instead of the golden motes.

He was closing the distance between them.

How can you be so cruel?

I am not cruel, Merida. I am nature.

"Go away," Merida told him. He stopped an arm's length away, his hands folded neatly in their gloves. He looked more like the Feradach she remembered from the trip to Keithneil now and less like the silhouetted god of Kinlochy, but she felt no friendlier toward him. "I have no interest in talking to you, and you have no business here yet. If I had my bow right now I would shoot you right through the eye; I don't care if you can be killed or not. I would do it for the satisfaction of pinning your face to the ground with an arrow."

"Is that fair?" Feradach said. "Is that fair just because you saw me doing what you know I do? Do you judge the Cailleach for calling up the seeds out of the ground? Do I judge you for what you are trying to do with your family?"

"I don't give a fig if it's fair or not, actually. I don't want to look at you. I don't want to see your face and picture you standing by those people as they burned to death!" She spit out the final words.

"What would you have me do?"

"I don't care what you do. I just don't want to look at you." She was angry to feel tears prickling at her eyes again, so she spun on her heel and marched back toward the guard tower she'd climbed up to get there. She had a horrible suspicion she had another big cry in her like the one she'd had by the well, and she couldn't stand to do that in front of him.

"Merida, I have to come here," Feradach said to her back. "The Cailleach says I must. That is part of the bargain, and not one I invented. And you—you have to see my work, too."

Merida turned back around. "Don't you think I've seen *enough* of your work this season?"

"You weren't supposed to be there. At Kinlochy."

"How could you not know that?"

"I don't know everything," Feradach said. "I only know the balance, unless I choose to go looking for answers, same as you. I don't track your every movement."

"You tracked me on my journey to Ardbarrach."

"That was different. That was the beginning. I was curious. I wanted to see . . ." He looked away, down the edge of the bracken-covered slope outside the wall, all the way down through the willow trees to the glittering gold water of the loch visible between them, the silhouettes of the DunBroch geese moving in the forever-dim summer evening. There was no sign of Harris or Brionn now. "Before, I made sure to choose the ruin I knew you would understand to show you. I chose ruin that was in the past, so you could see what happened after. I knew you could not see the value in it as it happened; how could you? Only a monster would love the destruction for its own sake. There is no glory in ruin; it only matters because of what comes after. I did not mean for you to see that. I do not know why you were there. Of all the places. Of all the times."

He fell silent.

"So you are here because the Cailleach demands it," Merida said finally. "And what have you found?"

"I see that your father is changing the castle," Feradach said. "And himself. I see that your brother Hamish has found himself. You are making progress."

But Merida already knew both these things, so there was no satisfaction in hearing him acknowledge it. "And yet if the others don't change in time, you'll do the exact same thing to DunBroch that you did to Kinlochy."

Feradach just shook his head, but not in the way that means *no*, the way that means *what do you want me to say?*

"Because the *balance*," she said coldly. "Because your *duty*."

"There are consequences to not keeping the balance," Feradach said roughly. "There are consequences to not fulfilling this duty. I have executed this duty for centuries. I have lived with these consequences for centuries. I am Feradach. This is my role. I will not be chastised by a *mortal*."

They stared at each other across the length of the high wall.

Feradach finally asked, "Will you come with me to see my work, as per the bargain? Tomorrow, if I return?"

"Do I have a choice?" But it wasn't really a question, any more than his had been a question. She had to see it. He had to see hers. She was angry that she had to do it, though, so she said, "I saw your stone. Feradach's stone."

His body went very still. "Did you now?"

"Yes, and you know what? No one remembers anything except your name. No one knows who you are," she said. "The Cailleach, they knew who she was. Not you. No one knows you exist."

How can you be so cruel?

Feradach looked at her for quite a long time then, his expression unreadable, his gloved hands folded in each other, and then he said, "You do."

23

CENNEDIG OF FIFE

MERIDA braced herself for Feradach's return, but he didn't come back the next day, nor the day after that. In fact, so many days went by that Merida began to wonder if she had succeeded in keeping him away, and if that would affect the bargain.

But nearly two weeks after she saw him on the wall, she woke in the morning (having had a ridiculous dream that foreheads were now considered vulgar and one had to brush one's hair across it in order to be considered decent in public), got dressed in the new riding dress her mother had completed while she was gone to Kinlochy, and managed to pick her way downstairs (which involved climbing up the stairs to the tapestry room and wending her way across the attic and then down through the remodeled music room and triplets' room, because of all the stairs under construction), and found that Feradach was not only already in the castle, but that he had already mingled with practically everyone.

In the kitchen, he had talked to her mother, who thought he looked like a nun and had talked to him about the holy well and his feelings on it.

In one of the stair towers, she discovered he'd had a spirited conversation on carpentry with the man who was working on her stairs, who had thought he looked like a very tall fellow craftsmen.

In the common room he'd played a game of Brandubh with Harris, who said he'd never seen an old woman so ruthless at the game and that surprise was the only reason why he'd lost.

In the music room Hamish had seen him, too, but as a fellow little boy who was also interested in the instruments and how their tuning had been disrupted by the changes to the space and to the weather.

To Leezie, he was an idle, unrecognized member of the kitchen staff, and had looked all through her pressed flower books with her, asking her about each.

In the garden, he appeared as a gentle old man who paused to help one of Aileen's staff pick peas.

In the stables, a stable boy found him a ruggedly built young man who left him comparing his muscles to the other stable boys' after he departed.

"Is there a single person in DunBroch you didn't speak to today?" she asked him crossly when she finally got to him. To her, of course, he looked as he always did, that young man with the tree-root brooch and the mane of light hair.

He smiled at her thinly and she had half a mind that all his conversing was entirely to be contrary about what she'd said before, about no one knowing him.

"They still all saw someone different," she muttered, but she knew it sounded more childish than properly mean.

"And what do I look like to *you*?" he asked. But she didn't intend to answer and he knew it, because he didn't wait for an answer before adding, "I'll need to borrow a horse. I changed my mind about what I want to show you and it's further than I expected to go."

"Borrow a horse! What use is there being immortal? Is there no magic way that you get about?"

"Not unless you'd like for me to beat you there by many hours. I could give you directions and a head start if you'd prefer."

"I would," she said.

But he simply stood around until she gave in. Eventually they set off, her on the Midge and him on a gelding that took quite a bit of kicking to go, because she didn't feel like giving him a horse he could appear noble on.

"Do you appear as something different to every horse, too?" Merida asked.

"I haven't asked them," Feradach replied.

She couldn't tell if he was being serious or not. "*Can* you talk to horses?"

"I assume they have a god of their own they'd rather talk to."

They rode due south until the landscape became a gentler one than that around DunBroch. Merida was unsurprised when their destination turned out to be a town just about as lovely as Keithneil, all the thatched cottages leaning in like good friends. There was farmland here, richer than around rocky DunBroch, and the prosperous village showed how much easier the fertile ground made life. Each little cottage had its own goats and ducks and herb gardens.

"I suppose now you're going to show me the time you killed everyone's children here," Merida said.

Feradach shot her a rueful look and instead guided her to a cottage that sat a little apart from the others. It was not quite the same as the others they'd passed. It was not that the cottage was fancier, it was just . . . as if the owner of it cared about it just a bit more deeply than everyone else cared about theirs, which was saying quite a lot, because the other houses were all quite tended. But the garden out front was larger, with more flowers, and the road leading to it was more meandering and bright, with stones intentionally placed all along the borders, and there was a martin house in the front yard for the birds, and the cottage's front door was painted red and had wind chimes hanging next to it. There was a hitching post cleverly shaped to look like two pigs tugging on an iron circle, which Merida and Feradach tied their horses to.

It was a very pleasant place indeed, and part of Merida wished she'd been told to investigate *this* place for possible joining as kin, because it all made her ache with its sweetness. But another part of her knew her feet would feel just as itchy after some time here.

At the front door, Feradach started to knock, but Merida said, "With hands like those, maybe I should do the knocking."

The door opened. On the other side was a man with an enormous head of white hair that was teased very high, and no beard, which made him seem a little like a very tall child. He eyed his visitors with both disbelief and humor. Who knew what he saw Feradach as, but Merida knew what he saw her as: the princess of DunBroch. Even her riding-out clothes were finer than most people's finest.

"Cennedig of Fife?" Feradach asked. "I have brought the princess of DunBroch for a meeting with you. Do you have the time for it?"

"A princess and a dwarf wasn't what I was expecting today," Cennedig said, adding, with amusement, "Who among us is allowed to not have time for the princess of anywhere?"

"The princess," Merida answered at once.

"Oh, you're witty," Cennedig said, with respect. "Come in, Your Highness."

The very first thing Merida saw inside his home was a beautiful harp that Hamish would have given his back teeth to play. The sound box was massive and gnarled, like a living tree, like a crouching animal. The strings were glittering and inviting, even to Merida, who could only pluck out a few pathetic dance numbers at her mother's long-ago insistence.

The rest of the cottage was not quite as impressive as the harp, but it was still homely and clearly loved upon. The walls were hung with carved spoons like the one Brionn had eaten back at Christmas, and everything that could be painted brightly had been painted brightly. Children had drawn big swirling patterns like those on Feradach's stone on the dirt floor; both Feradach and Merida were careful not to disturb them. In the backyard, Merida could see a group of youngsters tousling with a dog and—she had to squint a bit to confirm—a pig.

"Does the princess require a meal?" Cennedig asked, again sounding amused, and also directing the question to Feradach rather than Merida. He seemed to be both comfortable with Merida's being royalty but also well versed in the rules of royalty; he was not self-conscious in her presence, but he knew to give her some deference. This was someone who had not always been in this village, Merida decided. He had spent time in court.

Feradach said, "The princess enjoys berries of all kinds."

"How wise the princess is," Cennedig said, "considering my garden is overfull of them right now. Give me a moment to fetch some."

"Take your time," Feradach said. "We imposed."

As soon as Cennedig had gone out, Merida whispered, "The princess doesn't care one way or another about berries!"

"I know," Feradach said. "I needed him out of the house. Quickly, come to the harp."

Together they returned to the harp. Feradach leaned it over and gestured to the bottom. "Look down there."

Merida gathered her skirts and knelt, but she already suspected what she was going to see. Sure enough, on the bottom of the harp's sound box was a handprint.

"Quickly," Feradach said again.

Merida was too curious to even hesitate this time. She spread her fingers in that handprint, noting with interest that this one fit hers almost perfectly; whose face had Feradach been wearing when he put this print here?

"Harp," Feradach whispered, "show her what you've seen."

Merida just had time to think, *Oh, that is why I couldn't tell what Feradach's stone had seen,* and then she was taken through a life, all seen through the lens of this harp. First she saw a much younger Cennedig acquire this harp and learn the tunes he would play all over the land on it. It required many hours of lessons with an older harper and then even more hours of quiet study, but Cennedig didn't seem to mind. He practiced over and over again without tiring.

And it paid off: he became a famous harper. A worldly harper, a well-traveled harper. She saw him playing at DunBroch on several feast days. She saw herself, in fact, as a wee thing, barely heeding the musicians. At the next image of DunBroch, she saw wee Hamish, doing nothing *but* heeding the musicians. She saw Cennedig in similar celebrations in many feast halls. She saw him carrying the harp east, north, south, west. Everyone knew his name. He played before kings and more kings and more kings. He traveled overseas and played for Norse warriors and Moorish nobles, for French courtiers and Breton dignitaries.

She saw Cennedig travel to so many places that he could barely remember where he was at each. She saw him drinking and eating and talking and drinking and eating and talking and never, ever stopping. He was always making merry. He was always laughing. He was never quiet. He moved and moved and moved.

Then, as Cennedig was distracted, making merry with strangers he'd never see again, Feradach arrived. He did not look like what he looked like now, but Merida nonetheless recognized those fine gloves with the oxblood stitching.

Feradach removed a glove. He placed a hand firmly on the harp.

Things went wrong.

Not with sickness, like in Keithneil, nor with fire, as in Kinlochy.

Instead, it rained and rained. Cennedig, already on his way to the next place, bundled his harp into his cart and tied down blankets over it to try to protect it. Still it rained. It rained as he traveled north. It rained as he lost his sense of humor. It rained as the bridge beneath him and the cart washed right away in the rain-mad current.

The bridge joists went one way. The cart went another. The horse went a third way. Cennedig hesitated, trying to decide to swim for shore or for the harp. In the end, he picked the harp.

He had always picked the harp.

Cennedig swam against the current, his arm looped through the harp, and clung to the edge of the floating cart. He'd done it.

Just then, the current swirled capriciously. The cart

spun. Cennedig clung on. The harp looped round his arm gave the spinning cart propulsion and weight. The current and the harp pushed the cart hard.

As the rain kept falling, the river smashed the cart up against the rocky shore, Cennedig crushed between heavy cart and immobile rock. Cennedig's *hands* crushed between heavy cart and immobile rock.

The sound of them breaking was complete and terrible.

"Being forced to stop was the best thing to happen to me," Cennedig said.

Merida leapt back guiltily from the harp.

Cennedig stood in the doorway watching Feradach and Merida. Merida saw now that the hands holding the basket of berries were still somewhat bent and misshapen, still shaped like the trauma Feradach had visited upon him. Her heart was beating fast. Just as before, time seemed to hang like honey in the air, slow and luxurious in comparison to the time line she'd just whipped through.

"It's got a life of its own, that harp," Cennedig said. He seemed to think Merida and Feradach had simply been admiring the instrument, which suited Merida fine. "To not be able to play it anymore . . . Well, the kind way of putting it was that I moped for months and then settled down here, and that's when I finally remembered what it was like to be bored, and to train hard, and to fall in love. That's when I got my family. I miss the music itself terribly, but being able to stop, having to stop, not having to wonder if I should be going back out on the road—I didn't realize it at the time, but that was a miracle."

A miracle. All that disaster, a miracle.

Merida did not know if gods gloated, but she didn't look to find out. This whole trip had been set to make Feradach look as good as he had after the trip to Keithneil; none of the immediate agony, all of the happy ending. No screaming people, no hands reaching for the sky. If he thought she would so easily forget what she had seen him do in Kinlochy, he had another thought coming.

She stole a look anyway.

He was gloating.

She curled her lip at him before giving Cennedig a nicer smile. "It's a beautiful harp."

"It is," Cennedig said, "with or without me. My old friend. Now why did you come all this way, princess? Was it for these berries?"

This time, Feradach didn't answer for Merida. He simply gave up his gloating, lowered his gaze, and looked at his deadly gloved hands held inside one another. He offered up no excuse for why they'd be standing in this man's house. It was up to Merida to come up with one.

An idea dawned on Merida. "How would you feel about taking on a student?"

24

THE GIFT

ERIDA didn't put it all together at first, and when she did, she felt very thick about not seeing it in the moment. Cennedig, the weather that came after she returned to DunBroch, all of it. But she was so busy preparing for the long journey to Eilean Glan that she'd barely had time to heed the weather, much less mull over connections. Later she would remember the spate of late afternoon summer thunderstorms and the blustering winds in a time when the weather was usually getting drier as autumn approached, but at the time, all she thought of was how best to pack as many creature comforts as possible so that Elinor would not be put off by the travel.

She didn't want to be slowed down with a cart, especially since the roads to the far north were supposedly even poorer than in the rest of the country, so she enlisted the help of some of the craftsmen to help her construct

cunning wicker baskets for the pack ponies to carry. Then
she stocked them with blankets, feather pillows, and spare
pairs of dry boots. She pressed the kitchen into coming up
with ideas for food that would journey well. She planned
on devoting one pack horse entirely to bringing ale and
water in bladders. She tried to think of any time she had
ever been uncomfortable while traveling and what would
have improved the situation, and then she made a plan.

Merida vowed there would be nothing to make Elinor
dread travel.

She also took her time to blackmail Harris into going
with them on this last journey. She'd thought about it for
a long time, how best to convince him, and ultimately
decided to simply play his own game. It was easier than
trying to imagine how to persuade him to talk. She'd collected all the precious things in DunBroch that Brionn
had put chew marks in, beginning with her Christmas
spoon and ending with her mother's wedding shoes, and
threatened to bring them to their parents with an assess-
ment of Harris's dog-training skills unless he came along
and promised to take care of any errands Elinor might
have during the trip.

Harris actually seemed grudgingly appreciative of her
blackmailing efforts.

In any case, he agreed to go.

It was right in the middle of these preparations that the
harp arrived.

"What is *that*?" Merida asked with astonishment.

The harp was set right in the middle of the Great Hall,

and set right behind it was Hamish, his eyes shining with feeling. There were many other things in the Great Hall, too, like baskets of cloth and buckets of turnips, but mostly Merida had eyes for the harp. It was plainer than the one in the music room, but also newer, lighter, sturdier looking, a harp meant for going places. Behind it all, the grand doors to the hall stood open, revealing a merchant cart driving away through the early fall weather. The kitchen help trotted after it, throwing buns and joyful shouts.

"Little Bear's new harp," Fergus said grandly. "Just in time for his first trip to Cennedig of Fife!"

Merida was just as shocked by this as she was by the harp's appearance. Harps took a very long time to build, and even if this harp had not been built specially for Hamish, things took a very long time to make their way across the countryside. "You arranged for a harp?"

"I wish I had, but I can't take credit," Fergus replied. "This one rolled in by accident. The merchants were headed to Moray and said the floods kept pushing them further and further off their path till finally they just washed up here and decided to see if we wanted anything they had. And did we, boy?"

Hamish's smile was bigger than his face.

Harris, behind him, rolled his eyes. "Everything in this place is an accident."

"Hold your wheesht," Merida told him, "and spit those lemons out. You'll be out of this place tomorrow."

"Is it tomorrow we're going?" Elinor asked, sounding quite harried.

Merida felt a pang of anxiety, and then a pang of irritation, and then another pang of anxiety. Elinor couldn't back out now, could she?

Of course she could. She had fooled Merida before and she could still do it.

"It's the date you set yourself, ma'am," Ila broke in. She had appeared from nowhere, a stack of linens piled in her arms. "And Ms. Leezie would be quite upset if you moved it."

Leezie had declared tomorrow's date fortunate by some arcane calendar she had found. Three priests had come to the blackhouse village, and she'd used most of her spending money to buy a tiny statue of a frowning saint from an exotic country to the south. The saint statue was supposed to grant safe passage over water, which they would need to get to Eilean Glan.

"You don't all have to stare at me like that!" Elinor exclaimed, color coming into her cheeks. "I just lost track of the days!"

As Merida hurried out on her way to check the kitchen supplies one last time, she exchanged a grateful look with Ila.

They were going. They were really going. One last journey. One last triplet. One last season before autumn rolled into winter and Christmas came with its doom or salvation.

It was a wild last day and night. Aileen made a grand going-away feast. Fergus gifted Elinor a fine new cloak for her jouney, lined with shiny black fur. Elinor gifted

Merida a third dress to replace her dress worn at the elbows from shooting. Hamish played his new harp without stop. There was no sign of the slump-shouldered, uncertain triplet when his long fingers were on the harp. This was the boy who had saved his father as the world crumbled beneath him.

Old friend, Cennedig had called his harp.

Merida had no doubt Hamish had just met one of his own.

Later that night, after Merida had checked and double-checked and triple-checked their preparations, she'd settled down into bed for her last sleep in a good bed for many days. She lay there in her bedroom, listening to the mice have their way with her things under her bed, looking at the familiar shadows of all her childhood things, wondering if her mother was still going to back out at the last minute. She thought about getting up to find a cat to quiet the mice, but then she thought about how she would have to find something to quiet the cat. And then she thought about the trip some more.

And in the midst of all that, out of nowhere, as she ran out of things to think about, she realized the harp had to have been Feradach's doing.

She felt stupid at once for not immediately putting it together. Feradach knew Hamish wanted to be a harper, because he had come to see her directly after their return from Kinlochy. He'd had an entirely different proof of ruin to show her, which he'd altered after seeing how upset she was; the trip to Cennedig was clearly an improvisation, hence the delay in his return and the need to borrow a horse. Why take her to Cennedig of all people? Yes, the harper's story was a kind one, but in retrospect, of course he had meant for her to secure an apprenticeship for Hamish. And now, freak flooding had directed this harp right to their door just the day before she left. When had merchants ever accidentally found themselves at DunBroch? It had never happened before.

The hand of Feradach was all over the situation, minus the visible handprint.

Put together, it made sense.

But it also *didn't* make sense.

Feradach hadn't done a thing to save those dying people in Kinlochy. But he'd moved rivers to make sure Hamish's change was well and truly complete before Merida left for Eilean Glan.

Why?

But deep down, she knew why. Just as clearly as she remembered the horrors of Kinlochy, she remembered Feradach's shock when he saw her there at Kinlochy. His downcast face as she'd shouted at him on the wall. He knew what she could bear seeing and what she couldn't, and he'd tried his best to shield her and failed.

What could he have said to Merida to change her feelings about how it had all happened?

Nothing.

But Feradach could do his part to help save one of her brothers. From him.

It was an odd little gift from an apologetic god.

PART IV

FALL

25

A Royal Trip

IN THE end, Elinor astonished all of them.

All those days of planning on Merida's part, all her worries that Elinor would back out at the last minute, all her preparations to hopefully keep Elinor comfortable enough to forget the woes of traveling—it turned out to be for nothing.

Because when Merida, Harris, and Leezie assembled to leave the following morning, they discovered that the courtyard was absolutely full to madness. There were horses, people, and carts everywhere. Soldiers milled. Women hurried by with supplies. Aileen bellowed orders.

And at the helm of this ship of moving parts was Elinor, queen of DunBroch, looking as effortlessly regal as she did while doing anything else. Only what she had done in this case was, for the past several weeks, quietly put together an enormous retinue of the shape and quality that would be appropriate for a royal traveling through the countryside.

This was not Merida's slow trundle through the winter countryside with a pony cart. This was not Fergus's off-the-cuff trip with two of his children. This was suitable for diplomacy, for looking at from the outside.

Elinor had assembled a contingent of soldiers to protect them from bandits and neighbors who might mean them ill (these were the soldiers who'd kept Merida from her game field). She'd hired a group of hunters to protect them from wolves (why hadn't Fergus done that!). She'd had Aileen coordinate a mobile staff of women to carry and prep food. Stable boys stood at alert beside the pack ponies and the supply carts. Laundresses and their apprentices finished pressing the tools of their trade into rush baskets and wooden crates. An entire cadre of scouts had saddled up to check out the way ahead and set up the sleeping tents (tents! What luxury while traveling). There were ponies to carry heather mattresses and ponies to carry heather ale. Ponies to carry all the things they wanted to take with them and ponies to carry all the things they might want to bring back. At Elinor's side during all of these preparations was catlike Ila, smiling her private smile and holding Elinor's journals and ledgers for her.

Merida would have been more put out that all her own effort was for naught if she hadn't been so impressed. She didn't think there were that many people still even living in DunBroch. All the hustle-bustle in front of the newly renovated DunBroch made the entire castle seem brand-new.

Ardbarrach could not call this the work of a rural pretender, she thought.

She hadn't known her mother could be like this.

"That's my traveling queen," Fergus said. "Don't get into trouble."

"I'll be back before you know it," Elinor said. She looked not at all like Merida was used to seeing her, but rather pink and flustered and excited. "And you'll have Hubert back here in just a few days, just in time for the Hunt for the Unnamed."

This last bit was perhaps the biggest, boldest evidence that Fergus had changed. There was quite a bit of hunting at DunBroch. They hunted for food: rabbits, deer, grouse. They hunted for fur, and to cull the weasel population lest they devour all the eggs in the henhouses. They hunted for protection, against the wolves, on the years when the mercenaries didn't come to collect money for pelts. They hunted for justice: a few years back, a man down in the village was accused of smashing his brother-in-law's head in with a rock, which was not ideal, and then a few months later he stabbed a bunch of villagers with a sword and then ran off into the woods shouting that he was going to raise an army of fairies to kill everyone else, which was even less ideal, and finally the sister came to DunBroch in hopes of bringing him to heel. Fergus put together a hunting party of several hundred men and eventually the villain was found in the bracken and brought to trial.

But for the longest time, the most famous hunting at DunBroch was the Hunt for the Unnamed, an annual tradition that had dwindled only to memory over the past few years. Neighboring kings and their men arrived, and for one day and one night, they hunted through the forest with their dogs, crawling all over and making a huge racket. They never returned with a carcass. They returned, instead, with stories of the Unnamed. Each year it seemed to have grown. It was the size of a pony, then the size of a horse, then the size of an ox. It had ten points then twenty then forty. Its rack was like an oak tree's branches spied over a hill. No animal had existed like this. How cunningly the stag had evaded them this time, jumping over a fence, a boulder, the moon.

It had taken Merida a bit of time to realize that they never intended to catch the stag. It was possible the stag didn't even exist, as men had been holding the Hunt for the Unnamed ever since she was small, and surely the stag would be old and feeble by now, eating gruel and complaining about the days of its youth rather than leaping over moons. But it didn't matter. The point was the hunt. The finding. Not the catching.

This year, Fergus had organized the Hunt for the Unnamed once again, to take place while Merida was on her own pursuit in search of her own unspeakable task.

This autumn season felt weightier than the others that had come before it, Merida thought. The gift of time the Cailleach had given her was running out; she'd been pouring and pouring that syrup onto her cake and now there was only a very little left.

In the castle's newly renovated chapel, Merida prayed to Leezie's little saint statue. *Please let there be no disasters.*

But she knew that wasn't what she needed. That was just what she wanted.

She sighed and prayed for what she really needed out of the trip.

Please let this change them.

They set off into the wild.

Traveling with her mother was nothing like traveling with her father. Traveling with Fergus had been rough and ready, no expectations, no promises. No comforts, no delays.

Traveling with her mother was like traveling from one floor of DunBroch to another, like they had packed every bit of their lives back home to take with them. Courtly rules still applied. Merida's hair still had to be up. Meals were taken on schedule. Prayers were performed as before. Harris had to spend part of the day in a cart in order to continue his schooling, even while on the move. Every village and croft they passed by was greeted and questioned as Elinor nodded and made little notes in her ledgers.

No wonder her mother had wanted to put it off. This was no lark. This was work like Merida had never seen before.

But, oh, the nights were wondrous. At night, the company pitched massive tents and lit huge fires to keep the animals away. Guards stood at the ready. Musicians rolled out their instruments. Bards began to recite. Elinor, queen of DunBroch, held court.

Even better than that, though, were the quiet hours that happened after the festivities, because that was when

Elinor, Leezie, Harris, and Ila retreated into the large royal tent for drowsy, intimate conversation around candlelight. The subject matter ranged far and wide, unhindered by logic or duty because of the dwindling of the candle and the proximity to sleep.

It was several days into this journey that the topic of the Sight came up once more.

"As I said," Elinor said, "there are two kinds of people. There are people who seek the magic, and people the magic seeks. Which are you?"

"The first, ma'am," Ila said.

"The second," Merida added.

"Me as well," said Elinor.

"Neither," Harris retorted. "I'm the kind of person who thinks this is a stupid conversation. I'm going to sit with the guards. I wish I'd stayed home."

He stormed out, as much as one could storm out of a tent.

"Boys," Elinor said, unbothered. "Leezie, surely you're the first kind."

"I wish I was the second," Leezie said wistfully.

"Why?" Merida asked. "It seems much more fun to be a knight of magic than the rabbit the magic springs upon in the night."

Leezie didn't elaborate, though.

"You have to believe in yourself to be the first kind of person, ma'am," Ila said. "You have to be powerful in the Sight, or you will just chase nonsense your whole life and it will ruin you and people will make fun of you and you will believe them. You have to decide for yourself what matters and what doesn't, because there aren't enough people like that to compare yourself to or talk to. The second type of person, the type the magic comes to, they aren't necessarily powerful. They are just the recipients of power. They haven't chosen anything. It's chosen them."

This was the longest speech Merida had ever heard Ila make. She delivered it in a very matter-of-fact way, with no self-consciousness, as self-possessed and elegant a little girl in a candlelit tent as she was in the castle. For the first time, Merida truly believed that Leezie was right: Ila did have the Sight.

"When you say it that way," Elinor said, with a gentle laugh. "I wish I was the first type of person! Leezie, why are you wishing you were something else, that's Merida's job."

"Hey!" said Merida.

"It's easy for you to say you wish you were the first kind of person, the person who has to be powerful," Leezie said. "Look at all you do. All this tent, these people, this travel, that's what you do when you do a thing. You're always powerful. I'm just, just Leezie. I chase nonsense all the time."

Merida leaned on Leezie's shoulder. "Nonsense *and* cabbage."

"Merida," chided Elinor, but Leezie gave a watery giggle and punched Merida gently in the arm.

The candle was guttering down. The conversation was running out in the way it does when it gets too late or too serious.

"You know you have it," Ila said eventually. "You know you do, Leezie Muireall. You told me your mum had it and you know you have it, too. Aren't we all a lot like our mums here in this room?"

There was a deep silence. Merida was not sure this was at all true. Elinor didn't sound like she thought so either when she said briskly, "All right, girls, that's time for sleep, I think. If we go on like this we'll be up all night, and we have an early morning. Off to your tents."

Merida and Leezie nipped off to theirs, pattering quickly around the dying embers of the fire that had cooked their dinner, lifting the heavy flap of their tent, and getting into their bedrolls after checking to make sure no other creatures of Scotland had gotten into them first. They were far more comfortable than any bedrolls Merida ever traveled with because of the heather mattress Elinor had packed to go beneath each. It would have never occurred to Merida to make room for such a thing during her travels.

In the dark, Merida said, "Do you think it's true, what Ila said, that you're like your mum?"

Leezie didn't answer right away, and Merida wasn't sure if this was because she had fallen asleep, or because she didn't know, or because if it was too difficult to talk about. Leezie's mother had been dead only five years, which felt like both a long and a short time. Merida had never known her; they came from different worlds. Leezie had lived an entire childhood down in the blackhouse village before coming to work and live at DunBroch and managing to somehow become an honorary member of the family DunBroch along the way.

"I don't know," Leezie said at last. "People said she was a silly person. They say I'm a silly person, too, I think."

"You are a little silly," Merida said. "But in a Leezie way."

"It's the only way I am, so I don't know any other way to be."

"If anyone says it in a mean way, I'll pull their hair for you." Merida tried to remember all the things Leezie had ever said about her mother. She had never really said much except that she'd been a midwife. "Your mum had the Sight?"

Leezie was quiet again for a long time, and again Merida thought perhaps she'd gone to sleep. But then she murmured, "She believed people came back again and again. To life. In different bodies. She heard about it from a bald man from somewhere in the south. She always said the first thing a bald man says when you meet him is always true and the last thing he says is always a lie."

Merida was amused. "And the first thing he said was people come back again and again?"

"Yes, that Mum'll come back in another baby and do it all over again, which sounds like a lot of trouble," Leezie said. "But nice to get to taste things for the first time again, though, I think."

"What was the last thing the bald man said to her? Did she tell you?"

" 'You'll have a nice Christmas this year,' " Leezie said. "She died at Samhain."

Two months before Christmas.

"I'm awfully sorry," Merida said.

"Thanks. I always wanted to meet a bald man to see if it was true, but they're harder to find than you'd think. Oh, that monk we went to Keithneil with—do you think he counts as bald?"

Feradach. Merida asked, "What was the first thing he said to you?"

"That Keithneil wasn't far," Leezie said. "That was true."

"And the last?"

Leezie thought about it. "That he hoped we'd meet again. Well, that's dull."

The tent fell silent then. Merida turned on her side to go to sleep, but she didn't go to sleep.

"Good night, Ms. Leezie," whispered Merida.

"Good night, Ms. Merida," whispered Leezie.

Merida kept turning the conversation over and over in her head. It felt important to understand Leezie and what she had been moaning about this year, but because she and Leezie were so different, putting herself in Leezie's shoes was always a multistep process. By the time Merida understood what had motivated Leezie to do one thing, she was on to her next thing and Merida was having to understand her again. Until now, everything she didn't understand was easy to sweep under the *just Leezie* heading.

If she wanted to help Leezie change, that wasn't a good enough understanding of her.

I'm running out of time, I'm running out of time.

She thought she would never sleep, but she must have, because she got woken by a sound, and one can't get woken without sleeping first.

She opened her eyes, but there was nothing to see but blackness in the dark tent.

Then the sound came again, from just outside: *"Hsst."*

26

Consequences

"*H*sst."

It was a very intentional sound. A sound meant to pull the occupants of the tent outside. But who would be *hss*ting to them? Harris was not the sort to *hsst*. Ila surely couldn't manage to *hsst* without adding a *ma'am*.

Who could it be? she wondered. *It's almost the middle of the night.*

It was *exactly* the middle of the night, actually.

Merida quietly got up. She didn't need to get dressed or put on boots, as she had gone to sleep wearing everything she'd been wearing during the day. This was not only because it was cold overnight, but because she was used to traveling without Elinor's comforts and fail-safes, which required one to be on one's toes at all times. Perhaps Elinor was content leaving safety to the soldiers, but Merida couldn't get used to it.

With a glance back at the other motionless bedroll, she pulled aside the tent flap and looked out at the camp.

There was no one there. The remains of the fire outside the largest tent smoldered red. The sounds of horses snorting in the night were nearly inaudible over the sound of the drying leaves on the trees hissing against each other in the breeze. Not too far off, Merida could hear one of the soldiers stamping his feet against the cold at his post.

So who had *hssted* at her?

In the woods, she saw a flash of movement, then a flash of light.

At first she thought it was *na Fir-Chlis*, that strange green glow of the Cailleach, of the will o' the wisps, but then she saw that it was just the reflection of the firelight in an animal's eyes.

Brionn.

"Brionn," she hissed.

But of course he didn't listen.

The wiry dog looked at her with that addlepated, distracted expression, his eyes pointing off in two different directions as usual. Then he turned and bounded into the woods. A few yards in, he paused, looking over his shoulder, waiting to see if she was giving chase.

Merida thought about going to get Harris, but then she also thought about that sound. *Hsst.*

Two types of people: the sort who seek magic, and the sort that magic seeks.

A *hsst* outside a tent was a little like a knock on a door.

These woods were different from the snowy forest she'd followed Feradach through at Christmas, the first time they'd met. These were crisp autumn woods, full of clawed branches and dry thorns. Her pursuit disturbed red deer and owls, and the sounds of their flight were loud as they sent dried leaves rustling. Every so often one of these stags let out their terrifying roar, loud as a bear. But like those woods, she was on the hunt. She was pursuing Brionn, who in turn was chasing—what? The Hunt for the Unnamed. What was he pursuing? She didn't know. But she had to find out.

Brionn's strides at last began to flag, and Merida realized with a shock that she had entered a dead clearing.

Not dead as in *bare*. Not dead as in *worn down*. Not dead as in *cleared by man*.

Dead as in dead.

Unlike the autumn woods all around it, this clearing seemed to have already proceeded well into winter. The ground was hard and frozen, and every tree had shed its leaves already, letting the moon light the scene.

Stepping farther into the clearing, she realized it was beyond winter dead. It was the dead of a drought, of a harrowing fire, of a disaster. Even the evergreen larches had dropped all their needles, and they should've kept them.

Merida shivered, but not with the cold. Tilting her head back, she looked up at the stars, half expecting to see the Nimble Men glowing early among them. But instead the stars seemed dull and far away. The entire night felt muted.

Brionn let out a little yelp as he found his quarry.

It was already downed, lying in a heap in the peculiar dead glen.

Merida recognized those fine gloves with their oxblood

stitching, although she had not seen them like this before, the hands limp against the dead bracken.

"What are you doing on the ground?" she demanded.

Feradach made an unsuccessful effort to roll himself onto his back, because he was not just on the ground, he was on the ground on his face. That was quite the worst of it, that he had clearly fallen. No one lay down that way. No one even gently gave up that way. No, to lie like he was, his cheek against the ground, back to the sky, arms stretched down and hands palm up on either side of him—he had fallen on his face, and he hadn't had the ability to hold his hands out to soften his fall.

"I thought you couldn't be hurt," Merida said accusingly. It was quite wrong to see her adversary like this, his mane of hair dusted with leaf litter, body weak.

She began to tug on his cloak to turn him over, to at least get him off his face.

"Don't—touch—me—" he said. "My hands—"

"Don't be stupid!" Merida replied. "You didn't kill the horse you borrowed the day we went to Cennedig. You've got your gloves on still; I won't touch your hands."

It was a little nerve-racking to touch him, nonetheless, as she turned him over, but she was right, and it didn't kill her. It took less effort than she had expected. His mane of hair and his big fur-lined cloak had made him seem bigger than he was, but the body he was in was truly just a young man's, no older or weightier than she was.

She asked, "What happened to you? Were you attacked?"

She couldn't see any wound. What she could see, though,

was that the moss beneath him was dead, too, and so were the little shoots of grass that had been growing around it. Mushrooms were withered to dry straws, too.

"Consequences," he whispered.

"Consequences of what?" Merida swatted Brionn away.

"Of . . . not . . . ruining." Feradach closed his eyes for a long second, and then opened them again, with obvious effort. His dark eyebrows were drawn close together. "Didn't . . . ruin anything . . . since we last . . . since I saw . . . Cennedig."

"You haven't ruined anything since you saw me last?"

Feradach shook his head a little. "Wanted to . . . give . . . them . . . a chance . . . and I . . ."

He gave up talking and instead clawed his glove over his own heart, breathing with effort.

Merida found herself quite unsure what to do with this information. She felt angry, first of all. How dare he be her enemy and then turn around and do something like *this*. First the harp. And now this, whatever this was, breaking the rules beyond both of them, trying to do what she had said he ought to do, instead of what he had always done. He was supposed to be a god, and she was supposed to be a girl, and her words weren't supposed to hurt him.

"This isn't how I want to win the bargain," she said.

Feradach's head fell limply to the side.

"Merida!" Leezie's voice carried. "Merida, what are you—Merida, that's *not safe*!"

Leezie stepped cautiously into the dead clearing. Her hair was mussed and her eyes half-lidded with sleep; she looked, as ever, like she needed a bit of help. But her voice was wide-awake, and Merida, when she looked at Leezie, saw a little flash of the Cailleach's green starlight in her eyes.

Oh.

The Sight. People who seek the magic.

Merida felt quite out of sorts indeed. "How did you find me?"

"I had a—I had a dream," Leezie said. "I had a dream you needed me."

And Merida did need her. She needed someone who knew something about gods to tell her what to do, and Leezie was the closest thing she had. "What do you see? What do you think I'm looking at?"

Leezie hesitated, and Merida could see that she was trembling a little, like Hamish. Leezie mouthed a word but didn't say it out loud, just like when she had thought about trying to read the stone at Keithneil, but decided against it. Finally, she whispered, "I don't want to sound like I'm chasing nonsense."

"I'm not going to judge you for nonsense, Leezie, believe me, not this year of all years!" Merida said. "Tell me what you see! What is this here in front of me?"

Leezie shook her head, as if she couldn't believe what she was going to say, and then she said, "A *god*. Or something mighty like. Nothing for the likes of us to tangle with!"

Merida looked up at her. She couldn't say anything back at her because of the bargain, so she just implored Leezie with her eyes.

"But you have already tangled with it, haven't you," said Leezie. It wasn't a question. "Och, och, Merida! What did you do?"

Merida couldn't answer this, either. Her voice sounded more desperate than she meant it to. "I don't know what to do."

"This is a bad, bad, bad idea," Leezie said, as she knelt down to study him. "You poor wee thing. Who are you, boy? Oh, you're frightening. . . . Merida, look at his gloves. They're like the monk that—oh."

She looked at Merida, her pretty eyebrows knotted, her mind working over this information and trying to make it work out. She pressed her hands to her cheeks. She looked very much like she needed help, but help was what Merida wanted from *her*. Feradach's borrowed face was beginning to look of a piece with the dead things around him, colorless and slack.

"Can you tell if there's anything we can do, Leezie?" Merida asked. "Any of your rituals or your prayers or your potions or your Sight?"

"I don't have anything that can help with this," Leezie said. "I can't see that well. I should get Ila."

"Leezie, please," Merida said. "We don't have time. Please just try. For once don't give up when it gets hard. I'm a person magic seeks, not the other way around. Please, it's *important and I can't do it*. I need you! Please!"

Leezie sort of steeled herself then, in a way Merida hadn't seen her do before. She swept her wild helpless hair back defiantly, and then she stood up. She began to twirl in one of her Leezie-ish ways. Her hands seemed to be feeling the air. The sound of the leaves in the trees was a little like the moan of the Cailleach's voice, and then she moaned along with it. She didn't look silly. She didn't look Leezie-like.

Her eyes glimmered again with the glow of the will o' the wisps.

"He's a god of . . . ruin," Leezie said, under her breath, and Merida felt goose bumps rise on her skin. "Yes. He's a young god, and he's made a mistake." Leezie opened her eyes. "And he's dying."

Merida snapped, "What else?"

"He is not the first god of ruin," Leezie said, and she sounded awed at her own knowledge. "There were others before him. And if he doesn't do his duty now, he will die, but there will be other gods of ruin after him."

"As in, he'll come back?" Merida asked. "Like your mum said? He'll be reborn?"

Leezie looked perplexed at the question. "Another one will be."

"But what happens to *this* one? The one in *this* body? Is that who comes back?"

Leezie hovered her hands over Feradach again, then dropped them down into her lap. "I don't know. I don't know how to say it, Merida! It's not really for words. It's just—he barely exists anyway, Merida. He only looks like this, he only has a body, just for us. So we have something to see. And when there's no mortal to look at him, he's just a . . . *feeling* again. All he is is his duty, and if he isn't that, I just . . . What else is there of him?"

"He'll just go away?" Merida said.

"And a new god will take his place, yes," Leezie replied. "This one goes away. It's not like us."

Merida found this absolutely intolerable to imagine. She had goaded Feradach on the wall about how no one saw him more than once, and he had said that *she* did, and now, in his attempt to please her, he was going to have even that existence snuffed out. An existence only she had ever known of.

And of course the balance, the balance. She knew now that she believed him: he ruined for a reason, and it was important to keep that balance in place so that the renewal could move in.

But that knowledge didn't feel as immediate as the dying god in his borrowed body. Dying because of her.

"What do you want to do, Merida?"

"We have to help him do his duty," Merida said. "Help me take him to where he needs to be. Help me take him to whatever needs to be ruined."

27

THE RIVER WILL FIND ITS WAY IN

AGIC was a very strange thing.

There would have been no way for Merida and Leezie to carry Feradach far in the body in which Merida saw him. Merida and Leezie were plenty strong, but the hills were steep and the woods thick.

But whatever Leezie saw him as was obviously quite small, because after they realized Merida could not carry him, Leezie did. And because magic was a strange thing, Merida saw him both as the Feradach she knew, but also as the Feradach Leezie must see. Just as the first night when she had chased him, he seemed to shift forms in the moonlight. When Leezie paused to shake out her arms and focus on where her Sight told her they were meant to take him, he appeared to Merida as the blond-maned young man she'd met. When Leezie carried him, he was a too-thin redheaded toddler with a pinched expression and permanently worried mouth that reminded Merida uncomfortably of Hamish.

In both forms he was clearly dying.

Merida tried to push down the bad feeling inside her by telling herself that the redheaded toddler was a child he'd killed, that was why Feradach had his face, but it was a complicated truth that no longer brought her easy relief.

Dawn was beginning to lighten the sky by the time they arrived at the place he was supposed to ruin, the place he had been resisting. Even though the strange, waxy feeling that had marred the dead clearing was still hanging over everything, it was a lovely scene.

A wide river cut through the woods. Willow trees dangled their fingers into the surface as swans floated in slumber. Russet grass and tall wildflowers sighed in the breeze beside a stone hut. It looked like a home out of a story, quiet and peaceful.

As Leezie carried Feradach (Leezie was starting to complain a lot by now: "My arm is falling asleep!"), and Brionn circled anxiously around her, Merida crept to the hut. She peered inside.

It was a scholar's hut. The walls were lined with shelves of books and scrolls. A table was spread with manuscripts, inks, quills. Books were worth a fortune; manuscripts took forever to ink. It was years of work visible just in the dim light of the window. The scholar was visible, too—a woman, to Merida's surprise, as she knew few women who could read and write as well as her mother, certainly not enough to have done all this. But this woman clearly belonged to this scholarship, and vice versa. She was sleeping at the desk, long hair streaming over her shoulders, her ink-stained fingers not far from her quill.

Merida wondered what the scholar had done to bring Feradach to her. She wondered, too, what her fate was going to be.

All she knew was that it would be fair.

"I'm sorry," Merida whispered, her breath fogging the window for just a moment.

"Is there someone *in* there?" Leezie hissed.

"Put him down here," Merida hissed in return, intentionally not answering the question. "And then take Brionn and stand back. Far back. I don't know how to do this part. Don't look at me like that! You've done so much and I don't want you to get hurt because of doing your job well."

Feradach was laid beside the hut, within reach of the wall, both forms of him mingling in Merida's view. Leezie retreated far, far back, barely visible on the edge of the river plain.

Merida took a deep breath to give herself courage, and then reached for Feradach's glove.

"No!"

She flinched. The protest was the first indication he'd given that he had any awareness left at all.

Feradach's eyes had come open, and Merida saw him once more as just the man she'd come to know. With effort he said, "Don't."

"We brought you to where you're supposed to be," Merida whispered angrily. "I understand what you were trying to do, but it won't work. The balance won't let it. I understand. Do your duty. I want you to do what you are meant to do."

"I will," Feradach said, voice thin and strained. "But don't . . . touch . . ."

She realized what he meant and sat back. With agonizing slowness, he began to worry off the glove himself. It took forever, and for a while, it did not at all seem like he would ever manage it, as he had to keep letting his hands fall to his chest to rest before trying once more.

Finally, as the sun just came over the trees and lit one thousand bright diamonds of light across the wide pacific river, he managed to get one glove off. Such an ordinary hand beneath it. Such a deadly hand.

He hesitated.

Merida reached for his elbow where it was safely covered by his sleeve, and lifted his arm for him.

Feradach pressed his hand into the side of the hut. His handprint sank deep into it.

Immediately Merida felt the day right itself. The strange, waxy feeling lifted, and everything seemed sharp and near again. Even though something dreadful was surely going to happen—she had helped make sure of that—the world no longer felt dreadful.

The birds kept singing. The swans kept floating. The river kept easing by. But it was different, somehow. What must it be like, Merida thought, to have a sense of this balance at all times? No wonder Feradach felt so compelled to right it. How strange it must be to endure DunBroch's wrongness for an entire year; no wonder he had winced at the concept of the bargain.

When Merida turned back to Feradach, she found he'd already put his glove back on and pulled himself to crouch. Already he, too, was being righted. He gazed at Merida with a most peculiar expression.

"What will happen to her?" Merida asked, to hide the fact that she, too, felt most peculiar.

Feradach said simply, "The river will find its way in."

He did not say thank you, and she did not say that they had saved him.

They just stayed there for a minute, caught in that peculiar feeling that had nothing to do with the shifting balance between ruin and growth and more to do with the shifting balance between a god and a girl, and then Feradach said, "You should go. There's not much time left for you to do your work."

28

THE ISLAND OF LOST GIRLS

EVERYTHING stayed peculiar after that, actually. It was not that it was bad; it was the opposite. Everything went perfectly. Logically, it seemed as if uncertainty should have set in the farther they got from home, the deeper they got into rural Scotland, the wilder the countryside became. Even if nothing had gone wrong at all, it was still a very long journey over very wild terrain, including a boat ride across a capricious autumn sea.

But instead it was idyllic. Timeless. Happy. Exciting. The royal retinue journeyed right to where the land ended, at a remote harbor called Tarvodubron, and then climbed into small boats for the crossing to Eilean Glan. Merida had never been on such a journey before and it seemed impossible, terrifying, wondrous, to be in the middle of the ocean with land visible on one side and land barely visible on the other and nothing but water and weather between.

Creatures as large as Merida but with slick gray skin and small, clever eyes leapt alongside the boats, thrilling and delighting and horrifying passengers. It felt to Merida as if she had traveled not to another kingdom but to a dream.

It became obvious the moment they landed at Eilean Glan that it was not at all a kingdom in the same way that Ardbarrach or Kinlochy or even DunBroch were kingdoms. There was no massive castle here, no court, no lairds, no tacksmen. There simply wasn't enough land or people for such a system. Eilean Glan was one of a handful of small bare islands rising from the ocean, their edges sheer pale cliffs. Everything was whipping grass and blazing sun and bare flat boulders. There were precious few trees; how could there be? The wind was continuous.

It was the most memorable part of the island, the wind.

But it didn't seem to faze Elinor.

From the moment she stepped off the boat onto the shore, she floated. Her eyes were wide, taking everything in. With complete surety, she led them all from the harbor, to a road cut deep into the ground and edged with hedgerows and stone walls to offer a bit of a windbreak, and right up to a community of low houses and buildings dug into the ground to keep the wind from unmooring them. It was a convoluted layout, but Elinor seemed to know it intuitively. She took them directly to the main building, which was large, but like everything else, low. They had to duck to get into it.

Inside, rushlights illuminated rows and rows of girls, their hair all pinned neatly up, eerily matching the way

Elinor's hair was currently pinned, the way it was always pinned beneath her wimple and veil. They were all bent over books, fingers trailing along the words. Some of them were also writing as they went. Merida had never seen so many girls in one place and certainly never seen so many readers.

At the head of the room was a light-haired woman about Elinor's age who was dressed just as neatly and tidily as the girls. She was tapping a dry quill in her palm absently, but when she saw Elinor, she said, "Oh! *Elinor!*"

To Merida's surprise, the two of them embraced like sisters, and the woman laughed and wiped away a tear that had come out with her laugh.

"Look at you!" the woman said. "Has Máel Muire seen you yet?"

Elinor shook her head, laughing and crying too.

Merida and Leezie exchanged puzzled looks. Harris's eyes narrowed in a question.

But there was no time for answers, not just yet. Instead the blond woman told the girls to continue working, and then she told them something else in a different language, and then she told them something else in a third language (or perhaps she told them the same thing three times, in three different languages), and then she whisked Elinor and the others out to see yet more. Here was a building where more girls with neat hair and neat simple dresses watched a woman carefully as she tugged and pressed bread dough. Here, a building where a group of girls picked very slowly at elaborate patterns in embroidery.

Here, a building where girls played a song on mandolins together. Here, girls learning to handle ponies, here, girls learning to speak clearly, here, girls praying, here, girls braiding other girls' hair, here, girls doing laundry, here, girls, girls, girls, all of them learning something new with diligence.

The girls glanced curiously at them as they came through, particularly at Harris, who was obviously out of place. He didn't return the stares. His mood had been cool ever since the conversation about the Sight, and it had only gotten chillier during the remainder of the trip. Partway through this trip, he made an excuse to sit and wait with Brionn and the other soldiers who had been escorting them.

Merida didn't have time to persuade him to be more engaged.

She would worry about him later.

"What is this place?" Merida whispered to Leezie as they hurried after Elinor, Ila, and the teacher, battered by the wind. And what role would she play here if she came? Teacher? Would she be like the woman gladly leading Elinor through the compound? Or would she be a student again?

"Orphans," Leezie whispered back.

Of course, Merida thought. Now that Leezie had said it, it seemed obvious. The way the girls were all ages, from all walks of life, some clearly more comfortable with the material and each other. This was an orphanage. A school. An island for lost girls. Of course Leezie would see herself in them.

Finally they came to a small room where just three girls were bent over worktables, laboring with intense concentration. One was carving. One was painting. Another was carefully fitting together intricately shaped pieces of wood. To Merida's delight, she realized they were constructing a Brandubh board.

The older woman who sat in this room with them wasn't carving alongside them; she was writing in fluid, familiar handwriting, each letter precise and lovely. Even though she was quite old, she had a younger woman's posture. That surety, that dignity, that strength. She still exuded power. She had a thin, plain circlet of gold pinned into her hair; she must have been the queen of this place, if this place had queens.

"Máel Muire?" Elinor said, in a very different sort of voice than Merida had ever heard her use.

"Elinor, my child," the woman said. "I got your letter only the other day, but I didn't dare hope you would follow it."

Standing, she held her arms out. She and Merida's mother clasped hands tightly and Elinor's eyes dropped down in a very abashed way and Merida realized—

Her mother had grown up here.

As Elinor and the woman talked in low voices, Merida did her best to piece together the time line in her head. She knew that Elinor's parents had died before Merida was born, but somehow, from the half-heard stories, she had always thought it was when Elinor was already queen of DunBroch, not that long before Merida was born. She hadn't imagined it might have been when Elinor was a girl. She hadn't imagined that Elinor might have been an orphan.

Suddenly she thought of how quickly Elinor had taken in Leezie. How quickly she had taken to training up Ila.

But her mother had come from a royal family, she'd had tutors in France—

"Merida," Elinor said. "Merida."

"You never told her," Máel Muire said.

Elinor said softly, "It's not that I was ashamed—"

Máel Muire broke in, "I have no hard feelings, Elinor. The future will always be more important to study than the past. And you're here now. Is it as you remember?"

"It's even better," Elinor said. "There are so many girls."

"Too many," the old queen remarked, leading them out of the little building. As she walked them to the buildings where the girls slept, she told her story to Merida. "When my husband the king died, I found myself with much to do on these islands and few hands to do it with. I decided to take on some of the orphan girls from Skara Brae, from Hoy, and then even from Tarvodubron. Then word got out that I was taking in girls and teaching them to read and write, to have a craft, to be ladies, and I began to get orphans sent from further and further on the mainland. I thought that hardship was confined to these islands, but it turns out that wherever there are children, there are parents dying. I got poor girls and lairds' girls and even children like Elinor, the daughter of a recently widowed queen who died in childbirth. Do you know where your sisters ended up, Elinor?"

"France," Elinor said.

"Yes, France," Máel Muire said. "Yes, that makes sense. So I train them, and some stay and help me train more, and there are always more motherless daughters."

Merida was staggered. She kept trying to fit this information against what she knew of her mother, and it kept bouncing off like an arrow that had lost its tip. Her mother, her perfect, queenly mother, had learned her love of reading and language and education not in a court in France but here. When she had spent all that time chiding Merida to do better and be more womanly, she was comparing her not to princesses and women in places like Ardbarrach, but to the hardworking and varied girls and women here. When she'd said she wanted the best future for Merida and tried to marry her off to have a family of her own, she was coming from a place that started with broken families with no gentle places to land.

And perhaps the most difficult part to process was the secret of it. It seemed impossible that there should be something this vast about her mother that Merida hadn't even guessed at.

Merida thought of how she'd fought with her before she'd left for Kinlochy.

How can you be so cruel?

Her cheeks burned.

Máel Muire said to Elinor, "I know you came here to offer me Merida as help, and I will take her if she wants to come, but I have another proposal for you, if you will listen."

They had come to a low, small building that was closer to the shore than the others. Beds were built into all the walls, and little sewn animals were tucked here and there on them. Elinor sighed deeply; her gaze was far away. "Oh, my old quarters."

"Elinor, my fellow queen," Máel Muire said, placing her hands on Elinor's shoulders. "It would do me much favor in my old age if you would take some of these girls with you to DunBroch and raise them."

Elinor spun to face her.

"I know you can do it," the old queen said before Elinor could speak. "You were always fearfully good with a pen and paper. Your manners are impeccable. You are resilient as stone. I would not trust my girls with many, but I know you would do well by them if you had the room and the time."

Elinor turned to Merida and Leezie. Her face was both shining and confused, warmed by the praise and overwhelmed by the request.

"Don't even pause to think about it. Say yes," said Merida. She looked back at this wonderful elderly queen who made her suddenly understand so much about her mother. "She'll be ever so good."

"Yes," Leezie said emphatically. "Yes!"

"It's what she's made for," Ila added.

Of all the things that were said, this was the one that made Máel Muire smile. "Yes, I know."

29

THE DÁSACHTACH

HE journey back took longer than the one there, but Elinor had planned for this; she had known the weather would already be harsher and the days shorter by the time they turned around. She had constructed their trip based upon what she remembered from her last journey to Eilean Glan and what she had researched. She had each day's distance and each night's stop planned out.

By now, Merida realized that Fergus had been wrong about why Elinor hesitated to travel. It was not that she needed things to be nice. She needed things to be perfect, and it was hard to make travel perfect. She had lost faith in her ability to do it. Now she was remembering.

The return trip began well. They traveled through the dense forests without luring the wolves out. They camped in clearings that overlooked secretive little rivers. They ate meals nearly as fancy as the ones at the castle, augmented by salmon from the fast rivers. They told stories around fires. They saw wondrous vistas from atop high bluffs, and

Merida was overcome with how beautiful the world was. The sun went down and mist crept out; the sun rose and banished the mist and off they traveled again.

It remained very fortunate weather, although the crisp edge and the smell of oak leaves made Merida nervous, reminding her Christmas was soon coming.

"Something's going to go wrong," Harris told Merida. "It can't stay like this."

"When did you become such a toad?" Merida asked. "Is this a new thing or have you always been a toad? She's doing a good job."

"This isn't about Mum," Harris said in his cool tone. "Not everything is criticism. I was trying to have a conversation, but I should have known better."

"Here's something better for you," Merida said, and pulled his hair.

He bit her.

"Oh, very adult," Merida said.

"You're just sorry you didn't get me first," Harris said. "Brionn, come *on*!" His dog, as ever, didn't listen, and continued to wreak havoc among the pack ponies.

"I see something going wrong right now," Merida said, with a meaningful look at Brionn. "Clean up your own house before you start trashing others."

But Harris was, as Harris often was, right. Or at least not entirely wrong.

At first it was a day when they didn't cover quite as much ground as Elinor had planned.

Then it was a day when their intended campsite had been flooded and they had to camp several miles farther out.

And then, on the third day, they came across a completely destroyed town.

"What happened here?" Elinor demanded. Merida could tell her mother was becoming more upset because she became ever more rigid and queenly. The less she understood what was going on or how to fix it, the more rules and orders she was likely to deliver. "I want an answer!"

Her question was all the more ridiculous because it was obvious what had happened. The town had been razed to the ground. The doors had been barricaded. The roofs had been set alight. The livestock had been slaughtered. The pine trees for timbering had been felled and splintered. The wells had been salted. Anyone left behind was dead, and horribly so. They had been made to die slowly. It all smelled of destruction.

So the scouts who had alerted her to the destroyed town didn't answer her. And they didn't have an answer to the real question, which was *Who did this?*

As they picked through the town, Merida felt her stomach churn. She had blamed Feradach for Kinlochy's destruction before this, but now that she saw how cruelly this town had been cut to bits and tormented, she understood the difference.

He was nature.

This was human.

Feradach had ruined that town only as much as required. This town's destruction had far more in common with the initial brutal invasion of Keithneil. It had been pillaged in such a way that did not consider the future at all.

Finally Elinor waved a hand to spread the soldiers who had gathered close and protective around their queen as she investigated. She asked the unanswerable question. "*Who* did this?"

A clear voice came from among the few pine trees still standing. "I did."

Merida looked up and saw a man sitting on horseback, shoulders thrown back, head held high. In the half-felled trees behind him other warriors were visible. One of them wore a cloak made entirely of wolf tails.

"Name yourself," Elinor said, and her voice did not falter at all.

"I am Domnall mac Alpin," he replied.

Harris gave Merida a knowing look. Things had gone terribly wrong.

He was the Dásachtach.

Merida had not expected the Dásachtach to be young. For some reason, she thought he would be an old, jaded warlord, powerful and wizened. A man who had compassion once, perhaps, but lost it. A man who had slowly acquired the respect or fear of all the people around him.

But he was young.

He was barely older than her, perhaps, if even that. His face seemed pleasant. Earnest. He seemed less like someone you would cower from and more like someone whose favor you would like to have.

He did not, however, seem to have that effect on Merida's mother. She said, in her same imperious tone, "Explain yourself."

He did not posture and say he didn't have to answer to her or anyone else. He didn't ask her to prove her status and right to demand anything of him. He just did exactly as she asked. He explained how this kingdom had been fussing with its neighbors for generations. Stealing cattle. Stealing daughters. Refusing to help when the Norsemen came. Letting reformers come through and harass the clergy. Cutting down their resources and wasting them without sharing them with others. The trees on this rock wouldn't last forever, after all.

"I asked them to comply again and again," the Dásachtach said. Now he looked grim. Depressed. "Just a little show of loyalty. Anything, really. Send me sons; marry their daughters to the neighbors who were so fearful of them. Give us a choice. Anything. But . . ."

He held out his hand helplessly and showed them the ruined town as if that was the only option he'd had available.

If there hadn't still been smoke roiling off the town, it might have seemed more compassionate, but as it was, it remained a hard sell for the queen of DunBroch.

"This is no way to change hearts," Elinor said. "There are many other ways."

As they'd been speaking, more men had come into view behind him among the trees. It was not an entire army, but it was certainly enough to take out the DunBroch travelers if it came to a battle. Unlike the rigid dignity of Ardbarrach's regiments, the Dásachtach's group was a somehow free and organic mass, sinuous and fierce. If Ardbarrach's forces had been like a well-trained machine, this was like a nest of snakes, coiling and turning over each other. They were cunning and mobile and somehow seemed much more dangerous.

Harris watched them intently.

"If only that were true," the Dásachtach replied sadly. "If *only* that were true. Dear woman. You have not told me your name."

"Elinor of DunBroch," Elinor said, and Merida was proud of her mother's mettle. She was not having any of his fairy-tale spinning. "We have just returned from a journey to Eilean Glan, as per our discussion with your man, and have arranged for foster girls to come to DunBroch."

"How excellent to hear you are working toward unity," he said. "This must be your daughter. And oh—who's this?"

A dog was scurrying around his horse's legs, its tail up and curious. Very few horses like to be meddled with by strange dogs, especially in wolf season, and the Dásachtach's mount was no different. It whirled and tossed its head and kicked out, but the dog was like warm jelly and simply trickled out of harm's way.

"Tsssss!" Harris hissed through his teeth.

Because of course the dog that had crossed the distance to them was Brionn. Of course.

"Harris," hissed Merida.

"One of yours? What a fine-looking creature," the

Dásachtach said. He had calmed down his horse without getting flustered himself, and now he slid off and grabbed Brionn's wide collar in one smooth motion. Brionn twisted, his expression silly as usual, eyes pointing off in all directions, tongue lolling, but he could not free himself from the Dásachtach's grip. The warlord cast his eyes over the group and seemed to discern even at a distance of several yards who was at fault, because his gaze flickered to Harris and stayed firmly there. "It's all right; come get him."

Harris stalked across the expanse, his head up, shoulders back. If he was embarrassed about Brionn—and Merida knew he was—it wasn't visible in his walk. As ever, he looked much older than his years as he strode across the expanse under the attention of both Elinor's royal retinue and the Dásachtach's men. He looked neither left nor right. His fingers did not twitch to betray uncertainty. That was not the Harris way. He simply walked straight up to the warlord who had just slaughtered an entire town and inclined his head in understated gratitude.

The Dásachtach did not immediately relinquish Brionn. Instead he stood there and cocked his head and took in the sight of Harris of DunBroch. Harris remained unflinching, wearing, as always, his cool, slightly superior expression that gave very little away.

"This is your dog?" the Dásachtach asked.

"He was a gift," Harris answered in his distant way.

"Do you not think a dog's behavior reflects its master?"

"I do."

"And do you think this dog reflects you well, boy?"

It was a critique, and Harris did not generally take critique well unless he respected the giver very much, but all he said was, "He will."

This made the Dásachtach smile. He held a hand out as if displaying Harris to his men. "Here now is a fine creature. I can see the quick mind shining out through the eyes." He looked at Elinor. "Is this one of your sons? Boy, wouldn't you like to ride with us now? We have a horse just your size."

Merida thought she might throw up.

"Thank you for the offer," Elinor said coldly. "But we have already sent one son to Ardbarrach and we must consider if we want to send off another, as we have our own borders to think of."

"Indeed," the Dásachtach said. "How well you illustrate my point. You send a son; I send a son. You will not be unprotected. Together we are a family. You would not think twice to send your son to family to spend time, nor would you be sad to receive and host family in his place for a time. Does family always get along? No, family does not always agree. But they take care of each other. I am making a family. Are you sure you do not want to send him along? We are doing quite a lot of work on this trip and I think he'd enjoy seeing it."

At a subtle gesture from their queen, Elinor's soldiers had stood at the ready, hands tight on hilts and spears. Her voice had metal in the back of it, too. "He is not coming with you."

"Suit yourself," the Dásachtach said. He leaned and whispered something to Harris, whose face did not change. Harris took Brionn's collar and wrapped his fingers through it as Brionn panted and tried to lick him, and then he walked stiffly back to the retinue of DunBroch.

Then the Dásachtach snapped his fingers and said, "Thistlekin."

"What did you say?" Elinor demanded.

"I was trying to think of where I had heard your name before," the Dásachtach said. "Elinor of DunBroch. You were the diplomat queen, were you not? The Peacemaker. They still tell tales of you. And wasn't that the phrase you used back then when you settled the tribes? Thistlekin. They stick each other, but they stick together. You and I are not that different."

Merida, Leezie, and Harris looked to Elinor to see her reaction.

But just then she looked quite a bit like Harris. Remote and cold.

"Goodbye, Domnall mac Alpin," she said in her most regal of voices. "I do not expect to see you again."

The Dásachtach smiled.

30

WAR AND PEACE

ERIDA was not the only one who was quite shocked to hear of this other, famous side of her mother. First the surprise of her mother's upbringing, as told by Máel Muire, and now this. Merida was beginning to feel like she didn't know who Elinor was at all.

When they camped that night, just far enough away from the town so that they could not smell the awfulness of the Dásachtach's work, she and Leezie were united in trying to find out more about it. They gathered at the fire just outside the main royal tent and tried to get Elinor to talk about herself.

She would not, at first. At first, all she did was deal with the fact of the encounter with the Dásachtach. She sent a scout galloping back toward DunBroch to tell Fergus, and another scout galloping south to inform Ardbarrach of the burnt town. She sent yet another to a village she said was near, to find out if they had survived and to arm themselves against the Dásachtach, if they had not, just in case.

She was a queen.

This wasn't to say she wasn't still very lofty and flustered during all of this, and she calmed herself down by giving Harris a lengthy lecture about his dog's behavior and how badly that could have turned out and how it could have just as easily ended with his dog's throat being cut before his eyes or *his* throat being cut before hers to teach a lesson, and if he had seen the things she had seen!

Harris endured all of this with his usual stillness, and finally Elinor was calm enough to be sat by the fire with some food before her and Ila sitting beside her carefully plucking thorns out of her skirt. Which was when Merida and Leezie set in asking about her past, and she set about not talking about it.

But then one of the soldiers leaning on his spear near the fire straightened a bit and said, "My sister's named Elinor after your mum, Princess."

"I still remember what she looked like riding through our village after it was liberated," said one of the other soldiers.

"There's a song in my hometown about how she made Clan Gregor and Clan Concobar stop murdering each other!" said one of Aileen's kitchen helpers merrily as she refilled Elinor's glass.

Elinor pursed her lips and said, "Exaggeration."

But the stories kept coming in, and getting longer and more elaborate, until eventually nearly the whole of the retinue was gathered around the fire, telling Merida tales of her mother before she'd become a mother, and finally Elinor was laughing sweetly and pitching in details they forgot.

"They called us War and Peace," she said, breaking a cake into polite-sized mouthfuls. "When your father and I were engaged to be wed, no one believed it! Him spending his youth stirring up fights and me spending mine putting them down!"

"You were my age doing all that?" Merida asked in disbelief.

"Aye," Elinor said. "Sometimes it feels like an entirely different me. Like I've lived two lives entirely. Ah, it was a time."

Merida couldn't believe that her mother had been riding around Scotland at her age. Merida had ridden all over, yes, but no one was going to sing songs and recite ballads about her just because she'd read some books at a convent and raised some cows and tagged along with mapmakers.

She was uncomfortably reminded of that phrase that kept haunting her, in Feradach's voice: a storm that moved no roofs. Her mother had moved roofs.

And all this time, Merida had been judging *Elinor* for inaction.

She closed her eyes and thought about the ruined town and the odor of carnage. She thought about how the Dásachtach had salted the wells to keep them from being used in the future, and how he had ruined the good trees nearby to keep them from being used to rebuild new life.

How completely opposite that was to the searing, purposeful destruction of Kinlochy, or the brutal, incisive destruction of Cennedig's hands.

Feradach's ruin left a door open for the new; the Dásachtach had intentionally slammed all the doors shut with his.

"But why don't you still do it?" Leezie was asking. "Obviously we still need it! There's that madman running around instead having his way of things."

"It's not a task for someone with a daughter and three little boys!" Elinor said. "I was a mother."

"You could've strapped me to your back," Merida protested. "I would've been glad for it."

"I'm sure you would've," Elinor said, "but that was back when I was still believing you'd grow up to be a proper lady." She smiled to soften the blow. "And the triplets . . . well. It was hard enough to get them into the world, and it's a whole job keeping them here." She smiled at Harris to soften these words, too, but he just sat across from her at the fire as he always did, his eyes giving nothing away, his mouth still.

Merida badly wanted to know what the Dásachtach had whispered to him, but of course he'd just gone all scornful and silent when she asked. Harris had liked his secrets before they left, and he hadn't changed a bit since then, now that they were almost back.

And there just wasn't much time left.

31

Autumn Changes

 MERIDA found herself quite out of sorts after they got back to DunBroch. Part of it was just that everything was so very different. By the time they returned from Eilean Glan, the seasons had decidedly changed and it was well into the skinflint days of late autumn, each hour of daylight meted out with a miser's sneer. The sun had changed, too. It stayed low and sulky for the entire day, barely appearing in public before vanishing again. It gave everything a forever evening cast, a sense of always waiting, never receiving.

With the lack of sun came chill, of course, and the smell of peat burning as smoke piped out the top of the blackhouse village chimneys and from the tacksmen's houses down in the fields. Blazes rose up high in DunBroch's fireplaces, altering it even more than it had already been altered. Merida knew the physical changes to DunBroch were a big reason why she felt out of sorts. It was clear

Fergus had put all hands on deck to get the transformation done by the time his queen arrived home. Every room sparkled. Every beam that could be replaced had been replaced. Every tapestry that could be cleaned and repaired had been cleaned and repaired. Every staircase was new. Everything that was supposed to be straight was straight, everything that was supposed to be a perfect spiral was a perfect spiral. The tables in the great room were new; the beds were all new. The kitchen had new cupboards and bins; the armory was full of new weapons sized just right for Hubert.

The common room wasn't even smoky anymore. The furniture had all been moved back in from its temporary home in the music room, but it still looked different because the air was sparkling.

Oh, and the glass, the *glass*! Fergus had sold who knew how many cows and furs in order to have glass put in every window in the castle. Before, only the rooms that welcomed guests had glass. Every other window was open to the air, covered with one or two or four tapestries to keep the midges out in summer and the cold out in winter. But now there was glass, actual glass, in every window, often in pretty colors, too. It made the castle warmer than it had ever been before, but it was also disconcerting, because one could no longer hear everything that went on outside in the courtyard as clearly as if one were standing outside. Instead, there were two DunBrochs: inside and outside, two worlds one now could only traverse through a door rather than sort of existing in both.

The courtyard was paved and sharp, too, of course, and the stables and outbuildings had been shored up. Fergus had also wanted to show off for his old friend the king of Ardbarrach and all the other royals who had come in for the Hunt for the Unnamed, which hadn't hurt in quickening and expanding his efforts. And it was a good thing he'd renovated all the outbuildings, too, because two young orphans the triplets' age were coming from Eilean Glan in just a few days, and three times as many as that would arrive in addition before the weather turned, and Elinor needed every bit of space she could get to put them up. Aileen, to her delight, got upgraded to the newly finished attic, which had always been the warmest place in the entire castle. And the family DunBroch gave up all pretense that Leezie was anything less than a DunBroch, too, and also that she'd ever do anything like housekeeping, and moved her bed into the tapestry room above Merida's. Official papers were sent off making her part of the proper family line and they had a cake to celebrate it and everything.

Leezie no longer talked about falling in love; instead, she talked about the holy well, and gods of ruin, and the Sight, and because she could not find any priestess to teach her more about this, she began to sit in with Elinor's students to learn how to read so that she could read the books Elinor had on it instead. She still gave up on a great many things halfway, but she didn't give up on *all* things halfway: she had changed.

Hubert was home for the season now, and to Merida's great relief, he was not horribly altered. He was not the

Hubert she remembered—he was far more dutiful and less boisterous—but he was still good-humored and had his old enormous laugh, and he set the dogs loose upon her in bed the very first day he was back, so she did not think she had entirely lost him to a rigid, premature adulthood.

Hamish, on the other hand, was often not home, as he traveled with Gille Peter to Cennedig to train for a few days at a time, when Cennedig did not come and stay at DunBroch. Strangely enough, Hamish had become a little bit more like Hubert—the old Hubert. Now that he was no longer pressed so small by fear, he got sillier and louder and bigger. He still looked like he'd been kept out of sunlight for too long and like he might float away if you didn't tie him down, but his smile lit rooms dark with winter.

The entire castle was alive and bustling. It was changing, it was changing.

Except for Harris. She was no closer to knowing him than she had been at the beginning of this.

"You're so fidgety," Aileen complained one evening. "Why are you pacing round my kitchen?"

"I'm just looking for something small to eat," Merida said.

"You've seen six somethings small to eat. Pick one. Pick them all. Just get out."

Merida hovered her hands over the bread. The roasted nuts. This time last year, Leezie had been thinking she was about to get married. Merida wondered where the Cabbage was. She wondered if she needed to take Harris on another trip somewhere. She wondered if the Dásachtach would be satisfied with DunBroch taking in foster girls, or if he would be upset that she hadn't yet picked a kingdom to move to.

If Harris doesn't change, none of it matters, and I can't ask anyone for help. I'm so—

"Merida!" Aileen snapped. "You're wearing me out! Stop pacing! Pick something! What are you waiting for?"

What indeed? She felt exhausted with waiting. Strung out with waiting. She felt listless and faint with it.

"I tell you what, I am going to walk these drinks into that Great Hall and take my break and when I come back, I expect you to be out of here with whatever you put your mind to," Aileen said, and she stormed out with the drinks.

Merida didn't pick something to eat, though. Instead, standing in the pantry, she started to cry. Just a little. It was so unlike her to cry, to crouch in the pantry with the flour and the turnips and the barley and the little pantry moths, to be far away from the evening merriment of the rest of DunBroch, to be unable to turn her situation into a game or challenge of some kind; she had not cried since the day beside the well, months and months and months before.

It was just that the castle felt so full, and yet she felt so apart. They didn't know that if she didn't figure out Harris, they were all going to die. And this feeling inside her, this waiting, this waiting, this waiting.

Tap, tap, tap.

There was a knock at the door.

It was polite. Without urgency. *Pardon me,* the knock said, *is there anyone there—?*

She wiped the tears from her face. Leezie always said she enjoyed a good cry, but Merida felt as if her face had been kneaded and left to rise. Puffy and clumsy—when she rose, her sleeve caught a bag of oatmeal and knocked over a jar of cloves. Elinor and Leezie must have been putting them into oranges for centerpieces—Leezie never could be bothered to put the lid on anything tightly. The odor surrounded her. Christmas, it shouted, Christmas. Christmas and the end of everything, maybe.

The door.

She went to it, and before she put her hand on the door pull, she thought about that snowy night almost a year ago and she had half a thought that she would open it and there would be no one on the other side.

But tonight, when she opened the door, there was someone standing on the other side of it. A familiar figure: That mane of hair. The broad-shouldered cloak. The hands in their gloves with oxblood stitching held carefully in each other.

"*You*," she said.

But her mind thought, *Finally.*

This was what she had been waiting for. This was who she had been waiting for.

The very first flakes of snow of the year swirled behind him. She could hear the wind howling something fierce, nearly as strong as it had been on Eilean Glan.

It was the beginning of the end.

"Will you show me what has changed?" Feradach asked.

32

A FAMILIAR FACE

"YOU don't need me to show you," Merida told Feradach. "You can just feel it, can't you? You could probably tell me more than even I know just from standing in the courtyard."

Feradach replied, "The Cailleach says you're meant to show me, so I think you should show me."

"I think you just want to come in out of the cold."

"May I?" he asked.

Merida let him in. He stood in the kitchen, looking quite ordinary and mortal as he had when he had talked with Aileen two seasons before. His eyes flitted over all the things he saw there and she wondered if he remembered it well enough to see how even the kitchen had changed. She wondered if it mattered, anyway. External change wasn't what interested him.

"Do you want some bread? Do you eat?" she asked him. She felt shy around him now for some reason. He had been dying when she saw him before.

"I eat," he said. He looked around. "It's warmer than before."

"Glass in all the windows," Merida said. "Doing it right this time, my father said, welcome to the modern world. All the candles are beeswax now, too—no more smoky cow-smelling tallow candles, and oil lamps in the Great Hall and common room. The future is brighter!" she joked.

"It has changed," Feradach agreed. "Show me more."

"There are many people here," Merida warned. "You'll have to be quick on your feet as they see your changing face."

"I always am."

Yes, she supposed he was used to it. "Do you want to hang your cloak there?"

"I have always wanted to know what it looked like," he said, and then he removed it and looked at it as if seeing it for the first time.

And he was, Merida realized with an odd feeling in her stomach. He did not know what he looked like, he said, until someone told him enough to remind him whose face he wore. His appearance was in the eye of the beholder. Merida had made that cloak that now hung with the others behind the kitchen door, in a way.

Magic, magic.

But the cloak was not enough to tell him whose face he had, because she saw him furtively touch his fingers once more to his jawline before he turned from the cloaks, trying to identify it. She could see from his expression that he was unsuccessful.

"Come see what you'd like to ruin," she told him.

"I don't *want—*" he began, before he realized she was merely ribbing him. He caught a bread roll as she tossed it, and then let her lead him into DunBroch for a third time.

This was nothing like the first time, when she'd pulled him fearfully from Aileen in the kitchen, unsure of how the game was going to play out. Now, in many ways, he was her closest confidant. Certainly he was the only one who knew what she was living through. It was an odd push-pull. Familiarity; caution. Shared secrets; opposite goals.

Who knew of his existence? She did.

Who knew of hers? He did.

She gave him a proper tour.

In each room, she tried to describe how it used to look, and what had been improved with her father's renovation, but she found she frequently got sidetracked. When trying to think of good ways to describe how the room had been in the past, she often remembered stories that had happened in it, instead, and only realized partway through she hadn't said anything about change.

"That summer, Dad told the triplets he'd give them a lump of sugar for every rat tail they nailed to this board under their name," Merida said, in one of the hallways. "Seems positively violent to tell it to you now, but you have to understand, that summer of rats, they were everywhere, they were under the blankets with you in bed, they were taking supper with you, you'd reach down to pet a dog and you'd be petting a pile of rats instead." Hamish hadn't killed a single one, she was sure, but nonetheless he'd had just as many rat tails nailed up for every inspection, and Merida had once seen Hubert and Harris carefully splitting up their spoils in order to section off some for Hamish's board. "Who knew what they squeezed out of Hamish for such a favor, but I thought it was kind of them anyway." Merida shook her head. "I haven't told you what this room used to be like."

"The stories are fine," Feradach said. "I can see the change. I can feel it."

So she continued to tell him a story in each room. In the common room she told him how Mum had first found Leezie sleeping in her comfortable chair, right next to the fire, one of Mum's pressed flower books in her hands, back when they had first hired Leezie on as a housekeeper's assistant. She told him how Harris had once climbed out the window of the tower to the music room and hung on a rope there, trapped, for several hours, too proud to call for help. In the tapestry room, she told him how she and her mother had fought viciously over her right to her own hand in marriage, and of the mended tapestry that still hung there on the wall as a vow they'd never let themselves be separated by anger like that again. In the Great Hall, she showed him where all the tattered animal heads used to hang on the wall, horribly maimed, as she had, as a child, brought her bow and arrow in there and secretly shot at them for hours every night when she was first learning archery. She told him stories of Fergus and stories of Hubert and stories of Hamish and stories of all of them together, and he listened to all of them as the night outside grew deeper and the wind began to howl louder.

And then a remarkable thing happened.

They didn't realize it was remarkable until after, though.

At first, Elinor simply said, on her way up to the attic with the two orphan girls trailing behind her, "Merida, who's this fellow here so late?" She squinted at his expression and Merida could see her suspicion wash away with whatever she saw.

Merida thought fast and went with a version of the truth. "This is a fellow we met on the road to Ardbarrach. He gave us directions; he was passing through DunBroch and wanted to see how we'd fared."

The girls with Elinor had been looking at Feradach, too, as much as they could while remaining polite. Merida hoped that whatever they saw him as, it wasn't a woman or blind beggar, at least, so that the story held.

"Well, make sure he gets some warm ale in him," Elinor said. "It's quite a night out there. Those are splendid gloves, sir."

"Thank you," said Feradach. "They were a gift."

The remarkable thing had happened, but Merida and Feradach still hadn't realized it. They didn't realize it when they ran into Fergus and Hubert and Gille Peter in the armory, where they were all having a loud and boisterous time repairing handles on spears and telling tales round their lantern as the dogs gnawed bones (the castle's dog was already in the process of vomiting her bone back up to chew it once more, as she always did).

"What can we do for you, my love?" Fergus asked as Merida held the door shut enough to keep the dogs from escaping past her legs (yes, there was a door now! Gone was the chest that had been pushed in front of it for years).

"Er, I," Merida started.

"Oh, I didn't see you there," Fergus said to Feradach. "Your brooch—is that Breadalbane you're from?"

Feradach followed Fergus's gaze to his chest, and then his fingers touched the brooch Merida had seen him wear all this time, the circular pin with a tree on it, both its branches and roots visible. He felt it and only she could tell that he was feeling it for the first time, although it was clearly not a specific enough description to tell him whose face he wore. He just said the thing he had said many times: "It was a gift."

"What's the weather like outside?" Fergus asked him. "I thought I could hear the wind howling."

"Weather's coming fast," Feradach agreed.

But Merida and Feradach still didn't realize the remarkable thing that was happening.

They didn't realize it in the music room either, where Hamish was listening raptly to Cennedig tell a story of his traveling days, both of their harps resting upon their shoulders as if they might play at any moment. They looked up at Merida and Feradach. Hamish had seen Feradach before, of course, in a body with a scar on its face, but he showed no recognition now.

"We're just passing through on our way up," Merida said, hoping to draw attention from Feradach and any mismatch the two of them might have in how they saw him. "Don't let us stop you."

"I say," Cennedig said. "Young man, do you have family near Cairnlee? You look like a family I used to know near there, just in the eyes and that wild hair, of course." He smiled and touched his own wild hair.

"I've heard I do," Feradach said.

"Excuse us," Merida said, and hurried him through before any more probing questions could be asked. It seemed inevitable that they'd get tangled in conflicting backstories very soon.

It was only when they ran into Elinor again that Merida and Feradach understood the remarkable thing that had been happening. That was still happening. She'd been coming the opposite way down the hall; there was no escape. Merida would have to explain how she had come to have a second visitor on a wild night like this.

But to Merida's surprise, when Elinor walked up with her girls, Ila in tow behind them now, she just said to Feradach, "The weather has truly turned; you'll be staying the night, then, surely? Did you say you were from Ardbarrach, or headed there?"

"Neither," Merida said, slowly. "We met him on the way to Ardbarrach; he gave us directions."

Elinor was seeing him as the same person she'd seen before.

"Well, unless he's from the village he's not going to get far in any direction tonight," Elinor said. "Have you looked out a window?"

They hadn't; the tapestries were pulled tight across them. But now they did and discovered that the courtyard had been transformed to a gleaming bright landscape. Snow covered everything, and it was still coming down.

"The Cailleach is washing her robe for sure," Feradach murmured.

Elinor, to Merida's surprise, laughed. "I haven't heard that for ages."

"What's it mean?" Merida asked.

Feradach said, "There's a legend that when the first storm comes in like this, it's the Cailleach washing her robe in Corryvreckan, and when she's done, it's snow white and so is Scotland, and it's winter."

Elinor gave Feradach a rather complimentary smile then, pleased with him and his storytelling. "Ila, could you put up a bed for him in the solar?"

"Of course, ma'am," she replied.

"What's your name, then, I missed it, I'm sorry, I'm doing three things at once," Elinor said.

Neither Merida nor Feradach had the faintest idea how to answer.

"It's Feradach," Ila said.

Merida looked at her with surprise.

"Feradach, yes?" Ila repeated. "We met before."

Feradach looked quite undone. Merida had not seen him properly speechless before. Finally he assembled his features and said, "I'm sorry, I'm being rude. I was trying to remember where; I'm sorry."

"You looked a little different, I think, sir," Ila said, and she gave Merida that private cat smile. "And I did, too. I wasn't always this age!"

"Yes, our Ila is ancient," Elinor said. "And she'll take

care of the solar for you. Merida, I trust you'll make sure he's sorted. Feradach! Like the stone; a good name. Sorry, I've got to run or I'll never get to settle tonight. After this we're all going to gather a nip of whipkull and craic in the common room, Merida, if you're in the mood. Come on, girls."

Off they bustled, leaving Merida and Feradach quite confused. They had the shape of the remarkable thing in their head now, and it was only confirmed when they ran once more into Cennedig as he retired to the guests' quarters off the Great Hall.

"I'm older than I was," he told them apologetically, from the doorway, "and can't stay up hobnobbing like I used to. This old man likes his sleep. You know, you really are the spitting image of the MacAuslands of Cairnlee; they had an absolute litter of sons who all looked like you."

"Did they?" Feradach asked faintly.

"Don't take it so hard, lad," Cennedig said, laughing. "It's a compliment; they were handsome. Good night, you two."

As he closed the door, Merida and Feradach retreated back to the empty Great Hall and stood before the fire there.

In a hushed voice, Merida said, "They recognized you!"

Feradach shook his head, but it was clear it was shock, not disbelief.

"They saw you the same more than once," Merida insisted. "*And* I think they're all seeing you the same way. The same way as I do."

"It's not possible," Feradach said, but his fingers were

on the brooch that Fergus had pointed out in the armory. "It's never happened before." He narrowed his eyes at the window. "I wonder if this is the Cailleach's doing; she is tricky."

"How could this be a trick?" she asked.

He shook his head again. "How do you see me?"

Differently than she used to.

"I guess DunBroch's not the only thing changing around here," she said.

33

FERADACH, FERADACH

FERADACH stayed.

It snowed and snowed and snowed, and Feradach stayed. Surely the snow wouldn't have stopped him, but he stayed.

He stayed and stayed and Merida could see his face go still and expressionless every time he heard his name—which he did, again and again, because the magic that had allowed them all to see him the same way before this kept on happening. So it was "Feradach, do you want to play a round of Whips and Hounds with us?" "Feradach, have you ever been to Hoy?" "Feradach, do you need more to eat?" "Feradach, can you play the flute at all? We need someone to do the melody for us." "Feradach, you probably will be stuck here for days, I hope your business will hold."

On each of the snowy evenings he joined the family in the common room, partaking of their ritual of telling stories and drinking sweet creamy whipkull and enjoying all the recipes Aileen was testing in advance of the big Christmas banquet. Every evening Merida watched him hold his gloved hands tightly against himself as he listened to his name again and again: Feradach, Feradach, Feradach.

"You're very good at this," he said, a few nights in. He was playing a game of Brandubh with Merida, the first time she'd played the actual game in ages. They had a lovely new board now, to match the new castle. It had come along with the orphan girls of Eilean Glan.

"She's banned," Hubert said. "She always wins."

"Always?" Feradach asked.

"Yes, she's a cheater," Harris murmured, not looking up from his book.

Merida, remembering very well what Feradach thought of the Cailleach's cheating, said as she moved a piece, "I am not! I'm just very good at it."

"I'm very good at it too," Feradach said, moving one of his as well, his hands still safely gloved. "I've never been beaten."

"Enjoy suffering," Harris said.

But Merida did not win. Or at least, not right away. She played her pieces out as she usually did, and Feradach played his pieces, and there was some jaunting back and forth without reasonable gains on either side. Harris and Hubert gave up their own diversions and came to crouch on either side of the board to watch. The game went on.

Elinor arrived. "Who's winning? Oh, Merida's playing, I know who's winning."

"She's not!" Hubert said.

"I'm not losing, though," Merida said. She and Feradach battled back and forth.

Hamish and Fergus arrived with their drinks. Fergus saw Merida at the board and said, "So we've decided to drive Feradach into the snow, is that what we're after?"

"She's not won yet," Elinor said. "It's touch and go."

Leezie appeared in the doorway with a great Yule shawl she'd made of prickly-looking plants wrapped around her. "I thought Merida was *banned* from this game! Oh! Is she not winning?"

At just the same moment, Merida and Feradach moved their pieces in such a way to unlock the Black Raven.

"Impossible!" Hubert and Hamish roared.

"Improbable," corrected Harris.

Feradach lifted his gaze to Merida over the Brandubh board, eyes merry. "Evenly matched. What now?"

At just that moment, Brionn burst into the room. With an uncanny sense, he leapt straight at the object every human and god in the room was looking at: the Black Raven piece.

He snatched it up and darted from the room.

"Brionn!" Harris said, leaping up, as his brothers laughed hysterically.

"It looks like you've both been bested by a wolfhound," Fergus said to Feradach and Merida. "Who knew just how to employ the Black Raven. Better luck next time."

"It's nice to see Merida evenly matched for once," Elinor said.

That night, Leezie paused in Merida's bedroom door and whispered, "Is Feradach the god, Merida? The one we rescued in the woods?"

"You recognize him?"

"Of course I do!" Leezie said, indignantly. "I've been studying about gods and magic. I'm starting to read a little about it."

"You're reading!" Merida was delighted.

"The letters still wander," Leezie replied crossly, "but not as badly. Do you know why Feradach is here? Is he just grateful we saved him? Will he give us a wish? Sometimes grateful gods can give wishes."

Of course Merida couldn't answer the reason, because she couldn't talk about the bargain. And actually she wasn't sure that the bargain was the real reason he was still there at the castle.

"I don't think he's the wishing sort of god," Merida said, because that seemed safe. "He has that stone, not the well."

"Do you think he'd be offended if I asked him about the stone?" Leezie answered herself: "Probably I should pretend I don't know what he is. In the stories they seem to prefer that unless they're going about telling everyone who they are. I'm just going to leave an offering for him. They like that too."

"Leezie—" Merida started. "Never mind. Do what you think is best. Do you like it up in the tapestry room, by the way?"

"Of course," Leezie said. "The ghosts are very nice in there."

She didn't explain this; she simply twirled away, Leezie-like.

But in the morning, Leezie's offering seemed to have done something, because Merida searched all over the castle and found Feradach only just in time; he was getting his cloak from behind the kitchen door and putting it over his shoulders. He hadn't put it on in the last several days; there was something conclusive and fatal about how he put it on now.

"Are you going?" she asked.

He whirled at her voice, and she could tell he had indeed been intending to sneak out.

"You *are* going," she said. "You stayed and stayed without a reason to stay and now you're just going without so much as a word!"

"I can't stand it," he said, very simply. He went out into the snow.

Without hesitating, Merida snatched another cloak and leapt after him.

"You've got no *shoes*," Feradach said, sounding quite agitated. "Why are you always chasing me through snow in your bare feet?"

"You're not just going," Merida challenged, keeping up with his long strides as he crossed the courtyard. Her feet were freezing, of course, but never mind that. "You're running away!"

He ducked his head and continued to walk purposefully

away from DunBroch, right through the gate. "I understand now. I understand why I didn't look the same to
anyone before. I can't stay here. I can't stand it."

"That's what it took? People knowing you? I told you
that you didn't understand family! I told you that you didn't
understand time, what it was like to exist. It's not something you can learn by *watching*. It's different when you're
in it."

Now he whirled again. They were just a few yards outside of the gate, and he was partway into the woods she'd
first chased him through. Only now he was still quite
human looking, his ankles sunk deep into the snow. "And
what of it, Merida? What good does it do me? I can't *not*
do my duty. Does it bring you joy to know now that it will
hurt me? Imagine, if you will, that you win this bargain.
Then you will go on with your life having escaped ruin,
unchanged. Now imagine I win it. Imagine I have to put
my hand on DunBroch now! Imagine the next village, the
next person. Does it make you happy for me to know now
what I'm destroying? Does it—"

Feradach fell silent. Sometimes, even gods are failed
for words. And he didn't look much like one then anyhow,
his mane disheveled, his face tired and anxious. Before
he hadn't earned this face because he only wore it for the
minutes he faced Merida, and then he was something else,
something insubstantial, as soon as he turned away. But
this was now a face that belonged to Feradach. A body,
lived in. All the laughs he'd had over the past few days, all
the sleep he'd shorted—it was becoming shaped like him.

Merida felt abashed again, even though she wasn't the one who had somehow made him wear this face for more than one person to see. She felt as bad as when she had shamed him into not doing his duty.

"Of all the things I've seen you be this year," she said, "a coward isn't one of them."

He drew himself up, recognizing his words.

"Are you going to be a worthy adversary or not?" Merida said. "If you don't hold up your part, you'll die, and it won't matter, because another god will come along to render ruin after you're gone. So it might as well be you, knowing what you know. Now you can go if you want, but you haven't done your part of this visit yet."

Feradach's expression was threadbare. "And what part is that?"

"You came to see how much change happened here, but you didn't show me your part. You're supposed to show me something you've ruined as well."

He simply let out a sigh.

"I want to see the scholar," Merida said. "I want to know what happened to her."

"Her quarters and her life are several days' journey away, even without this snow," Feradach replied. "And you don't have that much time before the end of the bargain, and Harris is still unchanged."

This stung, even though she knew it was true. "You said before there was a way you traveled quickly, though; you said you could beat me on one of the journeys if I went on horseback and you went that way."

"Yes."

"Can you travel like that and take me?"

Feradach frowned, judging. "I think so. But I will be taking you out of your body. Do you trust me to bring you back?"

"Can you do it or can't you? You could have killed me many times before now, so trust is beside the point."

Feradach's face looked amused for the first time that day. "I can do it."

"What do I have to do? Is it a thing where we have to spin, like a Leezie ritual, where we—"

But she didn't say anything after that, because she had already been ripped right from her body and up into the sky.

34

A Girl Made of Air

THEY were air.

Merida couldn't think of any other way to make it make sense to her. It wasn't that she was an invisible body, floating, flying. She was simply present. Her thoughts, her self, her purpose. She was air. She was everywhere. She did not need to travel to the scholar's hut, not exactly, because in a way, when she was like this, without a body, she was already there.

It was easy to see everything about the situation when she was like this, because she didn't have to see (she had no eyes), nor hear (she had no ears), nor feel (she had no skin). She didn't have to translate any of those feelings into a story of what had happened in her mind, because, as a girl made of air, she was already aware of the entire tale, beginning to end and back again.

As Merida-the-girl-made-of-air, she saw the scholar's hut once again. She saw how the hut had previously been full of not just letters, but calculations, observations, endless documents of studied truths about the natural world. Now, however, it held nothing. The peaceful river that had lived within its wide banks for decades had risen up at Feradach's command and ruined the hut. All the precious parchment, all the precious data, had been scattered far and wide by the flood. Even if they could be gathered back up again, they were all out of order, and the water had soaked away much of the writing.

The scholar had lost all her work.

But she hadn't died; her body wasn't one of the things ruined in the flood. Instead, Merida-as-the-girl-made-of-air sought her out where she was now. It was a journey she'd made herself, in her physical body, not so long ago, and it had taken much longer. But as air, she made it to the island of Eilean Glan in no time at all. In a way, in fact, Merida-as-air was already there, as she was all places at all times.

She saw, in the way that she saw-heard-felt-was everything, what had happened to the scholar. The tattered scholar, having lost everything, had swallowed her considerable pride and come to these islands. Máel Muire knew her! She knew her very well; they were peers, though the scholar was much younger. They'd worked together while Máel Muire's husband was alive. But then there had been a familiar, dull sort of story: an indiscretion, an improper kiss, a scandal, a shipwreck, a widow. The scholar and the queen feuded and the scholar, exiled, became a hermit. She had retreated into her studies and her bitterness, and both her heart and her scholarly conclusions had become narrow as a thread.

Until the flood ruined it all.

Now the scholar returned, resentful, broken, prepared to beg for mercy and a roof over her head. But years had healed everything in the same way that being air healed Merida of needing her sight and touch; she was above all that when she was air. All the past hurts likewise seemed unimportant. Máel Muire welcomed the scholar back and granted her rooms full of willing future scholars to listen to her. Just a few months before, there would not have been room for her and her studies, Merida saw, in the overrun island compound. But a queen named Elinor had only recently taken away close to a dozen orphans and made room for newcomers.

Merida found herself back in her body, standing back in the woods just outside DunBroch.

Her teeth were chattering. Her feet were freezing. Her mind was reeling with the experience of being outside her body. Her heart was thudding with the hugeness of the ruin and renewal that she'd just seen. That she'd been part of. Time was moving slow and mortal around her again.

Merida and Feradach looked at each other across the snow.

Finally, Merida said, "We make a good team, for enemies."

Feradach nodded.

"You asked me if I understood why you did what you did," Merida said. "At the beginning of all this. I didn't. But I do now."

Feradach swallowed. He nodded again.

"You asked me what you looked like to me," she added. "At the beginning of all this."

He stood as motionless as a hunted stag in the woods. He did not ask.

But she answered, "You look kind, Feradach. I didn't want to tell you, because it made me angry. Why should you look like that when you do what you do, I thought? Yes, it's not all you look like, of course. You have a bushy light mane like a highland pony, but your eyebrows are dark. Your eyes are blue. You've got a pock scar just there, and when you frown, your lower lip goes like this." She demonstrated the pout. "You look like someone girls would fancy. But that's just the body, isn't it? The face you're wearing. The kindness is you, though, no matter if you're in that body or out of it. That's Feradach. And now I understand, and I don't mind telling you."

Feradach had touched the brooch very lightly as Merida began to speak, and then, even more lightly, he touched just the pock scar, and she knew he remembered the face that he was wearing. She wondered if he remembered, too, the young man's fate. Probably, she thought, remembering what it had been like to be Merida-as-air. Probably he remembered everything.

How strange his existence must be. How even stranger it must be now that he had walked for more than a week nearly as a mortal. Time moving slow as honey for her, swift as air for him.

"I understand now why you do what you do, too, Merida of DunBroch," Feradach said. "But I am still your enemy, and I cannot stay, because I don't care if it makes me a coward. I'm not as brave as you. I cannot bear it. Change your brother before it's too late and I have to do what I was made for."

And then she was alone in the snowy woods.

35

WOLFTAIL

ARRIS, Harris, what to do with Harris? For as long as Merida could remember, Harris had been the chilly triplet. The know-it-all triplet. The calculating triplet. The snottily bored triplet. The triplet who was too grown-up to engage in the childish rough-and-tumble of his siblings. Everything seemed to be below Harris's regard.

Who was Harris of DunBroch?

A whippersnapper, that was all Merida knew. A whippersnapper whom she'd seen walking through the woods with Brionn, storming from her mother's tent on the journey, and accepting a secret whisper from the Dásachtach.

She didn't know how to know him anymore, not like she once had.

And even though it seemed like supernatural ruin should have been the most important thing, another, more mundane threat managed to loom larger.

It came in the form of a very familiar visitor as the castle counted down the days until the Christmas feast.

Wolftail.

He wasn't alone, of course; he had his flanking assembly of soldiers that he brought with him, but for all intents and purposes, the Dásachtach's right-hand man might as well have been the only one visiting, because like before, he was the only one who spoke.

"I'd been hoping to never come here again," snarled Wolftail in his gravelly voice, and the rest of the pack watched him. "I have heard instead that your daughter is still here just as before, and rather than sending your remaining two sons to mac Alpin, you have kept them here."

Merida had a good view of him, because she and the triplets all hid in the same place she'd hidden before to eavesdrop the Christmas before, on the balcony of the Great Hall. Elinor and Fergus looked very royal sat in their thrones with their guards arrayed to one side and Elinor's neat foster girls arrayed to the other. It was pleasing, she had to admit, to see how much the Great Hall had improved. It looked much more impressive now. Much less like a place you could just come in and kick tables over and expect to get away with it. It looked like a place Mistress mac Lagan of Ardbarrach would find suitably royal.

"Then what you've heard is unfair," Fergus rumbled. "My daughter visited Ardbarrach, Kinlochy, and Eilean Glan; even one of those journeys would have been impressive in the span of a year, much less three."

"It was her proposal, not mine," Wolftail said.

"Yes. And she fulfilled it. Moreover, you and I both know Kinlochy burned to the ground this year, so there was no way my daughter could have found a home there. One of my sons is fostering at Ardbarrach and is only home for the winter. And I'm quite sure you can see for yourself the many foster girls we have taken in from Eilean Glan."

Elinor's voice was very crisp. "If your master's goal is uniting the kingdoms, we've more than done our duty. But if that was never his goal, now's when we'll find out."

Wolftail said, "Of course that was his goal. What a thing to doubt."

There was a heavy silence in the Great Hall, a silence Merida felt was punctuated by the memory of that burned-down town.

"Then I believe we can agree that my daughter's work is done," Elinor said.

"And DunBroch's commitment is unquestioned and responsibility to your master complete," added Fergus.

Wolftail licked his lips, and then he said, "Truly mac Alpin will be more than delighted to hear that he can rest easy this Yuletide. Will you introduce me to the fosters, and may I speak to your son about Ardbarrach, so that I can take this news back to him? And perhaps I can see all you have done to the grounds since last we came. Then I will return to him before the weather gets more poor."

"Very well," Elinor said. "We would be pleased to show you what we've accomplished."

Up in the balcony, Hubert whispered, "That went well."

Because it was Hubert, it was not much of a whisper at

all, since even his whispers were quite loud, but it didn't matter, as Wolftail had already been escorted from the Hall into the courtyard.

Merida was more relieved than she could say.

She didn't know what she'd expected, but not this. She had had half a thought that the Dásachtach would have held a grudge for the way Elinor spoke to him outside the village, or been annoyed to not simply get the triplets sent to him as he asked.

But now it was over, and she could just worry about Harris.

"And now you get to show someone else your muscles," Hamish told Hubert.

"And Mum can parade her clever girls for him, and we can get on with Christmas," Merida said. "What a relief."

Harris let out an irritated breath and stormed off. A few seconds later, there was a chaos of clicking and scratching as Brionn noticed that Harris had gone by and went careening down the stairs to follow him. They said that dogs became ever more like their masters the older they got, but there was no sign yet of Brionn closing the gap between his personality and Harris's.

"What's his problem?" Merida demanded. She couldn't mention the bargain, but she felt safe enough asking, "Do you think he wants something he can't say?"

"Yeah, to run away with the Dásachtach," said Hubert.

"What?"

Hubert stood up to go. "We heard Mum tell Dad how the Dásachtach tried to get him to come with. We were eavesdropping. You remember Harris's face, Hame?"

Hamish nodded grimly. "He was still all torn up about it. You should have seen it. He wouldn't talk to us for the rest of the evening. I heard him throwing stuff in the room, even."

"He thinks we're all idiots," Hubert said. "It's pretty obvious. He thinks the Dásachtach has it right and Mum and Dad are just messy and old-fashioned."

Uneasily, Merida asked, "He said that?"

"You've seen him," Hubert said. "Come on."

She didn't like thinking about it, but it didn't seem impossible when she did. Join the Dásachtach? Did Harris really want that? And if that was what he needed in order to change, was she willing to make that happen to save the rest of them?

She thought about the destroyed village. The salted wells. The mutilated trees. Ruin for the sake of punishment, of warning. Ruin for the sake of ruin. Nothing she stood for. She might not have liked Ardbarrach, but at least they weren't training their boys to pillage for the sake of pillaging alone.

"There's got to be a way to talk to him," Merida said.

"Oh, nobody has problems talking *to* Harris," Hamish said. "It's getting him to talk back."

36

LEGENDS ARE LESSONS

SHORT days bled into long nights, which then became more short days and even longer nights. The more Merida tried to show she wanted to talk meaningfully with Harris, the more scathing and remote he became. Often she'd make a plan to corner him individually after breakfast and find that as soon as he got up from the table, he had taken off. Literally running, surely, because by the time she got to the door, she'd see him and Brionn off in the fields, a tiny speck already.

It was difficult not to resent him when so much was hanging on his existence. He didn't know, of course, and she couldn't tell him. It all weighed on Merida, and no one else in the world knew except Feradach, and he was hidden away until he found out if he was to destroy them.

And then, all at once, it was the night before Christmas.

The entire castle was outfitted for the feast for the next night, and just as it had the year before, it looked splendid.

There was no snow this year, only frost, and so all of the newly renovated castle was undisguised and elegant, glazed with a shimmering layer that only emphasized how far it had come in a year. Lanterns glowed in the windows. Beautiful, intricate bowers braided by Elinor and all her foster girls hung heavy around each threshold. The air was scented with exotic, sharp Christmas spices. The guest rooms were full of Cennedig and his family, lords Fergus had reconnected with after the tragedy at Kinlochy, ladies Elinor had invited to see how to teach their own children. The castle was full as it hadn't been since Merida was a child.

But Merida couldn't celebrate. She felt she would go mad being the only one who knew on the last day that it mattered.

She retreated to the wall as the sun went down, watching the last of the golden glow shimmer across the loch before it vanished into darkness.

Just like last year, there was an enormous moon.

As she looked out over the moonlit forest, she heard familiar barking. Brionn. His high teen bark had not changed with age, although he at least stuck firmly by Harris's side now.

This was her last chance.

She used her vantage point on the wall to spy her brother out across the game fields, walking. It was so bright under the moon and stars with the glaze of frost that she could even pick out his familiar, stiff walk.

Hiking her skirt, she hurried to the closest guard tower,

down the stairs, across the courtyard, out across the field. Thank goodness her father had ordered them cleaned out.

"Harris!" she called, catching up with him.

He didn't alter his stride, just kept doing that chilly, austere walk of his, his hands in his pockets, posture perfectly straight. He didn't say anything, either, but it nonetheless felt as if he found her silly and disorderly, because she was out of breath and running after him, and he was in control and walking away.

Merida grabbed his arms and stopped him. "Harris, stop. Stop and look at me."

Harris was stiff as a bathed cat as she turned him to her. He looked thin-lipped and irritated. As ever, he appeared far older than he was.

"Do you hate us, is that what it is?" she demanded.

His expression, if possible, seemed more scathing than ever. He waited for her to lose interest in him and release him.

"Tell me why you want to go with him," Merida said. "Give me all the good reasons, and I'll listen, and if they aren't totally stupid, I'll help you, okay? I don't like him, and I don't like what he does, but I'm not you, and it's not my life. If that's what you want, I'll help you."

Harris just stared at her. He repeated, "Help me go with him?"

"The Dásachtach, yes," Merida said. "Hubert and Hamish told me."

"They told you I wanted to go with him? That's what they think?"

Merida released Harris. "Y . . . es?"

This wasn't going the way she expected at all.

Harris made his little condescending huffing sound like he was about to laugh, and then he did it again, and then Brionn pressed his head close to his leg and Harris twisted his hand in Brionn's collar and started to cry. Just two angry tears, running fast down his cheeks.

She tried to reach for him to give him a hug, but he moved rigidly away.

"Harris," she said, "why are you so mad at me? We used to be such good friends, didn't we?"

"Why do you care?"

"Why *wouldn't* I?"

"You left," he said, very simply.

Merida opened her mouth and then closed it again. She thought of another thing she might say, opened her mouth again, and then closed it again. She *had* left. She'd gone off on her big adventure across the kingdom and not thought about the triplets staying behind, because they had each other, and they had her parents. She just figured they'd be back here waiting for her, unchanged, and they were in this entire predicament because, for the most part, they were.

Merida knew she'd miss home. She didn't think home would miss her.

She didn't think *Harris* would miss her.

"Don't say anything fake," Harris said.

"I won't," Merida said. "I'm sorry." Then she said, "Please let me hug you."

"It will only make you feel better, not me."

Merida sniffed. "I know. But I need to feel better."

He let her hug him. He was very unpleasant to hug, like hugging a chair, but he permitted it.

Afterward, he said, "You know what the Dásachtach told me that day? When you couldn't hear? That he was going to kill all of you. He said he was going to kill all of you no matter what you did, all of you except for me; I would watch, and then he would take me back to his castle, and I would be the best warrior he ever had, and I would hate him and love him for it because he could see it was what I was made for."

Merida fell silent. "Why didn't you tell anyone what he said?"

"He said if I told, he'd know, and he'd come back even sooner and kill everyone faster."

"Harris!"

He had been carrying this weight since that day by the destroyed village. Sometimes she forgot that he was just a kid, and that kids could easily get outsmarted by evil men whispering in their ears. "You're probably much more clever than any of us, and we don't understand you. And you probably will be a great man, and they'll sing ballads about you. But you're an idiot! You should have told me. Or someone. There's no way he could have known you told anyone. How would he know?"

Harris murmured, "There are all kinds of ways of knowing things. How am I supposed to know what he can see or can't see?"

"It would have been impossible for him to see you telling us that," Merida said. She tried to keep her voice soothing, but her mind was racing. Did this mean Wolftail had been lying—his visit earlier had been a sham? Was all of this just a game before the Dásachtach came to teach them a lesson? To make a lesson *of* them? Merida needed to get back to the castle to make a plan at once. "He can't see inside your head. People can't see inside other people's heads."

Harris pulled back.

"This," he said, and his face had gone just as cool and distant as before, "is why I never talk to anyone."

She didn't understand what she'd said wrong.

All she knew was that she'd had an opportunity to reach him, and somehow, he'd slipped between her fingers.

"Harris, we used to talk," Merida said again.

Suddenly her eyes were caught by shifting movement overhead.

A green glow was beginning to light the sky.

Across the field, blue orbs began to light the dry grass, just as they had risen through the pools a year before. They bobbed eerily, invitingly. She was meant to follow.

It was time for the bargain to be decided.

37

THE GIRL FROM NOWHERE

THE orbs led them through the night. Or rather, they led Merida through the night. She supposed they could be seen only by those with the Sight. But Harris followed Merida when she gestured for him, too, so they were still together when they reached their destination: the holy well.

Merida supposed that felt right.

Just as the waterfall and its shallow pools had been transformed under the moonlight and *na Fir-Chlis* a year before, the area around the Cailleach's well also looked very different from when Merida had visited it with her mother during the day.

The well itself was lit with starry wonder. The will o' the wisps that had led them there hung around it as if they were waiting to make their own wish, but there were also ever so many in the well, getting dimmer and dimmer as they got deeper and deeper, making it seem as if the well had no bottom at all. Perhaps it didn't. Perhaps it went straight through to a strange ocean that was only there on this night of all nights.

Merida followed Harris's gaze to Feradach's stone. As light as the well was, the stone was dark. It was as if none of the light could reach it. The stone towered, a black silhouette against the green-lit night sky, casting no shadow in the moonlight.

I can't bear it.

"It looks cursed," Harris whispered. He had his hand knotted in the fur at Brionn's ruff again. What did this look like to him? Merida didn't want to ask; she was still afraid of violating the terms of the bargain, even at these very last minutes.

He didn't sound afraid, because Harris would never let himself sound anything other than sure, but Merida held her hand out to him and ordered, "Take my hand, Harris."

Harris hesitated, and then he took it. He lifted his chin up as if he had meant to do it all along, as if it were ritual instead of terror that had led him to it.

"I'm glad you came here, finally," said a voice. "Harris of DunBroch."

A little catlike frame stood opposite the well from them, appearing bright and shining in the night. Like the well, lit from within.

"Ila?" Merida said, disbelieving. "What are you doing out here tonight?"

"It's time, isn't it?" Ila said. "For the bargain to be decided. To see if all the work you've been doing this year, Merida, has been successful, to see if you have changed

DunBroch's fate. To see if you have managed to change enough to escape . . ." She looked at the dark, sinister stone that stood off by itself. "Feradach."

Harris frowned from Ila to Merida. "What is she talking about?"

But Merida didn't have an answer. Or rather, she didn't have an answer for *why* Ila was talking about it. Even in the cold, she could feel her palms sweating with nerves. "I didn't tell you any of this. I kept my word. I did everything alone, in secrecy."

Ila smiled her small, catlike smile. "You did. You have acted most bravely."

"What is *happening*?" Harris demanded.

"Tonight is the night that magic changes DunBroch's fate," Ila told him. "And your sister has been working alone on it. But no longer. You're both here now. With the magic. This isn't the first time magic has changed DunBroch's fate. Harris, do you know what the last time was?"

Harris shook his head, but in a way that Merida recognized well. That head shake didn't mean *no*. It meant *I don't want to admit that the answer is yes.*

"All the signs you've seen, Harris," Ila insisted. "The dreams. The wisps that have been calling you to the truth. Her journal."

"I didn't read the journal," Harris said stubbornly.

"Not even a little peek?" Ila asked. "The wisps led you right to it."

Harris shook his head.

"Now *I* want to know what's happening," Merida said. "What are you two talking about?"

Ila leapt onto the well's font. It seemed vaguely sacrilegious to do so, although Merida had never been told not to. She just could clearly hear her mother's voice: *Don't climb on the holy well, Merida!* But her mother wasn't there, and so Ila stayed there, precise and intentional. With all the light coming from inside her and from below, she looked like part of it.

"A little under a decade ago, magic came to DunBroch," Ila said. "Elinor, queen of DunBroch, was due to give birth to three triplet boys. How wonderful! How anticipated they were. But there was trouble. She had not been long at the delivery when she began to bleed, and although the midwife there did not tell the king, she suspected the queen—and her triplets—might not survive the birth. Luckily for Elinor, the midwife knew the old ways. She called in the handmaid, and put Elinor's coronation crown into her hand, her most prized possession because with it she had been crowned Peacemaker, acknowledging her accomplishments as a young woman before settling down, and then the midwife added her own most precious possession, a beaded belt she was very vain over, with a bead from every woman she had ever met who had appreciated her work. She bid the handmaid to run as fast as she could to this very well, and to throw these precious things into the water, and to ask the Cailleach for a miracle."

"The Cailleach!" Merida said. "The Cailleach saved our mother?"

"And the triplets, too," Ila replied. "And it was a good thing Leezie Muireall's mother put two things in the well that day, because the miracle to save mother and babies was a large one. First she saved Elinor, who, by all rights, should have bled to death that day. And then she saved one of the triplets, who had his cord tied right round his neck, turning him quite blue. You might have only had two brothers, Merida."

"Which triplet?" asked Merida. But she knew from the way Harris squeezed her hand which one it was.

"Saved by the other side, and now he can *see* the other side, but he doesn't want to look, does he?" Ila asked.

Harris didn't answer. He had his most still and remote expression, the one that meant he couldn't be badgered into speaking.

"Ila," Merida said, "how do you know all these things?"

"Harris knows," Ila replied. "He must. If he looks hard, he must."

But when Merida looked down at the most difficult of her triplet brothers, his eyes were closed fast shut and his mouth made a very straight, distressed line. When she glanced over at Ila, she saw that Ila was watching *her* instead, though, waiting to see what *she* did.

Because this was the last moment to change him.

But what could Merida say? The truth, she supposed.

She knew Harris wouldn't like it if she leaned down to his level, so instead, she used his hand to encourage him to step up onto one of the boulders next to the well. Now they were eye to eye. She fixed him with a hard stare, this strange brother of hers who had gotten older so much faster than the others. "I know it's hard to see things no one else can see. It's hard to know things no one else knows."

"You wouldn't believe what I've seen," Harris hissed.

His voice turned a little pugnacious, as if daring her to believe him. "Dad said it was in my head. Mum told me to stop trying to frighten the others. I saw DunBroch in ruins."

"I believe you," Merida said. "Trust me, I believe you. I see things too, sometimes. Look, Harris, you're very clever, you know that. And you're very brave. But you don't have to be lonesome. You can always talk to me about it, and I'll always listen. I might not know what to do about what you see, but I'll listen. And *believe*."

"Always?" Harris asked.

"Yes."

"Always?" he insisted.

"Yes."

Harris glanced over at Ila. For just a very, very brief moment, he looked just the age he was supposed to be, just a kid, and Merida thought she was learning something about what people looked like, how maybe it wasn't just Feradach who looked different depending on who looked at him.

Then Harris pointed at Ila and said, "She's the Cailleach."

Merida wanted to say *what!* But she had literally only just promised to believe him. So instead of saying anything at all, she just looked at Ila, who was once again wearing her secret catlike smile, and she nodded.

A familiar moaning sound, much like wind through rocks, or perhaps like a faraway laugh, began to sound.

And then Ila began to transform.

38

The Bargain, Part II

THE Cailleach stood on the font, lit brilliantly by the will o' the wisps all around her. Her one starry eye matched the round starry opening of the well beneath her.

"It was you all along?" Merida exclaimed.

I had to keep my eye on you.

Merida thought back to the very first moment that Ila had appeared in her room on Christmas morning, quite impossibly, in time to inspire her to action when she was feeling discouraged. She thought about how all these months, Ila had been teaching Leezie about the Sight and guiding Elinor toward the trip to Eilean Glan in the guise of an innocent little orphan.

"Feradach was right!" Merida said. "You *do* cheat!"

"I told you."

At the sound of Feradach's voice, Merida's breath got all stopped up in her throat. The Cailleach had turned her attention to the dark stone, and as Merida and Harris watched, Feradach stepped silently from the shadowed stone named after him. As he came just to the edge of the wild green light, she could see that he looked as he had all the other times. A blond-maned young man with a kind face and wonderfully made gloves with oxblood stitching. But there was something different about him now, Merida thought. A realness, a weight. He knew what he looked like now, and he had been seen like this by more than one person. He had lived in time, not simply watched it.

It had changed him.

When he ducked his head away from her gaze, it was with the sort of knowledge that came of knowing how one's body moved, knowing how much one's face could give away.

I did not cheat, Feradach. I was only present as much as you were.

"And when I kept this face for everyone who saw me?" Feradach challenged.

A gift.

But the Cailleach sounded amused with herself. He had been right about that, too, Merida thought. It had been a trick. She'd known it would end up with him in the courtyard, unable to bear what he needed to do. What else was a trick about her?

"You know what I am now, don't you?" Feradach asked Harris. "No more pretending you can't tell?"

Harris was very pale. He nodded. "You're . . ."

"You don't have to say," Feradach said.

Harris climbed down from the boulder he'd been standing on to press against Merida. He did not bother to hide that he was afraid now. He was trembling as badly as Hamish. "So what I saw was true."

Merida felt a terrible pit in her stomach. It had only just occurred to her that this was all coming to an end. A year had seemed like a very long time. Now there was no more time to try to change anything. There was only time to find out if it had worked. And then—what came after? She didn't know that, either. For an entire year she'd shaped everything around the journeys with her family and Feradach's visits, and she had forgotten what life used to be like before that. "It might be, or it might not. That's what we're about to find out, isn't it?"

Yes, the year has ended. It is now time for me to render my ruling.

The old woman on the rock tilted her blackened staff toward Feradach, who was as dark and motionless and still as the stone behind him.

Unless you have any objections to the way the bargain has been run.

"No," he said.

Feradach lifted his eyes then and held Merida's gaze. They were equals in that moment. Perfectly matched. The Cailleach had been tricking them both all this time. Whatever the ruling was would be whatever she had wanted it to be all along, Merida thought. She had been nudging both of them in whatever uncanny direction she wanted them to move; this was the trouble with magic, the trouble with gods. One always thought one had the upper hand, and then in the end discovered it wasn't even a game that used hands. Feradach, young god, had forgotten along with her, so nearly human as he was. Merida had the odd thought that during this judgment, Feradach should be stood on the other side of her, opposite Harris, holding her other hand, waiting for the ruling on their fate. But of course that was impossible. Illogical. His hand was the thing that would ruin them, after all.

Then let my verdict be witnessed, the Cailleach said. *Let the winds witness it and let the rain witness it and let the winter that is coming witness it and the summer that is past witness it. Let this land I live in and on and under and over witness it and accept it. Let all of them feel the balance that holds us all together in a dance as perfect as the stars overhead and below. Over the course of this year, I have watched every member of DunBroch and felt the balance shift this way and that, first in Feradach's favor, then in Merida's, and then back again, so on and so forth, until now, we come to the end and see where it has come to rest. If it is in the favor of change, Merida of DunBroch may go back to her home to live out the rest of her days as she pleases, so long as she still holds her tongue about the nature of this bargain. If it is in the favor of stagnation, Feradach must ruin DunBroch immediately on this night.*

Feradach looked away from Merida.

Merida closed her eyes.

But there was no comfort in that darkness, because in it she saw the burning castle of Kinlochy and the plague victims and the rising floodwaters. And even if she knew that whatever would grow after this would be good, because that was the nature of Feradach's work, too, she didn't want her family to die.

My verdict, the Cailleach said.

"Wait," said Feradach, voice rough. "Can I—"

DunBroch has changed enough to be spared.

Merida's eyes flew open.

Feradach stood with his hands clasped to his chest, glove tucked against glove, chin bent prayerfully. The Cailleach stood with her staff pointed high to the sky, sending the green that was threaded through the stars pulsing with fervor.

For a very long moment, Merida couldn't really believe it. She just gazed up at that night sky that looked the same as the night sky one year ago. How much had changed since then. How much indeed.

Merida seized Harris into a huge hug and spun him. He was about as rewarding as hugging a suit of armor, but she didn't care. She hugged him hard. "We did it, we did it!"

But disaster is still coming to DunBroch.

Merida stopped dancing at once. She looked hard at the old woman, waiting for her to clarify or change her statement, but she just pointed her staff toward the southern horizon instead.

"Is this a trick, Old Woman?" Feradach demanded. "What is it you want from me?"

Listen for yourself.

Feradach lifted his face to the wind, which raised his mane of hair. His eyes squinted, seeing something Merida couldn't, or hearing something she couldn't.

"Oh no," said Harris.

"Oh no," said Feradach.

Merida lost patience with all of them. Scouting for a way to get a better vantage point, her eyes landed on Feradach's stone. She crossed the distance with a few light strides and then threw herself upon it neatly as she would scale any of

345

the stones she'd climbed in her hikes around DunBroch. Her fingers and toes found purchase on the carved swirls and imperfections, as long as she went fast. And she was fast. The feeling of dread propelled her all the way up the dark stone to its top, where she perched sure as a rook in the rain, peering out across the landscape.

In the distance she saw glowing lights bobbing with movement. She heard a low roar, like there were lots of bodies moving. It seemed like they were far, but only because the dark erased all the finer details. Merida knew that if she could pick out the individual shapes of the torches, they were not very far at all. The lights were as far from Merida and Harris as Merida and Harris were from DunBroch, and marching steadily closer. Coming in the dark of night. Not in the bright, not nobly, not with diplomacy on their mind.

This is not Feradach's ruin approaching. This is no intentional restoration of balance. This is the razing that only humans can do to each other. This is destruction for the sake of destruction. This is ruin that means to stay ruin. This is . . .

Harris finished her sentence. "The Dásachtach."

39

THE BATTLE

MERIDA had grown up hearing songs and ballads of war and battles. The walls of her home were decorated with axes and swords and shields. She'd worn the armor, she'd shot the arrows, she'd learned to ride her father's war horse. She lived in a castle with walls thicker than a man was tall, and she knew that wasn't for looks. She had grown up in a life shaped by war.

She'd never seen it.

But she was seeing it now.

By the time they fled back to DunBroch, they discovered that Fergus's men were already arming themselves. They'd spotted the army, too. It wasn't difficult; the Dásachtach's men were now close enough to hear them. The clank of metal. The scream of horses. The bellow of men.

"What will happen?" cried Hamish.

"Nothing will happen to you," Leezie said. She was

holding a frying pan in what she must have thought was a threatening way. She wasn't even strong enough, however, to lift it with just one hand, so she simply looked as if she were about to fry an egg. She looked, as ever, like she needed help. "It will be okay. I see it. I *see* it."

Behind her, Hubert was uncharacteristically quiet as he suited up to fight. To fight! Merida couldn't bear that.

The orphan girls stood on the stairs, peering down, looking frightened in the way only those who have already lived through terrible things can. They knew all the ways it might not be okay.

"Take them away up into the attic," Elinor cried. "Merida too."

"No," Hubert said grimly, and for once he sounded as old as Harris. "You'll need us."

"I'm afraid he's right," Fergus said. "Merida, go with them, my love—no, don't protest. I need you there because you *can* fight, not because you can't. Get up into the rooms, smash out the glass if you must, and throw down whatever you can find below. We'll hold as best we can. This is all my fault."

"No, it is mine, too," Elinor said. "I baited him on our way back from Eilean Glan. I knew what I was doing."

But it was also Merida's fault, she thought. For making a plan with Wolftail, leaping into it, and then never really intending to follow through, because her eyes were fixed upon changing her family. Probably she could have been using those times to make friends with powerful allies instead. Being a little more like her mother and less like the girl she had always been.

"For DunBroch!" came the call from downstairs: Fergus's men getting ready for battle.

And then the Dásachtach's men were at the gate.

The fight began.

It wasn't anything like any of the songs or ballads Merida had ever heard about war. In the sagas, there were leaders. There was reason. There was a pattern, a flow. There was a goal. This was destruction; chaos. The Dásachtach didn't mean to take DunBroch as a stronghold; he meant to destroy it as a warning. There was the smell of fire from the woods; they were burning the trees, the woods, the game fields. Destruction for the sake of destruction.

At the base of the castle, the Dásachtach's men gathered in knots, smashing battering rams against the doors and flinging grappling hooks up toward the windowsills. This was where Merida and the triplets and the girls came in. From the music room, they threw furniture from the windows at the intruders down below as Merida shot arrow after arrow into the dark, knowing she'd run out of arrows long before she ran out of men to shoot at.

Crash! A mirror went out the tower. Crash! A lion-footed chair. Crash! The game table they played Brandubh at.

Hamish clung to the big harp, trying to decide if he could bear to throw it from a window and crack someone's skull with it. Merida couldn't decide if she could bear to tell him to.

"Don't, Hamish," Harris said seriously. He'd wrapped

a stone urn in a tapestry and now he lit it on fire. He did it with such skill that Merida suspected he'd thought about doing it for ages. "They'll remember this more."

His flaming stone dropped out the window. The shouts from below indicated he hadn't been wrong.

But then another set of shouts rang out. A tower! One of the guard towers in the wall! It was falling, terribly, in slow motion, the stones cascading over one another. The wall where Merida had walked with her mother so often.

With a sinking heart, Merida saw the army carrying the battering ram they'd used to destroy the guard tower. It was enormous; it required dozens of men and horses to move it.

It inched toward DunBroch itself.

"You earned this!" roared the Dásachtach. How was he audible over all of this commotion? "I was nothing but fair!"

It felt hopeless.

Think, Merida, think.

In this game of Brandubh, though, she could not think of what the Black Raven might be. The Dásachtach had no interest in peace. He was only interested in proving a point. They might be able to win if they had the support of all the people from the surrounding towns, but there had been no warning. And even if someone could somehow get out to them, there wouldn't be a way to get to them to gather any forces swiftly on a winter night like this.

It would take a miracle.

Merida thought about the story of the Cailleach saving

her mother and the triplets. The Cailleach had worked hard this past year to make sure Feradach didn't destroy them. Surely she didn't want the Madman to do the job instead.

Maybe she had another miracle to spare.

What had Leezie's mother done to ask for one? She'd given her precious things to the Cailleach's well. Merida could do that.

"Stay here," she told her brothers. "I'll be right back. Leezie, if anyone but me comes to this door, don't open it for anything!"

She hurried to her room. Her old familiar room, with all the things she'd had since childhood. She touched everything in it. But with each thing she picked up and put down in her room, she doubted that it was precious enough. Yes, she'd miss the toys her parents had carved, but they were just decorations now, and yes, she was fond of her old bow, but she could always get another. The scene on the tapestry was a memory that she'd still have even if the tapestry itself was gone. She had jewels to wear for public events, but she didn't care about them. She had perfumes she'd been given and rocks she'd collected.

Nothing in here was important to her, she realized.

It had been important at one time, but it wasn't important *now*. Nothing had been added to this collection for a long time. She hadn't even brought back anything from her travels before this year began.

What's precious to me? What's precious enough to trade for a miracle?

Her family was the only thing that she could think of, and they were what she wanted to save.

With a shock, she realized there wasn't anything else to her *but* how she felt about her family.

A storm that moved no roofs—

She could feel despair rising.

Think, Merida, think.

But she couldn't think. She moved from her room to the stairs, looking for anything that might be used to win a miracle from the Cailleach. She looked in the tapestry room. The hall closet. She went to the Great Hall balcony, but she didn't know what she was even looking for. Should she just go back to the room with the triplets, with Leezie and the orphan girls, to make a last stand there?

Hopeless.

To think that after all her work, this was how it would go. What a dreadful end. Ugly and desperate and very unmagical.

Then, in her quiet despair, over even the sound of chaos happening outside the castle, she heard hushed voices coming from the solar.

Feradach's voice.

And the Cailleach?

Here in the castle?

She drew close enough just to peer in the crack of the open door, and sure enough, she saw the two gods standing in the midst of the room. The Cailleach looked as wild as before, her powers unchanged by the mundanity of being in guest quarters. The greenish starshine that lit her continued to light her, and her single eye was like a candlelight in the room.

Feradach, on the other hand, looked supremely human. There was no terrifying power to him as he stood, shoulders slumped, before her.

"I knew you were tricky," he was saying, "but I never knew you were cruel."

I am not being cruel. I offer in earnest.

"Me, a mortal?" Feradach asked. "How would that even work?"

You know how that would work. You can see it. You can feel it. That body you are in would become your body. Those hands would be your hands. Those gloves would belong to someone else who would perform your duty instead. Another Feradach, the god. You would become Feradach, a man named after the god. You would live a man's life. You would die in the way all mortals do, at some point.

She paused and Merida drew back swiftly, silently, careful to stay out of sight.

"You would use your miracle for this?" Feradach asked. "Why?"

You have changed, Feradach. You have become something else. You have learned to love the continuity of humanity. You have learned to love belonging. You have learned to want to be seen as one person. You have learned to love that face you are wearing. You have changed the way you think about the world and that change, as you know, earns my attention. It is worthy of a miracle. I can make you human. You can have what you want.

"You cannot know what I truly want, Old Woman," Feradach said.

Take this body, Feradach, flee with Merida tonight, and you both win the bargain, in a way.

Merida held her breath.

Feradach echoed heavily, "Flee with Merida."

I know you have learned to love her.

Merida pressed a hand over her own mouth. It was to stop even the sound of her breath escaping, but instead, it made her think of the first time she'd seen Feradach remove his glove, the way it had been just an ordinary human hand beneath it.

Feradach again clasped his deadly hands to his chest. Merida could see them moving up and down with his uneven breaths.

In the silence, she heard the chaos of the army beating against her family.

"No," he said, finally.

Merida silently let out the breath she was holding.

No?

"You say my change has earned your miracle, is that right?" Feradach asked. "Then I still want the miracle, but not to have this body, not to run away with her. I want your miracle to help them defeat the Dásachtach. They cannot do it alone. They will be dead in a few hours. I want your miracle to drive him back so that he does not return, or if he does, it is not for years and years and years."

You have surprised me, Young Man. I misjudged what you wanted.

"I love her," Feradach said simply. "Which is why I cannot let her family die. They are everything to her."

Merida found that she, too, was standing with her hands balled up against her chest.

Even if you could become everything to her instead?

Feradach sighed, and in that single sound, Merida could

hear how deeply miserable he was. But he said, "I have watched ever so many humans. That wouldn't be love; it would simply be possession."

The Cailleach gently tilted her staff away from Feradach.

This is a very human thing you are doing, Feradach, even as you choose to say goodbye to this body you're wearing now and move on to the next and the next and the next. And I suppose some would say it is against your nature, to refuse change, to continue in your duties as before. But I think it is very fitting. You choose to ruin yourself to save the next generation of change, and that is exactly your nature. It will be done, this miracle you ask.

Feradach's eyelashes fluttered, and then he drew himself up. "Thank you, Old Woman."

The tide against DunBroch will turn before dawn. This is my miracle, if the land will grant it to me.

She banged her staff on the floor.

40

THE BATTLE, PART II

THE battle shifted, just like that.

The wall collapsed on a handful of the Dásachtach's men. The wind kicked up to throw dirt in eyes. The stable broke apart as the Dásachtach's army tried to burn it, but the escaping horses served only to spook the Dásachtach's horses. Harris and the triplets launched new pane glass at the army with cutting precision. The arrows found their mark. The doors held. The rain began to pour and put out the burning trees. And then, as the Cailleach's green fire receded in the night sky and dawn began to rise, the crofters and the townspeople suddenly appeared in a makeshift army, their weapons in hand.

There were people from outside the town, too, even people from Keithneil and, right before dawn, the men of Ardbarrach, their ranks glistening and precise and threatening. Never had Merida thought she'd be relieved to see those uniforms again. Never had she thought she'd be glad to see how disciplined and loyal they were. She fetched out more arrows from the armory and ran out with her bow to support them.

And in the breaking light, the boys of the Dásachtach's army began to recognize the families they had been taken from, and they began to break ranks. They ran back to fight with their families, and then not to fight at all, because there were not enough men left to fight DunBroch.

There was just Wolftail and the Dásachtach standing in the glittering green light of a new winter day, strangely warm, the rain dripping from the repaired roofs of DunBroch.

Merida wondered at how splendid the castle looked in this light, old DunBroch, a castle made new. The rising sun caught each of the panes of glass and lit them like spring fire. The ivy was green and lush. The berries in the Christmas boughs were bright as battle. It was a grand and welcoming and beautiful sight, vibrant and alive. Yes, there was smoking fire in the background and walls had newly been knocked down, but it was impossible not to see that beneath that, the castle had a live and beating heart. It had changed. It had earned its freedom from Feradach's destruction. It had become something new. Or rather, it was still DunBroch, but it was DunBroch, grown, changing, moving onward, and Merida was fiercely proud.

"Run away and never come back," Fergus called out to the Madman. "Because you told us to make friends with the neighbors, and we did, and none of us like you."

"If you never look our direction again," said Elinor, "we will never look yours."

"And perhaps one day we'll meet again," Harris hissed to the Dásachtach, and there was that strange old glint in his expression.

"Merida!" Leezie said, grabbing her arm, getting her attention. She was disheveled and pretty in the morning light, but for once, she didn't look like she needed help. She said, *"Feradach."*

Merida followed her gaze. Leezie was pointing to the woods. Brionn stood at the edge of them, tail up and fringey. Just behind him was a blue glowing orb, slowly fading to nothing in the morning light.

For the final time that year, Merida set off in pursuit of a god.

41

I Trust You

SHE found him at the pools. There was a good view of the castle from here, so it made sense. He stood there by the waterfall looking out at it with his mane of blond hair, his kind face.

"Feradach!" Merida shouted.

"You're an impossible person," Feradach said. "You're always chasing."

She tried to catch her breath; gave up. "I heard what you said. I heard the bargain you made. Is it true?"

"I wouldn't have said it if it wasn't true. I have only ever said things I think are true." When she didn't say anything, he added quickly, "Do not mock me for what I said, Merida of DunBroch. I couldn't bear it."

"I wasn't going to mock you," Merida said. She didn't want to mock him. She wanted to say earnest things to him, the sort of silly things Leezie talked about, things about love. She didn't know how to, though. She couldn't say them, only feel them. "You don't have to go. Or rather, you could come back. I know you can't stop doing what you do. This doesn't have to be goodbye."

"I would only be drawn here if there was stagnation," Feradach said. "And you would not want that."

"Then I could go to you," Merida said. "I could seek out places that need it, and maybe see you there."

"Is that what you want from your life?" Feradach asked. "To do as I do, to always be following your feet to places that are about to be swept away? That are at the ends of their lives? To ride all over this country looking for the worst of it?"

"Don't you want to be known?"

She saw from his face that he did want it. He wanted it very much.

And she wanted to know him. She knew Feradach the god now, but she wanted to know who he was, and who he would become, if he got to be known by at least one other person in the world.

"What a life that would be for you," Feradach said. "Chasing me forever. What a life that would be for me. Being caught again and again by a mortal. You *are* an impossible person."

"I wouldn't just be catching you," Merida said. "I could also be ganging up on you. I think the Cailleach would be happy to use me to trick you to save a few people here and there, and I don't think I'd mind that. If you wouldn't mind losing some more."

"The balance was corrected. I didn't lose at all."

Merida thought about what the next year would look like. Preparing for another year of journeying, adventuring far and wide on her irascible Midge. She knew she could do it, because she already *had* done it. And as soon as that thought crossed her mind, the uneasiness that she'd been feeling earlier congealed into an obvious and unsightly blob. She said, "*Was* the balance corrected? I was thinking about it, and that was the biggest cheat of them all, isn't it? The Cailleach let you get away with it, who knows how she did, but you must have known. You just didn't say, because you were biased, too. You were both biased. But there was one person who didn't change at DunBroch, wasn't there?"

Feradach didn't answer, so she knew she was right.

"At the beginning of all this, I was so busy, all the time," Merida said. "I traveled all over. And then I spent all my time this last year trying to get everyone else to change, and I didn't think a bit about what I was going to do with myself when it was all over. I just lived for other people this whole year, and that's okay, that's what it took, but I look at myself after all the things I've learned and I know I'm just the same old me."

"It doesn't matter now, though," Feradach said. "You have time to figure it out."

"I've had time," Merida replied. "I've had lots of time. I can feel how I want to stay the same, though. All my ideas are the same ideas I've already had. I'm a storm moving no roofs."

He recognized his own words at once. "That was very cruel of me to say."

"No, it wasn't," Merida said. "Or at least, it wasn't wrong. I wasn't changing. I still haven't. I don't really know how, still."

Feradach's gloved hands were in loose fists now.

"Which means I need your help," Merida said.

She gestured to his glove.

Feradach jerked his hand back.

"I'm not afraid," Merida said. She had seen all the ways his destruction could manifest, when he was the one choosing it. Sometimes it was the terrible fire, like at Kinlochy, but sometimes it was the flood, or the broken hand of a harper. She knew it was going to hurt, but she knew it would be fair. She knew in the end, she'd be like the scholar, like the harper. She would be a better version of herself. "Please."

"It won't be easy," he said.

"I trust you." *I love you.*

Feradach sighed, and then he looked at the palms of those gloves with the oxblood stitching.

"How do you decide?" Merida asked. "What it is that will happen?"

Feradach carefully tugged off one glove. Then the other. They were just ordinary, human-looking hands beneath, as always, but of course they weren't ordinary human hands at all. They weren't even really his. Just borrowed, for a bit. "It's instinct, I suppose. From watching humans for a long time. You think about what they think they want, and you take it away from them, so they have room to realize what they truly need instead. You cut out all the bits that are standing in the way of growth. The dead ends. The land that might have been good once, but now won't support another crop."

"Do you know what it will do to me?" Merida asked.

He nodded.

"You will heal," he said, and then he put his hand on her cheek. There was no feeling of dread, just the feeling of Feradach's hand on her.

"You will always be impossible," he added, and he put his other hand on her other cheek. There was still no sense of doom; of what might be to come.

"You will still be Merida of DunBroch," he said, and he kissed her.

Neither the mortal nor the god had ever been in love before. It is not every day or every week or every month or every year that one person meets another who is their perfect foil, and it is not even every century that the pairing is a mortal and a god. It's more than simply love when it is a pair like this: it is balance, perfect balance, the push-pull of opposite forces that require each other.

It is a sort of love that never grows old.

Magic, magic, magic.

Merida could feel the dread beginning to rise up in her.

Feradach pulled back just enough to whisper in her ear: "It is this: you will never see me again."

She closed her eyes.

When she opened them again, she was alone. There were not so much as a single footprint in the frost beside the pools.

Feradach's hands had done their destructive work. Her heart was broken.

She would never be the same.

EPILOGUE

THE KNOCK

THIS is a story about two gods and a girl.

The first god, the Cailleach, went about her business the way she had always done. Coaxing buds from trees, kits from foxes, crops from rocky ground. It is not that the Cailleach is incapable of change. It is just that she is very old, and will continue to get older, and so the scale of her change happens so slowly that it would be very difficult to capture in the space of a story like this. It is a bit like how you cannot tell the Earth is curved unless you're in space. It's just too big. She's just too old. Merida's story changed her a little, but so very little that we mortals can't see it.

The second god, Feradach, went about his business as well. The balance still had to be held. Destruction still had to be wrought. But his time with DunBroch had changed him. He was slower to incite ruin, and when he did, it was often less complete than before. He left humans room to make mistakes and to learn from them, and his destruction often threw people together in new ways, so that they could learn from each other without having to lose everything along the way.

The girl, however, did not go about her business as usual.

She had been a storm that didn't move roofs, but she'd spent a year watching storms that *did*. Instead of striking off on her own, as she'd always done, she decided to learn to listen.

In spring, she went to Eilcan Clan, and she listened to the old queen teach girls to heal.

In summer, she went to Ardbarrach, and as the bells rang, she listened to the value of order.

In fall, she returned home long enough for her mother to prepare for the journey, and then, as they rode around a new and fragile Scotland, she listened to her mother talk about peace.

In winter, she returned to DunBroch to think about all she had learned over the long, dark season.

"There's something I'd like to show you," Leezie told Merida.

The two girls—the two sisters—the two young women, really—took a chilly walk out to the standing stone known as Feradach's stone. It was dark and frostbitten and standing off by itself from the holy well nearby. The two sisters knelt until both were at eye level with an ancient handprint.

Leezie gestured for Merida to fit her hand into the print. She did.

"Stone," Leezie whispered, and her eyes glinted with the Sight, "show her what you've seen."

Merida thought for a moment that it would not work, and then, just like that, she was whisked to a long-ago time, in a DunBroch long before it was called DunBroch. There was a hunt afoot. This hunt did not yet have the name it would come to have later: the Hunt for the Unnamed.

There were two hunters pursuing the quarry that raced between the trees. Strange quarry it was, quarry without a body, just feelings, barely more than air, just gleeful odd beings that existed in all times over and over. These breathy entities could see everything, could watch everything, but that was about all they did. They did not harm the world, and the world did not harm them. They loved the world.

You can still feel them in the right places.

One of the hunters was a man, and although he was still pursuing aggressively, he would come away from the hunt empty-handed, as men always did. The quarry was too unlike him for him to even understand what he was chasing, and that's no way to catch anything.

The other hunter was the Cailleach, who was ancient even then. She was old and tired of doing unpleasant things; she longed to put the ugly work behind her and focus only on growth, and so she had a plan. She was tricky even then, and she used a trick to make one of the small pools of water she controlled become a perfect reflection of the sky. One of the strange carefree air beings got caught in it as it fled, and before it could make sense of the trap, the Cailleach scooped it out. The quarry was not entirely like her, but it was enough like her that she could hold it firmly.

Walking to the craggy standing stone near the pool, she pressed the being against the stone so that it was trapped between stone and skin.

"You will no longer be air," she said. "You will be a god."

The stone hummed with the power of it, with the transfer of the dread and the ruin. The airy creature cried out as it was given form for the first time. The Cailleach's hand sank right into the stone.

This was the first of the Feradachs.

"No," he said bitterly, understanding at once what his duty was to be. "There must be a way out."

The Cailleach smiled.

"Of course," she said. "But it will have to be a trick."

Merida sat back from the stone, her mind returning to the present day beside Leezie. Time moved sluggishly around her.

"Leezie," she said, her voice barely audible.

"I'll help you think of one," Leezie said.

The two sisters walked back to the castle, and joined the revelry there.

Later, as the snow began to fall on the shortest night of the year, as Merida went to the kitchen to get some fresh bread, as she stood there, looking in the fire and remembering, she heard a knock.

Author's Note

*B*RAVELY is "historical."

Note the quotes, if you will. "Historical," not historical. Don't get me wrong. Real historical fact leaps through DunBroch like a wolfhound, chewing spoons, breaking furniture, and curling up before the fire. Within these pages you'll find real historical figures (albeit somewhat displaced from their true time lines), real historical snacks (pulled from cookbooks with very old-timey spelling), and real historical struggles (sung in ballads, written in poems, found in graves).

I was a medieval history major, and I wanted to do my best to put as much history in here as I could. I am also a bagpiper and harpist who was raised in the peculiar pan-Celtic mixing bowl that is American Scottish-Irish diaspora, and I wanted to put as much of that culture in as I could, too. And finally, I am one of five children, and I wanted to also put in as much of the truthful chaos and frustration and joy of a large family as I could.

But at the end of the day, *Bravely* is a fairy tale, and it is true in the way dialogue in a novel is true. It would be dull to transcribe a real conversation. Better for the story to make the dialogue on the page *feel* like the real conversation.

My hope is not to trick readers into believing or doubting everything within these pages but rather to be curious enough to go hunting for the rest of the truth. Attentive readers will find the Dásachtach, the shiclings, and, if they are very watchful (or perhaps very unlucky), a cunning goddess named the Cailleach.

Acknowledgments

THANK you to my editor Elana for her intense enthusiasm, Lauren for early midwifing, Steve for letting me play in the sandbox, my agent Richard for his endless patience, Liz for allowing me to steal her dog, Sarah for the first read, Victoria for the middle read, Mom for the last, and Ed, always Ed, for the knock upon the door.